The Meaning of Life

ROBERT SCOLLO

Dedication

To my fellow conspirator and friend Mark who read the book whilst I was writing it, I thank him for his time, although his notes were impossible to read.

To my two son Matthew and daughter Megan, SURPRISE.

To my wife and brothers, they'll have to wait for the book to be printed in their native language, if that ever happens, for them to read it.

All roads lead to where we stand – Don McLean

About the Author

This is the author's first book, and he hopes that it inspires people to help one another. He lives in Melbourne, Australia, and has just turned sixty.

The author says, 'Frustration. We are constantly frustrated when we hear how badly we treat one another. We whine and complain. We turn our backs when people ask for help, or we ignore famine and prosecution, or we abuse the environment and leave it barren and toxic, or we slaughter animals to extinction, but no one does anything about it because we're a single voice in the wilderness. Apart from one impossible thing occurring in this novel, everything else is achievable. We just need enough of the right people to listen.'

The author hopes that more people than not will enjoy the book, and if they do, the main character James will return in a second novel.

Table of Contents

Chapter 1

'Chudo' James Shaw is eighteen years old, and sits alone in the house that his mother Elizabeth and father Charles built in a small town of around 4,000 people, eighty miles west of Los Angeles, California. The house stands on the top of a hill overlooking Lake Casitas just outside Oak View, and is set on ten acres of manicured gardens surrounded by natural forest. It boasts eight bedrooms, eight bathrooms, a theatre room, a gymnasium, a library, two kitchens, and a huge formal dining room for entertaining guests and clients. There are also several outbuildings, including a cottage where guests stayed over, a boathouse, and a stable where horses were once kept.

James's father spared no expense to design a home for his wife whom he cherished more than life itself, that is, until recently. The gardens are a little rundown although they are still maintained, and the horses are long gone.

To understand the events that took place that resulted in this tragedy occurring, and how it came about that his mother named him Chudo, we'll start back to when James's father Charles was nearing the end of his teenage years.

Chapter 2

The year was 1981. Charles lived in a normal home, in a normal neighbourhood, in a suburb of Los Angeles called Huntington Park. Although not a well-to-do area like Beverly Hills or Santa Monica, his parents were hard-working, and Charles, an only child, was loved by both of them.

He was a bright and intelligent student in his final high school year. Although he was in the top 5 per cent of his class, he was still undecided on what career path he would take and which university he would attend. His grades reflected his intelligence, with straight 'A's in English, mathematics, and the arts. Maybe that was why he was having difficulty in deciding on a career path.

People say that you are either a logical or creative person depending on which brain hemisphere is the more dominant one. People who use their right hemisphere are more artistic, show creativity, have greater imagination than those who use their left hemisphere, who are more logical, are more analytical, and use reason in decision-making.

Surprisingly, Charles appeared to have achieved what few people could. His artistic flair ranged from drawing images that were so realistic that they appeared to be photographs, right through to creations that, with so much imagination, art critics could critique them for hours if not days. He was comfortable in using oils, watercolours, and pencils, even charcoal.

On the other hand, he was seldom challenged in mathematics, from algebra to calculus. There was one time Charles questioned his mathematics teacher on an equation he was using to solve a problem, and after his teacher consulted his handbook, he had to acknowledge his error.

With his dilemma continuing and a decision deadline looming, he consulted his teachers, hoping for some enlightenment. He even met with the principal of the school who had been a notable lecturer before settling down to a less stressful lifestyle before retirement, but he came away more confused than ever.

As a final desperate attempt, he spoke with the only person he believed would give him the guidance and advice he was looking for—his mother. After explaining his dilemma, telling her that he was having difficulty in deciding what he wanted to be and do with his life, her answer was 'Why don't you do both?' He looked at her, puzzled and confused . . . again.

'What can I do that is both creative and logical?' he asked her.

'You love your art, and your drawings are out of this world,' she replied. 'I should know. We've got them framed and hanging on walls all around the house. I remember when you were little and you brought your drawings home from school. We used so many fridge magnets to stick them to the fridge, they even covered the fridge door handle. There were so many of them. They were so lovely, I didn't have the heart to throw them away. Although they're no longer on the fridge, I still haven't thrown one out. I've got them packed in the attic, and sometimes when I want to reminisce, I go up there and look at them again. They bring back so many wonderful memories. You can't imagine how many happy tears I've shed whilst looking at them. I've learnt now not to go up there without a box of tissues.'

Even now her eyes were beginning to well up, and she turned her head away so that her son didn't see her crying. Charles had a lump in his throat and was having difficulty speaking. He stood, gave his mom a big hug, and went to the kitchen to get them both a glass of water and some tissues.

When he returned and handed her the glass of water, he told her that he loved her. 'OK, so I'm good at drawing, but I don't want to draw or paint for that matter, for the rest of my life. So any more suggestions?' he asked.

'Well, I can't imagine you working for a company,' she replied. 'You're not that type of person, and you're too smart for that. So why don't you start your own company? I'm sure you can find some arty business you'd enjoy. Be your own boss. It would mean a lot of hard work, but you've got the stubbornness to do it.'

Charles sat there, thinking, *my own business—that's an idea.*

His mother continued, 'You've got to decide on what type of arty business you'd enjoy, and what people want that they would pay you money for. You know your father and I will always support you, and we've put some money aside for your college education. It's not a lot of money, and if you pick the right university that has the right subjects, and that's not overly expensive, you might still have enough to start your business.'

Charles was looking straight ahead, his eyes unblinking, his mind spinning at a million miles an hour. *My own business, something arty, something I'd enjoy.* His eyes widening, thinking. He wasn't breathing. And then it clicked.

'Thanks, Mom,' he said. 'I think I know what I want to do. I've got to check out some universities and the subjects they teach, but I think it'll work.'

He got up, gave her a big hug and kiss, and rushed out the door whilst saying, 'Love you, Mom.'

He headed for the school library where university material was held. There was extensive material on the surrounding universities, as well as material on the major national and international universities for those students who had wealthy parents where money was no object.

He scanned through each of the local universities and colleges, the subjects they taught, the cost of each subject, the pass rates, and the ratings given to them by the students who went through them. He narrowed his selection to two universities where the subjects he was interested in had the highest pass rate and student ratings. He finally settled on the University of South California where the fees were slightly less than the other.

He headed to the library's front desk and asked for an application form for the University of South California before heading back to a quiet corner of the library to fill it in, not that it was busy at that hour of the day. It was late afternoon by this time, and the library was nearly deserted apart from keen students wanting to better their education, or for those who needed to catch up as they were falling behind in their homework. After completing the application form, he placed it in the self-addressed envelope and handed it back to the library clerk.

'Only one application, Charles. At least you've finally made a decision,' commented the clerk, a middle-aged woman with thin features, naturally greying hair which she hadn't tried to disguise with colour, wearing bifocals which she was peering over anyway.

'Hi, Ms Thompson,' replied Charles. 'Yes, I've finally decided on the University of South California.' Charles had always been polite to his teachers and staff, even though he knew the librarian's first name to be Mary. Charles knew Mary quite well as he frequented the library often, and they had the occasional chat when she wasn't busy. She knew his dilemma about what he wanted to do after graduating, as they had had this discussion several times before.

'Good choice,' said Mary. 'I haven't heard too many bad things about them, and they have excellent teachers. I'm sure you'll be accepted. They'd be mad not to. I'll make sure I put it in the mailbag when I knock off so it gets to them sooner rather than later.'

Charles was about to walk off when Mary said, 'So don't leave me hanging unless you don't want to tell me.'

'I've decided to do a Marketing, and a Business Administration and Management course,' replied Charles. 'I'm thinking that if I do well, I want to start my own marketing firm.'

Mary's eyebrows rose. 'That's an interesting combination, and if anyone can pull it off, it's Charles Shaw. I wish you the very best of luck.'

With that, he said 'thank you' and left.

Charles spoke with his parents, telling them about his decision over dinner that night. Supportive as ever, they encouraged him and showed true excitement that he had a plan for his future. They discussed the cost of the four-year course, and although it exceeded their savings, they knew that they could make it happen. Charles noticed the slight pause in the conversation when he mentioned the cost of the courses, but he didn't want to press them on just how much money they had saved up for his university education.

He did, however, comment that he would be taking on a part-time job to try and save some money so that he wouldn't be draining their bank account and hopefully have a little extra to start the business. It was also a way of learning about just what a working life was like. There was visible relief in his parents' eyes when he said that he was taking on a part-time job. Since the university was local and only a ten-minute bus trip from home, they didn't have to pay for Charles to live on campus. They only needed to feed him, which they'd been doing for the past eighteen years anyway. The cleaning and washing was free, and with love.

The University of South California replied six weeks later, accepting his application, subject to Charles graduating, of course, which he did with flying colours. He achieved the highest grades in two of his classes, and he was in the top 10 per cent in the others.

His parents held a combined eighteenth birthday and graduation party since they were only one week apart and invited nearly fifty guests—friends, family, neighbours, and school friends. There wasn't an empty room in the house that night, with people spilling out from the front garden through to the backyard.

Chapter 3

The following year, Charles started university and, as promised, took on a part-time job after school at a café near the university, starting in the kitchen, washing dishes, and was gradually promoted to waiting on tables as well as being their barista. Working at the front of house, he made extra money on tips and, in most cases, made more money on the tips than his hourly rate. Apart from keeping a little pocket money, the rest he gave to his parents.

He worked five nights a week as well as Saturday night which was the café's busiest time. Somehow he managed, although he did look forward to Sundays when he had some free time to himself, apart from when he was helping his father with odd jobs around the house, and when he was able to tidy up his study notes so they made sense.

Most weeknights, his parents ate alone, although they tried to eat later in the evening so that they could try and have dinner with their son. When Charles didn't make it home for dinner, they would put his plate of food in the refrigerator, and if it was still there the next morning, his father would take it to work for lunch.

Occasionally, Charles would bring a girl home for a Sunday lunch or dinner, but it was rare, and they didn't see the same girl twice. Charles was more focused on his studies than dating girls, and when the girls tried to make it a serious relationship, he basically told them that he wasn't interested. They weren't happy with his response and moved on.

Four years later, Charles Shaw graduated from the University of South California with honours.

Over the next few months, Charles developed his plan on starting his business. He finally found a small ground-floor office in San Fernando where the rent wasn't too high, it was clean and tidy, and it was situated in a bustling commercial neighbourhood.

After paying his university fees, the combined money that his parents had saved, and the money they had put aside from his part-time job left him with just over a year's rent, just as long as he didn't spend too much on buying second-hand furniture to furnish the office, stationary and supplies, and a second-hand car. *You can't be visiting clients on public transport or paying for expensive taxi rides,* thought Charles.

Although he had never owned a car before, his father had given him driving lessons whilst he was in university, and he had a valid driver's licence, borrowing his father's car on the odd occasion he was taking a girl out.

Charles quit his job at the café and started his business. After rearranging the furniture in his new office several times, he finally sat at his desk, looking out the front window, thinking what had he gotten himself into. He had a marketing company, and the first non-paying client would be himself.

He had decided on the company name whilst at university but had yet to decide on the font, and style, and size, and colours, and the layout, and so on. Moving to his drafting table, he set about creating how the company name and logo should appear. By that evening, with countless designs rejected and balls of crumpled paper strewn across the floor where he'd missed hitting the rubbish basket, he was finally satisfied with the layout.

Before returning to the office the following morning, he stopped at a local paint store and purchased paints, brushes, and other supplies such as masking tape, solvents, cleaners, and even disposable overalls so that he didn't unintentionally paint himself.

After thoroughly cleaning the front office window inside and out, he began to stencil the design of the company name on the outside of the window before painting his company name from the inside, back the front. Surprisingly, he was finished early afternoon, and after re-cleaning the outside of the window, he admired his creation. A close examination of the paint strokes, he found no air pockets in the paint, the lines weren't overlapping, and the edges were clean and straight.

He stood back from the sidewalk close to the street and examined his handiwork again and then proceeded across the street to the other sidewalk, nearly getting run over by a car because he wasn't paying attention to the traffic. *Shaw Design and Marketing*—the lettering was legible and the colours distinct without being too gaudy or loud. He would wait for the paint to dry before cleaning the inside of the window and removing any smudges and handprints.

On the way to the office the next morning, he purchased several local newspapers and scanned them for the type of advertising they contained. He created his own ad and contacted two of the newspapers about advertising his business. He agreed on running his ad daily for a month and paid a little extra to have the ad appear within the first five pages on the newspaper, taking up an eighth of the page.

He faxed the newspapers a copy of his ad and mailed them a cheque for the first month of newspaper publication. A week later, his ad was appearing in the two newspapers. He also had flyers printed that he hand-delivered to companies in his area and paid kids selling newspapers in neighbouring suburbs to do the same.

Within the first week the ad appeared in the newspapers, Charles received several enquiries, and he made appointments to meet these prospective clients to discuss the type of marketing they wanted. Being the receptionist, secretary, designer, and owner of the company, he could only be at one place at a time. Every time he went out, he set his answering machine to record any phone calls received. 'Hello, you have contacted Shaw Design and Marketing. We are currently unavailable. Your phone call is important to us, so please leave your contact name and phone number, and we'll return your call as soon as possible.'

Within the first month, he had secured a dozen clients, and he was receiving more and more enquiries every week. By the end of the first year, Charles was renting a second office adjoining the first and employing one general secretary, a personal secretary, and two designers.

By the end of the second year, he had moved into a new office building in Santa Monica and employed six designers, two draftspersons, and four secretaries. Life was good and hectic, although he enjoyed every minute of it, frustrations and all.

At twenty-five years old, he couldn't believe how far he had come in just two years. He had visions of himself still sitting in his old office alone, his head in hands, and without a single client, struggling to pay his rent. The company now had over a thousand clients on the books. Most of them were from local businesses, but a handful were from other US states, some of which were large corporations. He was proud of what he had achieved and thankful for his supportive parents.

To celebrate his success, Charles's parents encouraged him to hold a party at the new offices, inviting his major clients, celebrities, and local officials. Surprisingly, the majority of people invited, including a few well-known actors and singers, accepted the invitations. Charles made sure that his parents were invited, since without their help and support, none of this would have been possible.

Chapter 4

Looking over the mingling crowd, with chatter and laughter and clink of glasses, Charles saw that the celebrities had separated and had groups of people mingling among them, trying to shake their hands and get their autographs. He felt sorry for them, considering they weren't getting paid for coming. He had to remind himself to go over and thank them personally later.

On the other hand, the mayor and deputy chief of police were standing alone near the bar, making small talk, and only got the occasional glance and polite 'hello' when someone couldn't wait for the waiter to come around and went to the bar themselves to get their own drinks.

With two hundred guests in the office, sipping on champagne and eating hors d'oeuvres, Charles waited for his parents to arrive before making his speech, as they were the reason he was here. Although it wasn't overly late, his parents were never late for anything, especially for something as important as this. He walked into his office and rang the home number. After a minute, the phone rang out, and all he got was a busy signal. He dialled again, but there was still no answer. Now he was getting worried.

He walked back into the main office where his secretary Linda asked if he was OK. 'I tried ringing my parents, but there's no answer,' he replied.

'I'm sure they're fine.' Linda chortled. 'And they're only thirty minutes late. Being such a special occasion, they probably spent more time getting ready, and they've only just left. If your mom is anything like me, thirty minutes late is being on time. Anyway, you should say something, even though you want to wait for your parents before giving your speech.'

Charles walked to the corner of the office, which had been elevated for when they were having presentations or displaying new products they were creating marketing plans for.

'Excuse me everyone!' yelled Charles to the guests. Once he got their attention and the crowd settled, he continued, 'I hope you're enjoying yourselves, and please feel free to drink and eat whilst we prepare for the speeches.'

Charles had become so nervous and worried that he had forgotten the microphone which had been linked to their Public Address (PA) system placed there specifically for the speeches.

Charles walked over to the window, looking in the direction of his parents' home. Being on the twenty-fifth floor, he had a clear view of the main thoroughfare his parents would be arriving from, hoping to see their old black Buick trundling in his direction. Nothing. He went back to his office and tried the home phone number again. Still no answer. He circled his office a couple of times, thinking. He was having trouble breathing. Maybe there was something wrong with the air-conditioning. He decided to go downstairs and clear his head.

Being so late, and a Saturday night, no other offices were open. The elevator had been locked so that only the twenty-fifth floor, the lobby, and the underground car park were accessible. As soon as Charles reached the lobby and the elevator doors opened, two police officers were heading in his direction, accompanied by Sam, the security guard who was escorting guests in when they arrived with their invitations.

'That's Mr Shaw there,' stated Sam to the officers.

'Mr Shaw, Mr Charles Shaw?' questioned one of the officers.

'Yes, I'm Charles Shaw. Can I help you?' replied Charles.

'I'm Officer Johnston, and this is Detective Bradshaw,' responded the officer. 'Is there anywhere where we can talk in private?'

Charles was becoming increasingly anxious. 'I'm afraid my office is full of people, so we'll have to chat here,' said Charles.

Turning to Sam, he said, 'Thanks, Sam. That'll be all. Please go back to the main door and see if more guests are arriving.'

Charles waited for Sam to start walking back to the front of the building before turning back to the officers. His mouth became dry, and he couldn't speak.

Detective Bradshaw started, 'I'm afraid to inform you that your parents were involved in a car accident and have been transported to LAC Medical Centre.'

Suddenly, Charles felt cold and began to sweat at the same time. 'Are they all right? How did this happen? Are my mom and dad OK?' shrilled Charles. Charles could see Sam turning his head in their direction with concern on his face.

'When we left them, they were being loaded into the two ambulances,' replied Officer Johnston. 'We were the first officers on the scene after the accident. My partner and I were patrolling the area and heard the accident. Your mom was still conscious. Although in pain, she asked me to come here and tell you not to worry and that she loves you. They'd been sideswiped by a drunk driver who had gone through the intersection on a red light at speed. The driver of the other car has been taken into custody and is sitting in the jailhouse, waiting to be charged. As I said, we waited for your parents to be put into the ambulance before heading straight here.'

'Are you trying to tell me that the other driver walked away without a scratch?' questioned Charles.

'Literally,' responded the officer. 'He was driving a reasonably new model Mustang with all the bells and whistles, and the airbags saved him. Unfortunately, your parents' car has no airbags fitted, and they felt the full force of the impact.'

Charles shook his head. 'Life's unfair,' he stated.

'No argument there,' responded the two police officers in unison. Surprisingly, Charles felt a calm wash over him and told the officers that he would be going directly to the hospital.

'We figured that,' responded Detective Bradshaw. 'We'll wait for you out the front and escort you to the hospital unless you want us to drive you there.'

'No, I'll be fine,' said Charles. 'It might be a long night. I'll head down to the car park and meet you out the front in a couple of minutes.'

Charles walked over to Sam and asked him to tell Linda, his secretary, that his parents had been in an accident and that he wouldn't be back that evening, before he headed to the car park.

Charles made it to the Los Angeles County (LAC) Medical Centre in record time. The police officers were in front of him, with their siren blaring and lights flashing. Charles parked haphazardly in one of the emergency parking bays, thanked the officers, and ran into the hospital emergency entrance since the main entrance was closed at that time of the night.

Charles was confronted with long queues snaking towards the two information stations, and the waiting area was crammed with people. He couldn't wait in line to speak to one of the receiving nurses, so he hastily looked around and saw two burly security guards standing behind the entrance he had just walked through. They were employed to make sure there wasn't any rowdy behaviour from impatient people waiting to be seen.

He approached one of the security guards and said, 'Hi, my parents were in a car accident, and they arrived here a little while ago. Is there any way that I can speak with one of the nurses urgently?'

The security guard looked him up and down and finally said, 'Give me a sec'. The guard headed to the front of one of the queues, leaned over, and spoke with the nurse. The nurse leaned around and looked in his direction before making a phone call. She told something to the security guard before returning to her duties.

The security guard came back over to Charles and told him that someone would see him shortly. Charles thanked the security guard and focused on the door next to the information station which led into the hospital. Two minutes later, the door opened, and a nurse in her white uniform and cap headed in his direction.

'Mr Shaw?' questioned the nurse.

'Yes,' responded Charles.

'Come with me,' said the nurse.

Reaching the door she'd just come through, she entered some numbers on the security pad next to the door, heard a faint beep, and pushed the door open. Charles followed her along a main corridor with curtained cubicles on either side. He could hear chatter and moans coming from some of the cubicles as he went past. Clearly, this was where patients were examined after being called by the nurse.

The corridor snaked left and right, and within several turns, Charles had become completely disorientated. Only intermittent lights were on in this part of the hospital since the corridors were seldom used this time of the night. They finally arrived at what appeared to be a waiting room near the main hospital entrance. The nurse asked Charles to wait there whilst she went to get the doctor.

Five minutes went by, and Charles was still waiting. He paced the waiting room and had some cool water from the drinking fountain. He was becoming more and more anxious by the minute. He looked down the corridor and noticed two metallic signs above two doors. They had a silhouette of a man and woman printed on them and realised that he needed to use one of the restrooms. He walked to the door marked 'men', stopped, and listened for any noise of footfalls to signal someone was nearby. Nothing. He pushed the lavatory door open and locked it in the open position so that he could hear any noise whilst he was in there. The last thing he wanted was to be in the toilet when the doctor arrived and possibly missing him.

He relieved himself, flushed, washed his hands, and dried them using the disposable paper towels before closing the lavatory door behind him and headed back to the waiting room. Ten minutes later, the doctor arrived.

'Mr Shaw,' started the doctor and shook Charles's hand. 'I'm Dr Timothy Rowlings, one of the surgeons called in to look after your parents. I'm sorry for keeping you waiting, but we were operating on your mom when the nurse told me you were here. I had to finish the operation before seeing you.'

'How are they?' asked Charles. 'When can I see them?'

'I'm afraid it will be some time before that happens,' replied the doctor. 'They have suffered extensive injuries in the accident, but we have three teams of fine surgeons taking care of them. We have a long night ahead of us as we have to perform several operations on your parents as quickly as possible.'

Charles was silent for a moment before asking, 'Will they be all right?'

The doctor gathered his thoughts for a moment before answering, 'Do you mind if we sit down?' Charles reluctantly did, and the doctor moved one of the waiting room chairs so he was facing Charles before he sat himself.

The doctor continued, 'Your father has the most severe injuries as he took the full impact in the accident. He has extensive breaks and fractures, a punctured lung, and other internal injuries. Although these are quite significant, my biggest concern is with his head trauma. He has severe swelling of the brain which we're currently operating on to relieve some of the pressure. We have two teams of doctors operating on him right now. One team is working on his head trauma, and the other team is trying to locate and stop the internal bleeding around his body. I know he's your father, and we're trying everything in our power to try and make sure he comes through. I know all the doctors operating on him personally, and they are some of the finest surgeons.'

Charles felt numb. He was leaning forward in his chair, elbows in his knees, hands clasped in front of him, looking at the carpet, unblinking.

'Your mother has less severe injuries, although still significant,' the doctor continued. 'She has a number of broken ribs, both her legs are broken, a shattered elbow, and her pelvis is broken in several places. She has a bruised liver, a punctured lung, and damage to her spleen and intestines. I was amazed that she was still conscious when she arrived in the operating theatre. She is one tough woman. My team are operating on her at the moment.'

Charles's throat felt tight, and he was having difficulty swallowing. He couldn't build up the courage to ask what the doctor thought their chances were. He didn't want to hear the news that he knew would come.

The doctor suggested that Charles go home and get some rest as there was nothing he could do here. The doctor would ring him tomorrow morning after the operations were completed and update him on his parents' condition.

Charles mumbled something like 'Thank you, Doctor. Please help them' before he was led to the front door of the hospital and let out. Charles walked around to the emergency parking area and managed to get into his car before he began to sob uncontrollably.

He finally managed to start the car and drive home, although tears continued to run down his cheeks. He opened the front door to his parents' house, and although he had lived there all his life, his sense of smell was so acute at the moment that the smell of the house flooded his mind with all the happy memories he had had. He saw his parents' faces and in each other's arms, smiling as they frequently did. That set him off again, and he began to sob.

It was now early morning. He felt wrung out and tired as if he'd just run a full marathon. His mind continued to race, and he knew he couldn't sleep. He went into the kitchen and put some milk in a saucepan to heat up. The phone rang. He turned off the stove and went to answer it.

He picked up the receiver and said hello.

'Thank God. I've been ringing for hours since you left the office.' It was Linda, his secretary.

'How are your parents? Are they all right?' Linda asked.

'They were in a bad car accident on the way to the office,' replied Charles. 'They were hit by a drunk driver who didn't even get hurt. That's fucked.' Charles seldom swore, especially in front of women. There was silence on the other end of the phone. Linda might have been in shock as she had never heard Charles swear.

Charles continued, 'They received a lot of injuries, and they are both being operated on right now.'

'I'm sure they'll be fine, you'll see,' encouraged Linda.

But Charles knew she was wrong. Unless there was some miracle, his parents wouldn't make it.

'Anyway, don't hurry coming back. We'll look after things until everything's OK. Just take care of yourself and ring me if there's any news,' continued Linda.

Charles couldn't think. He didn't ask how the party went, and he didn't care. He said, 'OK, bye,' and hung up.

Charles turned the stove back on to heat up his milk. He spooned out the film which had formed on the top of the milk whilst he had been on the phone and rinsed the spoon under the tap. Once he saw small bubbles appearing on the surface of the milk, he turned the stove off and poured the milk into a mug. He went to the cupboard and brought out a packet of chocolate powder and spooned two teaspoons into the milk. His mother had made chocolate milk for him when he was young, and she still made it for him now when he came home tired from the office.

He carried the mug of hot chocolate to the lounge room, sat in his favourite chair, and took a big gulp of the scolding chocolate milk. He placed the mug on the side table, put his arms on the armrests, tilted his head back, and closed his eyes.

The ring of the phone startled him awake. He looked at the wall clock and noticed it was nearly eight in the morning. He was surprised that he'd managed to sleep for nearly six hours. Disorientated, he leaned over and picked up the receiver. 'Hello?'

'Mr Shaw, this is Dr Rowlings from the LAC Medical Centre.' Charles heard an audible sigh as Dr Rowlings continued, 'I'm sorry to inform you that your parents have passed away. Their injuries were so severe that we were unable to save them. Although it means little to you at the moment, I am truly sorry. If you wish to see them, we can arrange for that to happen. You don't need to decide right now, but when you do, just ring the hospital and ask to speak with John Alexander. Take all the time you need. Do you have any questions?'

Solemnly, Charles said, 'Thank you Doctor, for all your help. I can't think straight at the moment, so I don't have any questions to ask. And no, I don't want to see them. I would rather remember them as they were rather than how they are now. I'll ring the hospital once I've made arrangements. Not having done this before, is there anything I should know?'

'The only thing you need,' replied the doctor, 'is their death certificates which I will prepare shortly. I suggest you contact your parents' lawyer, assuming they have one, as that will be required to prepare probate. If you have any other questions, give the hospital a ring.'

'Again, thank you Doctor, for your help,' finished Charles and said goodbye.

Charles went to his bedroom and picked out a change of clothes before showering and getting dressed. His parents did, in fact, have a lawyer, and he found his phone number in the Teledex next to the phone. Charles dialled the number and spoke with Tim Larson, his parents' lawyer. After the initial shock, Tim agreed to organise everything and would collect the death certificates from the hospital.

Charles organised to meet with Tim in his office the following morning where his parents' wills would be read. Since Charles was the only beneficiary in the wills, he was the only one who had to attend.

The wills were pretty straightforward. Everything was left to Charles, including the house and the small insurance policies they had. After the taxes were paid, along with paying out the mortgage, all Charles was left with was the house.

The funeral was small and solemn with only close friends and neighbours invited, along with Charles's work colleagues who wanted to attend. His parents were buried alongside each other, and Charles had elaborate tombstones made.

He told Linda, his secretary, that he would return to work in a week's time after he had cleaned up around the house and sorted out a few things.

Charles spent the rest of the week going through his parents' things and only boxing things that had no sentimental value so that he could donate them to the local charity shops. After gardening and doing any chores that needed to be done, he went back to work.

Chapter 5

It took Charles several weeks to get back into a routine, but he would never be quite the same again. Even his colleagues saw him in a different light. Although he was the boss and owner of the company, he was now physically and emotionally standing on his own two feet. He really had no one. He hadn't kept in touch with anyone from either high school or university. He wasn't even seeing anyone at the moment, and he hadn't developed close friendships with anyone.

Charles immersed himself in his work, and his company continued to thrive. He did, however, wonder what this was all leading to. Although Charles had leased the new premises, allowing for further growth, three years later, space in the office was at a premium.

Clients on the books continued to grow and now included a number of overseas companies, although small organisations. Shaw Design and Marketing had an excellent reputation.

In the fifth year since starting his business, Charles was contacted by a large and well-known clothing and leather goods company based in Italy. This iconic company's brand was known throughout the globe, but with cheap, inferior, and knockoff brands flooding the market, they were rapidly losing their market share. Gucci invited Shaw Design and Marketing to help them revitalise their brand and help them achieve their number-one status again.

Charles saw this as an incredible opportunity to further expose his company on a world scale and decided to personally take charge.

After numerous phone calls and faxes to Gucci's CEO Secretary, a date was finally settled for him to meet with the CEO in their offices in Florence.

Charles began to research Gucci's brand name, products, markets, and sales figures for the past ten years. He prepared a portfolio highlighting results achieved by his company for some of his major clients, as well as preparing a draft proposal on how he could market the Gucci brand. He had two weeks before the agreed meeting date.

Once the flight to Rome was booked, Charles contacted Angelica, Gucci's secretary he had been communicating with, and told her about his itinerary. 'You plan to do a bit of sightseeing before coming to our offices, I see, Mr Shaw?' questioned Angelica.

Angelica spoke with a strong Italian accent, and sometimes it was difficult to understand her. 'Yes,' replied Charles. 'Since I've never been to Italy, I thought I would look around a bit.'

'We can book a hotel for you in Florence and pick you up from airport if you like,' continued Angelica.

'That would be wonderful,' he told Angelica. He knew that Florence was around 170 miles northwest of Rome, and he had yet to decide the mode of transport he was going to take to get there, and where he would stay. At least that was two less things he had to worry about.

With the deadline looming, Charles felt that he was as prepared as he could be. He had decided to arrive in Florence two days before the scheduled meeting so that he could familiarise himself with the Italian culture since he'd never travelled overseas and to a country where the primary language was not English. It would also give him the opportunity to conduct further research on possible aspects of his proposal he might have overlooked.

Charles arrived at the Fiumicino, Rome's international airport, on Saturday morning, and after collecting his luggage and passing through customs, he headed to the main exit. A grey-haired gentleman in his late fifties was standing near the main doors, holding a handwritten sign displaying his surname. He was immaculately attired in a dark blue double-breasted Gucci suit. He approached the gentleman and introduced himself.

'Good morning, Mr Shaw. I am Vincenzo. I hope you had a pleasant flight.'

'Yes, thank you,' replied Charles. Vincenzo helped Charles with his luggage, and they proceeded to the car, which was actually a stretch limousine.

The trip to Florence took nearly three hours and was uneventful. Apart from some light conversation which was difficult to have as he was sitting in the back, he spent most of his time looking at the scenery. Although the countryside was picturesque, Charles couldn't believe that majority of available land—whether it was farmland, empty lots, or people's gardens—was covered in grapevines. On one of their occasional discussions, Vincenzo confirmed that Italians were infatuated with their wine.

'We drink the most wine of any country in the world, around 100 litres per person per year. That is why we grow grapevines wherever we can.' Charles did the conversion so that he could understand the amount of wine Vincenzo was talking about. That was over twenty-five gallons per person—for every man, woman, or child—a year.

When they arrived in Florence, Vincenzo pulled up in front of the Palazzo Magnani Feroni. This was a sixteenth-century palace converted to a hotel around the early to mid-twentieth century. Two bellboys briskly walked out, took Charles's suitcases out of the trunk, and carried them into the hotel.

'I've been told that you have a meeting at the Gucci office at nine o'clock, Monday morning. I will collect you at eight thirty sharp. Although the office is only a short distance away, traffic can be, let's say, unpredictable. You don't want to arrive late and make a bad first impression.' Vincenzo chuckled.

After shaking hands, Charles walked into the hotel to check in. Once the bellboys were told the room number Charles would be staying in, they used the service elevator to carry Charles's luggage to his room. By the time Charles arrived at his room using one of the main elevators, the bellboys had placed the luggage on the bed and were standing on either side of the door, holding out his room key.

Charles knew that they were waiting for a tip and, reaching into his pocket, gave them a 5,000 lira note each, equivalent to around $3. The bellboys bowed, smiled, said 'grazie tanto' (meaning 'thank you so much'), and headed for the elevators.

Charles closed and locked the hotel-room door behind him, unpacked, laid out some casual clothes, and took a cold shower to freshen up. Although it was just afternoon in Florence, it was early morning at home. He couldn't try and take a nap now or he wouldn't get to sleep tonight and would suffer for it the next day.

After speaking with the hotel's concierge and given a map of the local area with some of the main attractions highlighted, Charles headed out on his own on this warm and bright summer's day.

He turned left on Via dei Serragli and arrived at the famous Arno River. He followed the Arno River along countless cafés and finally selected one to have a light lunch and a strong coffee. After downing his second cup of coffee, he crossed the river and headed to Il Duomo di Firenze Cathedral or Florence Cathedral, making note on which direction he had come from so he didn't get lost later.

He spent the afternoon in the confines of the cathedral, admiring its design, statues, and paintings. Although it was quiet in the cathedral with only a few sightseers spread out throughout its large interior, taking photos and reading the plaques, he was thankful that it was also cool. He didn't realise how tired and sleepy he was until he stepped out into the warm afternoon setting sun. This was going to be more difficult than he'd hoped. He had to last a few more hours before getting some needed sleep.

He headed back to the hotel and walked into the empty dining room. It was six in the evening, and diners wouldn't be arriving for at least another hour since Italians usually had late dinners. From a distance, the waiter gave Charles a questioning look before coming over. Charles asked for a table for one, and the waiter sat him on a small table along one of the sidewalls.

The waiter walked off to his serving station and returned with the dinner and wine menus and a carafe of water which he filled his glass with. Thankfully, the dinner menu was both in Italian and in English. He selected a plate of antipasto for the entrée, and gnocchi in a tomato and basil sauce for the main meal, but no dessert. He also asked for a glass of their red house wine.

The dinner was delicious, but now his eyes were drooping, and he was feeling lightheaded, possibly a combination of being overly tired and the glass of wine he'd had with dinner.

In his room, he took off his clothes, put on one of the complementary dressing gown, and went to the bathroom to splash some cold water on his face. '*One more hour*,' he says to himself.

He took out his meeting notes and sat on the bed to read them. Now he felt drunk and found it difficult to keep his eyes open. He looked at the alarm clock on the bedside table—thirty minutes had passed. Good enough. Charles threw his notes on the table, took off his dressing gown, got under the cool sheets, and closed his eyes.

Charles woke the next morning, feeling refreshed. He had slept ten hours straight and felt the better for it. He showered and dressed and went downstairs for breakfast with his notepad and map of Florence.

After breakfast, with his notepad and map in hand, Charles headed to the main shopping district. '*Time to investigate*,' he told himself. He roamed the major department stores and boutique shops, taking notes along the way. They displayed their merchandise and the marketing signs in and around these stores. Tourists flowed in and out of the stores, their purchases in bags showing the logo of the stores they were purchased from or the brand of goods they had purchased.

He finally found the Gucci outlet and went in. Although there were a number of customers in there, less of them were exiting with purchases. Again, he took notes on their layout and marketing signs. It felt old and stale. It didn't feel vibrant or inviting. Their range of product was extensive, but they were poorly displayed and not appealing.

One of the salespeople approached him and asked if they could be of some assistance. Although he had clothes for tomorrow's presentation, he might win some brownie points if he was wearing Gucci clothes. Charles asked to try on a formal suit and possibly an accompanying shirt, tie, and shoes. The assistant was pleased to help and—after looking him up and down, taking neck, shoulder, arm, waist, and leg measurements—proceeded to search though the various racks for the clothing he considered appropriate and retreated to the change rooms with a suit, shirt, and tie in hand. He returned empty-handed and asked Charles for his shoe size. After returning with a box of shoes, Charles followed the salesperson into the change rooms where he was shown into a cubicle containing the clothes the salesperson had previously selected.

Charles was surprised how accurately the salesperson had selected the size of clothes. The shirt, a light aqua colour, was well fitting and not too long in the sleeve length. The trousers slipped on easily, but they appeared too long. Once he put on the shoes the salesperson had selected however, the trouser length was perfect. He threaded the tie under the shirt collar, made a Half Windsor Knot, and tightened it in place. He slipped on the jacket which fell onto his shoulders with ease, and he could just see the shirtsleeves peeking from under the jacket sleeves. He tried to look at himself in the full-length mirror, but being a small change room, he felt as if he were looking down at the clothes because he was too close to view them properly.

He stepped out of the cubicle so he could see himself from a distance and met the salesperson who had selected his clothes. The salesperson stood back and looked at Charles with one eyebrow raised. He put his hand on Charles's shoulder and spun him around, stepped back, looked, and spun him back. He leaned forward, undid Charles's tie, and made a double Windsor knot with it.

After the salesperson brushed Charles's shoulders down with his hands, he led him to the end of the bank of change rooms where it was well lit and a larger wall mirror stood. The salesperson disappeared again and returned with a black braided belt that matched his black slip-on shoes. After fastening the belt, Charles stood in front of this mirror and examined himself. He was amazed. To think that this was an off-the-shelf suit that he didn't require fitting for was astonishing. The dark grey pinstripe suit complemented the shirt and tie perfectly. Even the swirl of burnt orange and marine blue on the tie matched without being garish.

'I'll take it,' said Charles without asking how much it was. The salesperson smiled and nodded solemnly. He led Charles back to the change room so that Charles could change back into his original clothes whilst he waited outside. Once Charles was back in his casual clothes, he handed the suit, shirt, tie, belt, and shoes to the salesperson and followed him to the sales counter.

After placing the suit in a suit cover, folding the shirt and tie, re-boxing the shoes along with the belt, the salesperson proceeded to write up the purchase and handed Charles the receipt. Wow. Charles tried not to appear alarmed at the total purchase price, and he believed he pulled it off.

Well, that's the most expensive purchase of clothes I'll ever make, thought Charles. Charles retrieved his wallet from his front trouser pocket and handed the salesperson his American Express card. He was once told by one of his colleagues not to have his wallet or other valuables in his back trouser or jacket pockets as they were easily stolen. Charles quickly learnt to always carry his wallet in his front trouser pocket, with his hand either in the same pocket or over it.

The salesperson produced a flatbed imprinter from under the counter, positioned the credit card on the imprinter, followed by a charge slip, before passing the handle over the charge slip and back again. The salesperson entered the purchase details on the slip before having Charles sign it. After confirming Charles's signature matched the signature appearing on the credit card, he handed Charles back his credit card along with the carbon copy of the charge slip, and the sale was complete.

Charles walked along the sidewalk, carrying his purchases with the Gucci logo like countless of other tourists with their purchases.

Like they say, 'when in Rome'. It must be the same for Florence, thought Charles.

That night, Charles again had an early dinner in the hotel dining room, getting the same questioning glance from the same waiter. He spent the rest of the evening reading the notes he had taken during the day's excursion and revising his notes for tomorrow's presentation.

The next morning, Charles had an early breakfast in his casual clothes, read his notes a final time, showered, and got dressed in his brand-new and expensive Gucci suit. That was the last thing he did before heading down to the foyer. It would have been devastating had Charles gone to breakfast in his new suit and had someone spill something on it.

Charles waited at the front of the hotel, holding his briefcase and portfolio. He was early. He was becoming nervous. If he managed to win Gucci's account, it would be a big feather in his hat. At exactly eight thirty in the morning, the long black limousine he remembered came around the corner.

'Good morning, Mr Shaw. I hope you had an enjoyable weekend,' enquired Vincenzo as he got out of the limousine. 'Would you like me to put your briefcase and package in the trunk?'

'No, thank you, Vincenzo. I'll hold onto them if you don't mind,' replied Charles as Vincenzo opened the back passenger door to let him in.

Once settled in the limousine and they were on their way to the office, Charles continued, 'I did a little sightseeing and a little shopping.'

'I see you've been to one our stores based on the suit you are wearing. It certainly makes you look very distinguished, and it fits you very well,' replied Vincenzo.

Although the traffic was quite congested, they arrived at the Gucci offices in fifteen minutes. The four-storey building was painted all in white and was quite old with intricate designs around the windows and doors.

As Charles stepped out of the limousine, a slender woman in her mid-fifties wearing a floral dress approached him. 'Hello, Mr Shaw.

I am Angelica, Mr Gucci's secretary. It is nice to finally meet you,' said Angelica as she put out her hand.

Shaking Angelica's hand, Charles replied, 'Hello, Angelica. It is nice to be here. What a wonderful building.'

'Yes, it is,' confirmed Angelica. 'The founder Guccio Gucci purchased it in 1936. The style, as we say in Italian, is called cinquecento, and it was built in the sixteenth century. Although the outside remains untouched, there have been considerable renovations to the inside. Shall we go in?'

Charles followed Angelica into the foyer or the main reception area. He could see the extent of the renovations. The foyer was a huge room with a patterned marble floor, and the height of the ceiling was the height of the building. All the rooms and floors above the space they were standing in had been removed, and a massive chandelier, possibly half the height of the room, was hanging from the ceiling. The most impressive feature, however, was the glass wall behind the reception desk. That was also the full height of the room, with a large courtyard behind. All the rooms and floors were on either side of the building as it was shaped like a 'C'.

He continued to follow Angelica to the lift on the left side of the foyer, and they proceeded to the top floor. They continued down the corridor until they reached a room with double doors. Charles could hear some form of argument coming from inside the room.

'Excuse me a moment,' said Angelica as she stepped into the room whilst he waited outside. There was silence. Angelica returned and invited Charles to enter. Surprisingly, she didn't follow him in.

As he opened the door, he could see four men and a woman sitting at a large boardroom table. He could also see the courtyard he had viewed from the foyer behind them. He recognised the man sitting to the left of the woman instantly. He was the grandson of the founder Guccio Gucci and now CEO of the company, Maurizio Gucci. The woman was stunning. She appeared to be in her mid-twenties, with red hair tied back in a bun, a tight-fitting plain black dress, and glasses with large frames that accentuated her eyes. The three men to the left of Maurizio did not appear to be pleased.

'Please be seated, Mr Shaw,' said Maurizio without an expression on his face as if it were made of stone.

Charles sat opposite the group, placing his portfolio on the table and his briefcase on the floor next to his feet. Maurizio turned to the three men to his left and said something to them in Italian Charles didn't understand.

He noticed the woman again. Her features were exceptional. She could have been a model. She smiled at him, and he looked away. Maurizio turned to the woman and spoke to her briefly in Italian. Charles thought that if he miraculously won this contract, he might have to learn Italian.

The woman turned to Charles and began to speak.

'Mr Maurizio Gucci would like to thank you for coming all this way to meet with him and hopes that you can help his company become a leader in the marketplace again,' she began.

Charles's eyes widened. The woman was speaking in English but not with an Italian accent. He guessed that she came from an Eastern Bloc country, and his best guess was that she was Russian. He couldn't understand why a Russian-born woman had learnt to speak English and Italian to become an Italian interpreter.

The woman continued, 'My name is Elizabeth Orlova, and I interpret for Mr Gucci when he meets special English-speaking clients from overseas. Although Mr Gucci understands English well, his English vocabulary is limited and wants to make sure that there is no misunderstanding during today's discussions. To the left of Mr Gucci are his three advertising advisors, Mr Michele, Mr Ferrozza, and Mr Antoni.'

Charles turned to the three gentlemen and nodded. They returned his nod with solemn expressions. It was clear that they didn't want to be in this meeting and appeared nervous. Charles wondered why he had been invited here to propose a marketing campaign when Mr Gucci employed advisors of his own. He assumed that they weren't the ones who had recommended him.

'I see you wear Gucci clothes. You like?' enquired Maurizio Gucci with a genuine smile on his face.

'Yes,' replied Charles. 'I acquired a taste for them just recently, and I am considering upgrading my wardrobe with more.'

'Mr Gucci has heard a lot of good things about your company and is interested in your ideas,' continued Elizabeth, 'and although you have come here at very short notice, he hopes that you have some fresh ideas on how to market his brand.'

'I am humbled that Mr Gucci has asked for my assistance,' replied Charles, 'and I hope that I don't disappoint him. I've created a small portfolio with some initial ideas and proposals. As long as he is aware that they are still in the development stage, they will hopefully show him the design and marketing ideas that I have in mind.'

'Please proceed, Mr Shaw,' said Elizabeth.

Charles stood, opened his portfolio, and took out his notes. Over the next three hours, he presented his ideas to the group. Apart for the occasional question raised by Maurizio, Charles did most of the talking. At the end of the three hours, Charles felt mentally drained and exhausted as if he had gone fifteen rounds with Muhammad Ali.

Charles looked at his audience and saw Elizabeth smiling. The three advisors, however, appeared concerned. Maurizio stood and approached Charles, with Elizabeth following, and shook Charles's hand with enthusiasm. Clearly, he appeared pleased.

Maurizio spoke to Charles in Italian with Elizabeth interpreting. 'Mr Gucci is very impressed with your presentation and is excited about your proposals. Mr Gucci would like to invite you to dinner tonight at his favourite restaurant where you can celebrate your . . .' Elizabeth paused trying to think of the appropriate word. 'Association,' she continued.

'You mean he's giving me the contract?' blurted Charles.

'Mr Gucci does not waste time making up his mind, and he was pleased with your presentation,' replied Elizabeth. 'Obviously, you will draw up your proposal formally when you return home, but if you can deliver on what you have presented, you will have a long-term relationship with Gucci.'

'Will you be coming to dinner with us Elizabeth?' enquired Charles nervously. That was the first time he had spoken her name, and he loved the way it sounded. Charles thought that he would have to learn to speak both Italian and Russian.

'Of course,' replied Elizabeth, smiling. 'I am Mr Gucci's interpreter.'

Charles thanked Maurizio and shook his hand. He walked over to the three advisors and shook their hands as well. When he came back to where Maurizio was standing, Elizabeth put out her hand, and Charles took it. It felt warm and soft, and he didn't want to let go. Elizabeth appeared to blush.

'I will see you both tonight then,' said Charles. Elizabeth nodded with a faint smile on her face.

The limousine took Charles back to the hotel and collected him promptly at seven that evening. Charles dressed casually with non-Gucci designer clothing. He thought it would be crass to wear the same suit he had worn during the presentation. Thankfully, Maurizio wore casual clothing as well, although they did appear to be from the Gucci collection. Elizabeth, on the other hand, looked beautiful in a red dress that followed the contours of her slender body.

Although there were some discussions about the Gucci design and marketing plans, Charles spent most of the time chatting with Elizabeth about how she came to be an Italian interpreter. Maurizio was quite content in just listening to the chatter whilst he enjoyed the wines of the region.

Charles allowed Maurizio to select the courses they would have so that he could taste traditional Florentine dishes which used ingredients from the surrounding countryside. Some of the ingredients, however, Charles would have never dreamt of eating. Each course they had was accompanied by a complementing wine, and he had to admit they were delicious. The entrée consisted of slices of toasted Tuscan bread covered in a liver pâté mixed with chopped anchovies, onions, and capers and accompanied by a Brunello red wine. Although Charles was a little squeamish about eating liver and anchovies, the first bite won him over.

Charles felt similarly squeamish with the main course which was *trippa alla fiorentina*, which was a tripe dish sautéed in olive oil, onions, and tomatoes, topped with grated parmesan cheese. This was accompanied by a Vernaccia white wine. Charles loved every mouthful.

Dessert was a sweet Florentine cake called *schiacciata fiorentina* accompanied by a glass of *vin santo*, being one of the region's dessert wines.

By the end of dessert, Charles was feeling the effects of the wine he had consumed, although not as much as Maurizio who had consumed more of the wine because each wine bottle from each of the courses remained on the table. They were enjoying each other's company.

Charles discovered that Elizabeth was indeed Russian, born in a little town called Alexandrov. She had learnt English there and moved to Italy when she was eighteen years old. There, she had taught English whilst learning Italian. She still taught English classes but was employed by Gucci part time as their interpreter. Charles learnt that Elizabeth was indeed twenty-five years old, and she wasn't married or in a relationship. Charles was relieved.

'So when are you leaving for home, Charles?' enquired Elizabeth. The formalities were discarded earlier on in the evening, and now they called each other by their first names, including Maurizio. Elizabeth, however, still addressed Maurizio as Mr Gucci since their relationship remained strictly professional.

'I'm supposed to fly back tomorrow night, although I wouldn't mind staying a little longer since I haven't had time to myself since I started my company,' replied Charles, with the exception of the time he had taken off when his parents had passed away, but that didn't count.

'Well,' said Elizabeth, 'I have no engagements for the next few days as Mr Gucci does not require me to interpret for him, and I'm sure I can postpone my teaching classes. I would be happy to show you around Florence and the surrounding towns if you like.'

Charles tried to keep his excitement from showing. 'I would love that,' said Charles. 'I'll reschedule my flights, and I'll see you in the morning.'

After some further small talk which included Maurizio, they said their farewells. Charles shook Elizabeth's hand, and although Charles wasn't sure whether it was a tradition or whether it was the amount of wine Maurizio had consumed, when Charles tried to take Maurizio's hand, Maurizio pulled him in and kissed him on both cheeks.

'Grazie, Charles, for coming. I hope we work well together. See you again soon,' said Maurizio.

That night, Charles had trouble getting to sleep. His mind was racing, and his heart was beating through his chest. He was feeling something unfamiliar. Was he falling for this woman?

He set the bedside alarm clock and got into bed, with sleep finally taking him.

Chapter 6

The next morning, he had a light breakfast, rang the airline to change his flight to Saturday, and then rang the office, telling them that he wouldn't be back until the following week.

As soon as he got off the phone, the phone rang.

'Hello?' said Charles.

'Good morning, Mr Shaw. This is reception. I have a Signorina Elizabeth here.'

'Thank you,' replied Charles. 'Tell her that I will be down promptly.' One thing they hadn't discussed last night was what time Elizabeth would be picking him up.

Elizabeth drove a small two-door Fiat, and she was a surprisingly good driver navigating the narrow, winding streets of Florence with ease until they reached the narrow, winding roads of the country side. They travelled though small towns, stopping whenever they saw something interesting and having lunch at a café that appealed to them before continuing on. That evening, they returned to Florence and had dinner at a restaurant she liked before she returned Charles to his hotel. She kissed him on either cheek like Maurizio had done, but this time, he enjoyed it as it didn't feel uncomfortable.

The next morning, they headed in a different direction and continued their tour of the countryside and towns. The kiss that night wasn't on the cheeks. Charles tasted Elizabeth's sweet lips for the first time.

On the third morning, they greeted each other with another passionate kiss, and whenever they stopped the car to investigate an interesting town or view an interesting feature, they did it hand in hand. At one point, she surprised Charles by turning off the main road and onto a dirt track. The track climbed and meandered up a hill until they reached the summit. She parked the car under a tree where they both got out. Elizabeth went to the trunk of the car and retrieved a cane basket and blanket. The basket was covered so he couldn't see in side, but he assumed it was a picnic basket. Charles helped Elizabeth by taking the basket by the handle and followed her. It felt surprisingly heavy. They walked a little way down the hill until Elizabeth found a reasonably flat area where Charles helped her lay out the blanket.

They sat on either side of the blanket as Elizabeth began unpacking the basket. It looked as if she had brought enough food to feed a village. She pulled out a loaf of crusty bread followed by a platter of cold meats such as salami, ham, prosciutto, and cured sausage which had been sliced into bite-sized pieces. The next platter contained a variety of sliced cheeses, olives—both green and black—and sundried tomatoes in olive oil. The next plate contained pastry parcels which had been deep-fried until they were golden brown, containing potato, beef mice, onions, and cheese, called knish in Russian.

But the basket was still not empty. This was followed by a large plate containing a whole chicken which had been opened and flattened so the outside of the chicken was on one side. It looked as if it had been either fried or grilled because he could see the char marks on the skin, and it was making his mouth water. The dish was called *tsiplonak tabaka* in Russian. Another plate was produced containing a round cake which had been pre-cut into wedges, called a honey cake or *medovik* in Russian. Thinly sliced layers of sweet cake with sour cream spread in between each layer. The last thing she pulled out of the basket was a bottle of white wine and two glasses.

Charles opened the bottle of wine and poured each of them a glass. Elizabeth was smiling as she tore off a piece of bread from the loaf and offered it to Charles, inviting him to eat. The food was delicious, and he had to pace himself, or he would find himself with a stomach-ache. They ate in silence, enjoying each other's company, looking over the picturesque valley below which was covered in grapevines as far as the eye could see. Being late summer, the leaves on the vines had colours ranging from green to gold to deep burgundy.

That night, having dinner at the restaurant in the hotel he was staying at, Charles finally asked Elizabeth on what she wanted in life.

'To be honest,' replied Elizabeth, 'I've never seriously thought about it. Although I like what I do, I have no plans for the future. I work not only for myself but also for my parents who still live in Russia. My mother is frail, but my father still works, although he makes little money. And I try to send them money as often as I can. With the breakup of the Soviet Union last year, work has become scarce, and everything has become very expensive. They have a small garden where they try and grow their own vegetables, and they even have chickens for their eggs and meat. But after paying their bills and taxes, they have little money for food or clothes. I've invited them to come to Italy and live with me, but they are stubborn.'

Charles thought about what to say next. He had to be tactful without being too forward and frightening her away. 'Elizabeth, I like you . . . I've become very fond of you, and I don't want to return home without telling you what I think of you. Although we've known each other for a short time, I want to see if there is something between us that will grow. Please forgive me if I am upsetting you, and you can tell me to stop this conversation right now.'

'Charles,' responded Elizabeth, 'I am happy that you feel that way about me as I feel the same way about you, but there are many obstacles that will make it difficult for any relationship to blossom. Firstly, you live in the USA, and I live here—I'm guessing over 10,000 kilometres away. I need to work not only to support myself but also to help my parents. You are a businessman who, I'm sure, is very busy with his company to spend time and money to travel between the two countries just to see me.'

'I would rather come and visit you than Maurizio Gucci,' said Charles jokingly. 'My company is doing well, and they can look after things if I want to take some time off. Obviously, I will need to be involved with this Gucci contract, but once I'm happy with what we design, and it's accepted by Maurizio Gucci, my designers can look after it from there. I would say that, within a month, I should be in a position to formally present my contract and proposal to Mr Gucci, and once that's accepted, I'll have the time to concentrate on us.'

Charles gathered his thoughts before he continued, 'Please don't take what I'm about to propose the wrong way. What you see is what you get. I'm not a crazy person, although crazy people say that they're not crazy anyway. The only way we're going to find out if we can have a life together is if we spend time getting to know each other in a normal environment. I mean what I say, and what I am about to say, I truly, truly mean. Come to Los Angeles and stay with me after I've finalised Gucci's contract. You can stay as little or as long as you want. If at any time you feel that this cannot be the life for you or I disappoint you, you can tell me that you want to go home. As for your parents, and this is what I'm worried about you being offended with, I would be happy to send them money whilst you are with me. Please say yes because I would be devastated if you refuse.'

'Oh, Charles,' replied Elizabeth with tears in her eyes. 'That would be wonderful. I care so much about my parents because they are the only family I have. I have no brothers or sisters, or any other relatives that are close. I would love to come and see your country, and I hope that you will see that I am also not crazy.'

They spent the rest of the evening further refining their plans, and when they finally said goodnight, Charles felt elated.

Elizabeth picked Charles up the next morning and drove him to the airport. Although Charles had travelled light, it was a squeeze trying to fit his luggage into the small Fiat. Standing at the departure gate, Charles held Elizabeth's face in his cupped hands and kissed her. He looked into her eyes which, he could see, were welling with tears and told her that he loved her for the first time. Elizabeth put her head on Charles's chest and squeezed him tight, sobbing, telling him that she loved him too.

On the long flight home, Charles sat at the window seat, looking out the window, thinking of the past few wonderful days he had spent with Elizabeth, remembering how she looked at the airport when he'd told her that he loved her. Tears began to run down his cheeks.

Chapter 7

The first morning back at the office after arriving back from Florence, everyone could see that Charles's demeanour had changed. He appeared jovial and excited. Everyone thought that it was because his meeting with Gucci had gone well, everyone except for Charles's secretary Linda, that is.

'OK, I assume everything went well with Gucci,' questioned Linda, 'but I have the feeling something else happened whilst you were there, especially when you rang the office, saying that you were going to stay in Florence a little longer.'

'Well,' replied Charles sheepishly, 'I . . . I met someone whilst I was there, and she might be coming over.'

'She must be someone special if she managed our workaholic boss to take a break?' enquired Linda.

'That, she is, Linda,' responded Charles.

Not wanting to pry too much, she let Charles be. If this mysterious woman did come, Linda would see for herself what type of woman had managed to steal Charles's heart.

The next few weeks were hectic at work, although Charles made time every day at noon to ring Elizabeth as it was evening time in Florence, and to update her on how things were progressing and, of course, to tell her that he loved her.

Charles had every available designer helping him with finalizing his formal proposal and contract so that it could be submitted to Gucci. Charles and his designers brainstormed his original notes and ideas, and by the end of four weeks, they had created an extensive design and marketing plan that even Charles was impressed with.

The contract was couriered to Gucci, and within one week, it was returned signed by Maurizio Gucci accompanied by a cheque covering the first year's design and marketing services.

Two weeks after the Gucci contract was signed, Elizabeth landed at Los Angeles International (LAX) Airport, flying first class. She was struggling with four large suitcases, trying to manoeuvre them through the arrival doors on a trolley.

'I didn't know how long I would be staying, so I thought I'd bring extra things just in case.' Elizabeth smirked. Thankfully, Charles had one of the company cars, so he was able to fit two of the suitcases in the trunk and two on the back seat.

'So how did your meeting with Maurizio go? What did you tell him?' enquired Charles.

'He knew,' relied Elizabeth. 'I had my story all made up about me going to visit my mother because she wasn't feeling well and that I would be sending one of my students to help with any translations he needed, but he knew where I was going. All he said was to make sure that you looked after and, if I wasn't happy, to let him know and he would send for me.'

'There's no chance of that happening. You're here to stay for as long as you want, and I'm sure that I'll be taking the very best of care of you,' stated Charles.

They arrived at the house—his parents' house. It was late afternoon. Charles had made room in the closet and the chest of drawers in the main bedroom for Elizabeth to unpack her clothes into.

'Charles?' bellowed Elizabeth as Charles was in the kitchen, preparing dinner. 'Sorry Charles, but it seems that there isn't enough room for my clothes,' continued Elizabeth when Charles entered the bedroom.

'You must have brought everything with you except the kitchen sink.' Charles chuckled. 'No problem. There's a closet you can use in my old bedroom.' Charles carried the final suitcase and placed it on his old bed. Once Elizabeth finished unpacking, she joined Charles in the kitchen. She noticed two pots on the stove, and Charles was cutting tomatoes and cucumber for a salad.

'Something smells good,' complimented Elizabeth.

'I thought that you might be too tired from your long trip to go out for dinner, so I thought we'd have a quiet dinner at home,' replied Charles. 'I'm sorry it's nothing fancy, but I hope it's passable, and I don't kill you with food poisoning on your first night here.'

Elizabeth giggled. 'If it tastes as good as it smells, I'm sure I'll enjoy it.'

Charles placed the last of the sliced cucumber in the salad bowl before returning to the stove. He lifted the lid on one of the pots and gave the contents a stir before taking a teaspoon from the drawer and tasting his tomato sauce creation. Charles nodded. He covered the pot and removed the lid from the second pot. Wafts of steam rose from the boiling water. After adding a generous amount of salt to the water and a little oil, he gave the water a stir before placing a packet of tagliatelle into the water and stirred it again until he was satisfied that the coils of tagliatelle had fully separated.

Elizabeth appeared amazed. 'You seem to know your way around the kitchen,' she complimented.

'I like cooking,' replied Charles, 'and I don't like going out for dinner alone. Usually, I make enough sauce for several meals and freeze them in single portions. On busy days at the office, I can thaw them out when I come home at night and make myself a quick and easy meal. The last thing I want to do is pick some fast food on the way home because I'd be the size of a barn in no time. I've got several different types of meals in the freezer so that I'm not eating the same thing every night.'

'My, you certainly are efficient,' commented Elizabeth.

'I have to be, running my own business and all,' replied Charles. 'I've learnt to be methodical, thorough, and disciplined.'

'Well,' returned Elizabeth, 'I hope I can make you let you hair down, so to speak, whilst I'm here.'

'No doubt you will, and I'd like that,' replied Charles.

They had an enjoyable dinner accompanied by a mild Californian red wine. Elizabeth commented on how delicious the sauce tasted, but by the end of the meal, tiredness had set in, and she began yawning.

'OK, time for bed,' said Charles. 'There're some clean towels in the linen cupboard next to the bathroom. You can take a nice warm shower whilst I clean up.'

Elizabeth came out of the shower, wearing a warm and fluffy dressing gown and a towel wrapped around her damp hair.

Charles was standing near the bed, holding his own bath towels. 'My turn,' he said.

'Charles,' started Elizabeth, 'I know this is awkward, but I need to explain something. I hope you're not offended.'

Charles looked puzzled.

'I've been brought up in a religious family,' continued Elizabeth, 'and even though I've lived in Italy for a few years, I've never been with a man. Sure, I've kissed a few whom I liked, but nothing more. I believe that the first time should be special with the man I truly love, the man I marry. I want to give myself to him wholly and completely. Please don't be angry.'

'Elizabeth, I love you,' replied Charles, 'and I'll hopefully show you that as time goes by. If our love grows together, then I am willing to wait until we do bond our love in marriage.'

Elizabeth's eyes were damp with tears. 'Oh, Charles, I so much love you, and I'm happy that you understand. I hope that you sweep me off my feet sooner rather than later.'

That night, they slept together. They kissed, and she slept in his arms.

Charles was up early whilst Elizabeth continued to sleep. He checked his emails to see if there was anything urgent he needed to attend. He'd given the responsibility to Linda, his secretary, to screen his emails and forward them to the appropriate department to action. It looked like she had. All the emails in his inbox had little forwarding arrows, confirming that she had sent them on.

Elizabeth walked out of the bedroom, stretching and yawning. 'That was a wonderful sleep,' she said. She came over and gave Charles a big kiss.

'Would you like me to make you some breakfast?' enquired Charles.

'No, I'm still quite full from last night's dinner,' replied Elizabeth, 'but I wouldn't mind a coffee.'

'Easily done,' said Charles.

Charles walked over to the refrigerator and retrieved a glass jar containing ground coffee beans. He took out a percolator from under the sink and unscrewed the top from the bottom. Elizabeth looked on in wonder. Charles filled the base of the percolator with water, inserted the strainer and filled that with ground coffee, and screwed on the top half. He placed the percolator on the stove and turned the gas on.

'You amaze me, Charles,' commented Elizabeth. 'Just when I thought I'd seen everything from you . . . I'm lost for words. I was expecting some instant rubbish, the stuff you get at a cheap restaurant. You must be part Italian?'

'No,' said Charles. 'I just like good coffee. I grind my own coffee beans and keep them in the refrigerator so they stay fresh.' Elizabeth chuckled.

Elizabeth and Charles arrived at his office where he introduced her to Linda. 'Linda,' said Charles, 'I'd like you to meet Elizabeth.'

'It's nice to meet you, Elizabeth,' replied Linda. 'Charles has told me nothing about you. He's been keeping you a secret from us all this time. I now know why. It's a pleasure to finally meet the woman who has transformed him into a boss we almost like working for.'

Charles looked at Linda sternly. Then they all laughed.

Charles proceeded to introduce Elizabeth to the remainder of the staff, all of them nodding their approval in Charles's choice. Elizabeth was shy but proud of the man she was becoming to know.

'So how are things going?' Charles asked Linda.

'Good,' she replied. 'It's been busy, but we're coping.'

'Great,' said Charles. 'I'm going to be showing Elizabeth around for a few days, but if there's something you need help with, please contact me.'

A few days turned into a few weeks as Charles and Elizabeth started with day trips around Los Angeles, and then they began travelling from the East Coast to the West and everywhere in between. They travelled to the Grand Canyon, Niagara Falls, the Statue of Liberty, the White House, Mount Rushmore; they even spent a few days in Las Vegas, although this was probably their least favourite destination. Although they were impressed with the various attractions each hotel offered, they didn't enjoy the hustle and bustle of the crowds which were out and about every minute of the day and night.

By the time they returned home, they were happy to be back and more relaxed in their own company. They appeared truly in love. Elizabeth was happy, and Charles had to finally decide on how to move forward.

They were preparing dinner on their second night back when Charles turned to Elizabeth, held her hands in his, and proposed. 'Elizabeth,' started Charles, 'never having done this before, all I can say is that I love you with all my heart and soul . . . Will you marry me?'

'Charles,' replied Elizabeth, 'I've knew that I would love you from the first time you entered Mr Gucci's office. You are mine, and I am yours. I would love to be your wife.'

With that, they kissed passionately and with fervour. Reluctantly, they separated and continued preparing their dinner, forming their plans to get married.

'I don't think we should stay here,' said Charles. 'I want to start our new life together in our own home, something we could grow in and maybe start a family.'

'You mean build something from scratch?' asked Elizabeth.

'Why not?' replied Charles. 'Something that represents us— obviously, we would be entertaining guests from time to time—but also something cosy that we could grow a family in.'

Chapter 8

The next day, with a map of the surrounding area around Los Angeles, they headed west along Highway 101, stopping at towns along the way to see what land was for sale. They found nothing that interested them until they reached Ventura. One of the real estate agents there was displaying a ten-acre block of land near Oak View overlooking Lake Casitas. After having a late lunch in one of the cafés there, they travelled up Santa Ana Road until they came across a small display board at the start of McPherson Way, advertising 'Land for Sale' with an arrow indicating the direction it was located. They travelled along McPherson Way until they came across a larger 'Land for Sale' sign. They parked the car on the shoulder of the road and walked past the sign, up a gradual incline to the summit. The view was breath-taking. They could see the lake below, glistening brightly in the afternoon sun. But behind and to either side of them, the land was covered in oaks and maples and gums. They instantly fell in love with the area.

'It is beautiful, Charles,' said Elizabeth, 'but isn't it too far for you to travel to work every day?'

'Nonsense,' retorted Charles jokingly. 'Los Angeles is only about sixty miles away. It would take maybe an hour or so to get there, and I wouldn't mind the drive if I was coming home to this, and to you of course. Remember, I'm the boss of my company, so I can be there anytime I want.' Now he was boasting. Elizabeth knew he was trying his hardest to convince her.

'But what about keeping special appointments that you can't miss?' questioned Elizabeth. 'There might be times you need to be there, and you can't rely on getting to work at the same time. What if there's an accident on the way or there's more traffic than usual?'

'That's easy,' replied Charles. 'We keep the house in Los Angeles. If I need to be at the office early or I have an important meeting, then I can stay in the old house the night before.'

Elizabeth was running out of excuses, and she did love the area. 'OK, let's do it. So what do we do now?'

'We go back to the estate agent and make them an offer they can't refuse,' replied Charles in a poor impersonation of Marlon Brando in *The Godfather*.

Elizabeth laughed.

Charles made no offer when they returned to Ventura and met with the estate agent. 'How much?' asked Charles.

'It's $500,000,' said the estate agent.

'Sold,' said Charles. 'Where do I sign?'

And that was it. Charles wired the money to the estate agent the next day, and the land was theirs.

Charles did some online investigations and found a reputable architect in Burbank. He made an appointment to see them that afternoon. With site plans in one hand and Elizabeth's hand in the other, they strode in and began discussions on building their new home.

Charles was surprised when Elizabeth took control after they had sat to discuss their new home with the architect Tom Arnolds who was one of the two partners of the firm. Elizabeth had been thinking on how the house should look like ever since they began their search. Charles smiled as Elizabeth described the types of features she wanted in the house to the architect.

'Tom,' said Charles, 'I want you to work with Elizabeth in designing the house she wants. Spare no expense unless she starts asking for gold fittings or diamond chandeliers.' They laughed.

The next day, Elizabeth drove to the architect's office, and Charles finally went back to work.

Over the next eight months, unless Elizabeth asked Charles for some advice on certain features she was considering, he left all the decision-making to her.

When he arrived home at nights, Elizabeth was usually happy and humming to herself whilst she was cooking dinner unless she had hit an obstacle she was nutting out with the architect.

There were days late in the project when Charles arrived home and Elizabeth wasn't there. She usually rang him, letting him know she was running late because of some catastrophe or another they were trying to fix on the house.

Charles never went to see how the house was progressing as it was being built. He trusted Elizabeth, and she was enjoying the challenge.

The day came when Elizabeth invited Charles to see the house for the first time. He was excited. She drove as she had done countless times over the past eight months.

As they drove along McPherson Way, Charles could see a white picket fence which he assumed was the border of their property. Halfway along the fence, they reached a driveway. To the right side of the fence, the letterbox appeared to be part of the fence itself. All he could see was a rectangle cut-out in the fence for letters and a circle cut-out alongside for papers. The number of their house was below the letterbox in shiny bronze: 47.

The driveway itself was made from finely crushed red scoria which meandered up the hill with small cherry blossom trees planted on either side, spaced every ten or fifteen feet. The driveway ended in a huge circle that you could easily turn the car in. On either side of the entrance were parking spaces for when they had guests.

The house itself was white render, with two square pillars supporting the extended ceiling jutting out to the driveway. Small lights were embedded in the ceiling, leading to the double front doors which appeared to be made of natural oak. The doors themselves had geometric shapes cut into the wood, each door having four rectangle cut-outs similar to the letterbox, one above the other, which had been filled with frosted glass.

The windows on either side of the house had similar oak frames, and he could see the shear curtains behind.

Elizabeth opened the doors, and Charles stepped inside.

It was a large open space in shades of cream and white. The floor was marble, and straight ahead was a wide spiral staircase leading to a second floor. The steps were also made of marble, and the handrails appeared to be oak. On the left side of the room were double doors leading the formal dining room which continued into the kitchen and laundry and returned to the main entry through a separate open doorway. The bathroom was to the left of the staircase, and to the right was the toilet, each of which you could access from behind the staircase which was not attached to the far wall. Further along the right were three more doors. One was a large lounge and theatre room, the next was a study and library, and the third was a gymnasium room.

Upstairs were four bedrooms, each with their own bathrooms as well as another study area.

Charles looked puzzled. Although he loved what Elizabeth had done as it was perfect for entertaining guests and holding functions, he didn't believe that it was something that Elizabeth would classify as a home.

Charles turned to face Elizabeth, but before he could ask a question, she placed her index finger to his lips and led him back outside. She walked round the car and got in. Charles followed and sat back in the passenger seat puzzled.

Elizabeth started the car and circled the car park to an ambiguous driveway to the right of the house. Charles hadn't noticed this driveway as they had approached the house. A lattice wall disguised the entrance. They travelled along the side of the house which lead to another entrance. This one wasn't fancy like the main one. Charles turned to Elizabeth with a beaming smile on his face. She nodded.

This side of the house was warm and inviting—no high ceilings or fancy appearance. Although everything was new, it was homely and welcoming. It wasn't sterile like the main house appeared. It had four bedrooms, three bathrooms, a lounge and a living area, and the kitchen doubled as a family room. There was even a study for Charles to work in.

'I love it,' said Charles as he picked up Elizabeth and spun her around. 'I love you.'

Elizabeth giggled. 'I hope you like what I've done.'

'It is nothing like I've seen before,' replied Charles. 'It's perfect.'

'The architect thought I was crazy when I proposed this,' said Elizabeth, 'but he liked it too once he saw how it was coming along.'

'What other surprises have you got up your sleeve?' asked Charles.

Elizabeth led Charles to the lounge room where she pointed to the far wall. He looked, but all he could see was that it was made of wood panelling. He looked closer and saw a small round handle. 'Pull it,' Elizabeth said.

Charles pulled on the handle, and a door miraculously opened. It was so well disguised that unless you knew that it was there, it would have been overlooked.

The door opened to the study and library room in the main house. 'Amazing' said Charles, 'so we can access the other side of the house if we need to.'

Elizabeth nodded.

'OK,' continued Charles, 'are these all the surprises you have, or are there more up your sleeve?'

Elizabeth led Charles back to the front of the small entrance where they proceeded further along the house and to the back.

There was a stable, although there weren't any horses yet. 'I thought we could buy some horses and go riding in the woods, maybe with the children or by ourselves,' said Elizabeth.

There was a boathouse, although it didn't house a boat. 'Since we're near a lake, I thought we could go sailing.'

'You've really thought of everything, haven't you?' questioned Charles. 'And I thought I was thorough and methodical. Finished with the surprises?'

'One more,' said Elizabeth.

They walked another twenty feet to where the treeline began, and Charles saw the faint outline of a roof in a small clearing ahead.

'No,' said Charles, not in anger but in amazement. The small cottage was self-contained with two small bedrooms, a combined kitchen, a lounge and a dining area, and amenities such as laundry, bathroom, and toilet.

'Let's just say that it's a home away from home, or for when we have friends who want to stay a while or when the kids want to leave home.' Elizabeth chuckled.

'I am absolutely amazed on what you've done and in such a short time,' said Charles. 'So how broke are we? Do I have to sell the business to pay for all this?'

'Not at all,' replied Elizabeth. 'You gave me a rough budget to work with, and I've maybe gone over it a little. The good thing is that I got a discount from the architect as I've given him some new ideas to use. I made sure that he gave it to me too.'

'I'm sure you did.' Charles chuckled.

There was one more surprise to come that both Charles and Elizabeth cooked up.

Chapter 9

After moving all their belongings into the new house and had settled in, Charles invited all his work colleagues for a housewarming party.

The Saturday of the party was finally here, and the guests started to arrive. Charles greeted them and showed them around the main house until they were all present. They were impressed.

'No thanks to me,' said Charles. 'What you see are all Elizabeth's ideas. I just paid for it.' They all laughed. He hadn't show the guests their little home behind the big house.

The waiters Charles had hired for this occasion walked around the room, offering hors d'oeuvres and drinks to the guests. Chefs were in the main kitchen, preparing dinner for them.

"So where is Elizabeth?' asked Linda.

'She's probably still getting dressed. Last time I saw her, she was a little nervous and not knowing what to wear,' replied Charles. 'I'll go and see how she's going.'

Fifteen minutes later, Charles came through the study, wearing a tuxedo complete with top hat and cane. He nodded to one of the waiters to turn off the piped music.

'Ladies and gentlemen!' yelled Charles so that the guests could hear him over the chatter. They all turned to face him, some laughing, others giggling. Charles didn't join their laughter.

'I'd like to thank you all for coming and be part of this special occasion,' continued Charles. 'I'm sorry, but I've invited you here on false pretences. Although I told you all that this was going to be a housewarming party, what you are about to be part of is . . . a wedding.'

There was silence and shock across the room. Then everyone looked at one another and cheered.

'I know this is short notice,' said Charles, 'but it seems that I'm short on people to help in the wedding. I've managed to drum up a bride to marry and a priest to marry us, but I need to find a couple more. Linda . . . would you mind being Elizabeth's bridesmaid?' Charles could see Linda had tears in her eyes. She looked genuinely happy for him.

Linda nodded. 'It would be my pleasure,' she said.

'And, Russell, you've been with me since the early beginning of this rollercoaster ride. It would honour me if you would be my best man,' said Charles.

'The honour would me mine,' replied Russell. Russell had been one of the first designers Charles had hired after starting his business.

Charles began walking directly across the room, followed by Linda and Russell, creating a clearing between the guests. Charles turned when he reached the other side of the room, with Linda on one side and Russell on the other.

Charles nodded to the same waiter who started the music again. This time, however, the song that played was Minnie Riperton's 'Loving You'.

Charles looked at the entrance to the study just in time to see Elizabeth step out in her flowing white dress and a veil covering her hair and face. She looked frail and alone. The priest stepped out beside her, took her elbow, and guided her towards Charles.

The moment, the music, his bride coming to meet him overflowed in Charles, and tears began running down his cheeks. In unison, the music ended, and Elizabeth arrived beside him. She looked into his eyes, lifted her white gloved hand, and wiped Charles's tears from his cheeks.

There was complete silence as the priest gave the sermon and finally pronounced them husband and wife.

The guests cheered loudly. The men rushed to Charles to shake his hand and give him a pat on the back; the women went to Elizabeth and hugged her and welcomed her into the extended family. And then they swapped. The women went to Charles and gave him a kiss and a hug. The men went to Elizabeth to shake her hand; the more adventurous ones kissed her on the cheek.

They all wined and dined the night away until the early hours of the morning. Eventually though, they all left. Charles was going to be up for a more expensive catering bill as the waiters had to stay back much later than planned. *But you're only here once,* Charles thought to himself.

Whilst Charles locked up the front of the house and turned off the lights, Elizabeth returned to their little hideaway. By the time Charles walked into their bedroom, Elizabeth was showering. Charles started removing his suit and was glad to do so. Wearing new clothes—especially the shoes—for such a long time, he could feel all the pressure points on his body, including his feet. Charles slipped on his robe as Elizabeth stepped out of the bathroom in her own robe, rubbing her hair in one of the towels to dry it.

Charles kissed her and stepped into the bathroom to shower as well. When he came out, Elizabeth was standing in the middle of the room, waiting for him. She looked excited but nervous. She was shivering although the room was warm. Charles knew that the time had come. He hadn't been with a woman for so long that he was worried that it would be over before it began.

Elizabeth untied the sash on her dressing gown and let it fall to the floor. *My god*, thought Charles. She was more beautiful than he'd ever imagined. Her breasts were perfect. They were pear-shaped, with the nipples in the centre of her areolas standing erect, something that a part of his own body was also beginning to do. She was truly a redhead. Her pubic hair, although not trimmed, was fine enough that he could see her labia. Charles did the same and disrobed. He could see Elizabeth's eyes slowly moving down his body to his now erect penis. Her eyes widened.

Charles stepped forward and kissed her. Elizabeth kissed him back with passion. He lifted her and placed her on the bed, sliding alongside her. He continued to kiss her on the lips and then her neck. He slowly travelled down and began kissing and licking her breasts, rolling his tongue around her nipples. Elizabeth began to moan and sigh. Charles could see goosebumps develop around her breasts. He cupped one of them and continued to kiss and lick around the areola before moving to the other. Elizabeth continued to moan and wriggle.

He moved further down, kissing her stomach and licking her belly button, and continued further still until he was just above her pubic hair. He plunged his face into her pubic hair and breathed in her slightly musky and sweet scent. There was also the faint hint of the perfume she had been wearing when he had stood beside her taking their vows. He manoeuvred his body as he continued to rub his face in that glorious mound until he was below her. He then placed his tongue on her labial lips and lightly licked the outer edges, encouraging her to bend her knees, which she obliged. He inserted his tongue deeper and began to lick the length of her labia from her anus to her pubic hair. Her moans increased, and she was shaking slightly. He continued to roll his tongue in and around her labia, and he could begin to taste her juices. He moved his hand and slowly inserted his index finger into her vagina whilst he continued to lick her.

He could feel her tense, so he stopped moving his finger whilst he continued to lick her. She relaxed, and his finger continued its journey in. This time, she moved forward to take his finger as he slowly gyrated it inside her. Her moans were now guttural as he removed his finger and replaced it with a second. This time, there was little resistance, and he began sliding his fingers in and out of her vagina. She began bucking and swaying, and Charles knew that his body wasn't going to last much longer.

He slowly moved his body up hers whilst he continued to lick her body back to where he had started from, and kissed her on her moaning lips. He looked down her body to where his penis was and slowly guided it into her. As she began to accept it, he continued to enter her until their pelvises were touching. He stayed unmoving for a moment, not just for her benefit but also for his. He knew that if he lost control now, it would be all over. He concentrated on kissing her as she moaned and kissed him back. He began with slow movements in and out whilst her face moved away from his, and she began licking his neck and biting his ear. He could feel her hot breath on his neck and her increasing moans in his ear. Charles's thrusts became more urgent, and she moved her hips to accommodate his thrusts until she screamed. Charles tensed and came deep in her for what seemed like an eternity. He rested on her body whilst he gathered his breath and emotions and then slowly raised his head, looking into Elizabeth's eyes.

She was panting, and her body was pulsating every few seconds. 'Oh, Charles, more please,' said Elizabeth.

Charles chuckled. 'I wish it were that easy. It's going to take a little time for me to . . . wake up again.'

Elizabeth faked a pout, jutting out her lower lip. He moved alongside her again, and they spoke about how well the wedding had gone and how surprised his colleagues had been. Elizabeth got up to get a glass of water and asked if Charles wanted one too. As she moved away from the bed naked, he saw her from behind for the first time. *Her body is perfect,* he thought.

She returned and slipped back into bed. 'Ah, Elizabeth,' said Charles, 'you know what I said about taking time to wake up?'

'Yes.' Elizabeth giggled.

'I'm awake,' said Charles.

This time, their lovemaking was slow and long and tender, and they tried several positions before Charles came inside her a second time. Elizabeth, on the other hand, made it more than several.

They slept soundly in each other's arms until late morning. Being Sunday, they had the whole day to themselves. They weren't expecting any visitors, so they made themselves breakfast in bed, but by the time they ate, it was actually early afternoon. They even had another lovemaking session encouraged by Elizabeth who wanted to learn the art quickly. Charles, apparently, was a good teacher.

At dinner that evening, Charles asked Elizabeth what her next project would be as Charles would be at work.

Whilst they were planning their surprise wedding, Charles and Elizabeth had discussed whether they wanted a honeymoon after the wedding, but Elizabeth said that she would rather spend time enjoying their new house and her new husband.

'Now that the house is finished,' started Elizabeth, 'I'm going to start on landscaping the garden. I've got a few ideas about planting an orchard and a vegetable garden.'

'Sounds interesting,' replied Charles. 'Need any help?'

'I'll be fine for now,' said Elizabeth, 'but I'll be counting on you when I need someone to dig some holes for me.'

With Charles throwing himself back into his work, which he had neglected for over a year now, Elizabeth spent her days visiting plant nurseries and selecting plants for the garden. Shaw Design and Marketing continued to thrive and expand, and Charles was happier than he'd ever been. Even his colleagues were amazed in his change, and the atmosphere in the office, although professional, was an enjoyable place to work.

Charles left for work early each day so the traffic on the road was tolerable, although it usually took him an hour-and-a-half commute time, but he never let it phase him. He knew he had a wonderful wife to come home to, and she was more than he'd ever dream of having.

The times he had to stay in the old house overnight because he had an urgent conference or meeting with important clients, Charles missed Elizabeth greatly. He rang her before going to sleep, wishing her a good night and telling her that he loved her. And he rang her in the morning before going to work, asking her how her sleep had been and telling her that he loved her.

The garden was slowly growing, and Charles spent most weekends with Elizabeth, digging holes for plants and trees she had selected. By the end of the first year, they had an orchard with numerous fruit trees thriving in the soil she had prepared for them. There were several varieties of apples, oranges, and mandarins. There were fig trees and apricot and cherry and peach and plum—

the list appeared endless. Elizabeth had even prepared four large plots to grow a myriad types of vegetables. *All we needed,* thought Charles, *are a few animals, and we won't need to go food shopping ever again.*

'You do know that there're only two of us here?' commented Charles to Elizabeth. 'We can't possibly eat everything you're growing.'

'Nonsense,' replied Elizabeth. 'I can preserve them so we can have them when they're not in season, and you can take some to work for your colleagues.'

'I can't see myself walking into the office with a bunch of celery in one hand and a basket of apples in the other,' retorted Charles, 'especially since I'm their boss.'

'You are their boss,' continued Elizabeth, 'but they're also our friends. Remember, they did come to our wedding.'

'I suppose,' said Charles reluctantly, as if he were a little kid who had been scolded by his mother.

Chapter 10

Life was good for Charles and Elizabeth. Whoever said that there was a short honeymoon period before the rut sets in didn't include the Shaw family. They did everything together when Charles wasn't working. Charles even accompanied Elizabeth on some of her shopping adventures, looking for new plants to plant in the garden. Their love for each other never diminished, and their lovemaking was always passionate and exciting. By the end of their first year, they even purchased two horses and went riding in the forest behind their property.

During the second year, Elizabeth went to visit her parents in Russia for a month whilst Charles continued to work. Over the month that Elizabeth was away, Charles missed her greatly and often wished that he had gone with her to meet her parents. But he rang her every day, sometimes two of three times, especially on weekends when he wasn't being kept busy with work. Charles was glad when she returned as he felt whole again, like a limb had been reattached.

By the end of the second year, however, Charles could see a little melancholy appearing in Elizabeth.

'What's wrong, honey? Are you OK?' asked Charles. 'Are your parents all right? Have I done something wrong?'

'No, my love,' responded Elizabeth. 'I thought by now that we'd have our first child, and I don't know why we haven't.'

'Let's go see the doctor and see what he says,' encouraged Charles.

They went to see Dr Rowlings. Dr Rowlings had operated on Charles's parents when they were involved in that horrific car accident, and although he had since retired from being a surgeon, he had opened a little clinic adjoining the LAC Medical Centre.

After conducting numerous bouts of testing, the doctor said they were both healthy and that there was no reason they couldn't have children.

'I've done every possible test on you both,' said the doctor, 'and you're both in excellent health. Your sperm count is normal, Charles, and they seem to be strong swimmers. And Elizabeth's ovaries are healthy and appear to be productive. Some couples have difficulty conceiving, but I see nothing in either of you that would suggest that you can't. We can look at artificial insemination, but I believe it's too early to consider that option. You can look at monitoring Elizabeth's body temperature during her menstrual cycle to determine the best time to have intercourse. Here is some literature describing various natural methods you can try to help you conceive.'

The doctor handed Charles and Elizabeth several pamphlets. 'See how you go,' concluded the doctor. 'And if you have no success, say, in the next twelve months, come back and see me, and we can look at more options.'

Charles and Elizabeth were encouraged, but they had no luck in conceiving over the next two years.

Charles noticed that Elizabeth was eating less and less, claiming she was full after only eating a small portion of here meals. She was spending less and less time in the garden and feeling fatigued most of the time. When she started feeling severe pains in her stomach, Charles decided it was time to revisit the doctor to see what was going on.

After Elizabeth endured more blood and urine tests, various ultrasounds, CAT scans, and MRI examinations which were repeated several times, the doctor called Charles and Elizabeth in to discuss the results.

'I'm sorry for putting you through so many tests, Elizabeth,' started the doctor, 'but we needed to be sure of the results. We've diagnosed that Elizabeth has epithelial ovarian cancer.'

Charles was devastated. 'What?' shrieked Charles. 'Why wasn't it diagnosed earlier?' Elizabeth looked withdrawn and was staring at the floor.

'Unfortunately,' started the doctor, 'this type of cancer is only noticeable after it spreads beyond the ovary or fallopian tube. The good thing is that we've caught it early enough, and we can treat it with surgery and chemotherapy quite successfully. The only complication we have is that Elizabeth is pregnant.'

Elizabeth raised her head and looked at the doctor. 'I'm having the baby,' she stated.

'But we need to treat you now Elizabeth,' replied the doctor, 'because it's going to give you the best chance of survival.'

'I'm still having my baby,' repeated Elizabeth. 'You can treat me after I have my baby.'

'But the chances of successfully treating the cancer will not be as favourable if we wait that long,' said the doctor. 'And besides, the baby may not survive anyway. It's going to be a great risk to both you and the foetus because we don't know how the cancer will affect the baby.'

'I don't care,' replied Elizabeth. 'We've tried so hard for the last four years to have a child, and I'm not going to kill it. It's mine . . . ours,' she corrected.

'Honey,' interjected Charles, 'you've got to listen to reason. You must have the treatment now. I don't want to lose you.'

'You won't lose me, Charles!' exclaimed Elizabeth. 'I have faith in God in keeping us both safe.'

Charles didn't want to argue about whether there was a God or if He was going to save her. She was stubborn, and he knew that he wouldn't be able to make her change her mind.

'I have to abide by your decision Elizabeth,' concluded the doctor, 'but I suggest that we monitor your condition and the condition of the foetus monthly. And if we detect any deterioration, we operate.'

'Agreed,' responded Elizabeth.

Monthly, Elizabeth visited the clinic and was thoroughly examined. Her child continued to grow in her body, and apart from nausea, Elizabeth exhibited no noticeable effects of the cancer. Her appetite returned since she was eating for two, and the times she didn't feel like eating, she forced herself to. Charles helped and supported her every step of the way, taking on the chores she could no longer do, even cooking and tending the garden. He fussed over her and made sure she was comfortable and did not overly exert herself.

On the sixth month of her labour, they moved into the old house so they could be close to the hospital, just in case there was an emergency.

She nearly reached full term before she started feeling contractions and her water broke.

It was a long and difficult labour, lasting nearly twenty hours, and Charles held his wife's hand and encouraged her until the baby came, and it appeared healthy.

'It's a boy!' exclaimed the doctor.

The nurse picked up the child, cleaned and weighed him, and checked for any abnormalities. 'He's a healthy six-pound, three-ounce baby boy!' exclaimed the nurse.

'Can I see him?' asked Elizabeth, raising her arms towards the nurse.

Wrapping the child in clean blankets, the nurse walked over and placed the bundle into Elizabeth's arms.

'Oh, he's beautiful, Charles.' Elizabeth chortled. Charles looked down at both of them with eyes welling, proud but frightened, frightened of what the future would bring.

'I know it's still early, but have you thought of a name for him?' asked the doctor.

'Chudo!' exclaimed Elizabeth.

'What?' questioned the doctor.

Charles knew that it was a Russian word. 'It means *miracle* in Russian, Doc,' explained Charles.

'What a fitting name,' replied the doctor.

Charles didn't have the heart to tell Elizabeth that they couldn't name their child Chudo. 'I think Chudo James Shaw has a nice ring to it,' continued Charles.

'I love it,' agreed Elizabeth.

The doctor agreed for Elizabeth to return home for a week to settle the baby in until she had to return to hospital to be operated on and have bouts of chemotherapy.

Charles visited Elizabeth in hospital with the baby every day for the six weeks she was there. He was forced to become a father quickly, looking after the baby by himself, feeding, washing, and changing nappies, but the baby thrived and gave Charles little trouble.

Once the doctor examined Elizabeth after being tested countless times, he gave her a clean bill of health, and Elizabeth returned home.

Apart from Elizabeth returning to the clinic every six months for a check-up and some tests to make sure there was no recurrence of the cancer, the Shaw family, including the baby, resumed their routine.

With fervour, Elizabeth returned to tending the garden and keeping house, accompanied by her baby, and Charles returned to work. She wasn't going to let Chudo out of her sight, and she would keep him safe because she was never going to conceive again. The doctor had decided to remove Elizabeth's ovaries and fallopian tubes to ensure her cancer didn't return.

In the beginning, the child was confused and frowned when his parents called his name. His mother called him Chudo, where his father called him James. When he was old enough, he realised that he had two first names and answered to both whenever his parents called him.

At three years of age, Chudo, or James, accompanied his mother to the clinic so that he could also be tested to make sure he didn't exhibit any signs of abnormalities.

They were the ideal family. Their love for one another was unreserved and endless. Once James was old enough, they took trips together during the holidays to places children enjoyed, such as Disney World, Universal Studios, New York Zoo, the Empire State Building, the San Diego Zoo, and the Statue of Liberty.

Although Charles and Elizabeth read English storybooks to James at bedtime, Elizabeth taught him a little Russian and Italian, and by the time he started school, James could speak basic Russian and Italian quite well. She thought that if he ever travelled overseas, speaking other languages might be an advantage.

James was a bright and intelligent child, and his grades reflected that. He enjoyed school and liked to read whenever he wasn't doing homework or chores given to him by his mother.

They finally bought a boat and sailed around Lake Casitas, exploring all the little estuaries. At the age of ten, they agreed that James was old enough to have his own horse and purchased a young filly which had been trained by its owner before they purchased her. They thought that James and the filly, which James named Sugar, would grow up together.

Chapter 11

Life was wonderful, and with Charles's company continuing to thrive, it paid for the luxuries they were enjoying.

James flourished at school, and all through his high school years, he was close to the top of his class in every subject.

The big house was regularly used to entertain Charles's guests and prospective clients from interstate and overseas, and on one occasion, Maurizio Gucci was the guest of honour. Charles was proud to present Maurizio to Elizabeth whom he hadn't seen since she had come over to America.

'Just as well you did,' replied Maurizio jokingly. 'Otherwise, you'd be swimming with the fishes.' They all laughed as Maurizio attempted to impersonate Marlon Brando in *The Godfather*. Looking around, Maurizio continued, 'So this is what you've done with my money.'

Unfortunately, life continues to disappoint us and prevents us enjoying life.

As James turned seventeen, Elizabeth's latest visit to the clinic identified some abnormalities in her blood. Dr Rowlings called Charles and Elizabeth to see him after receiving the latest test results.

'We've identified a few discrepancies in Elizabeth's blood sample that I want to keep an eye on,' started the doctor. 'Your platelet and neutrophil counts are below normal, and I am concerned that you may be susceptible to infection until we stabilise them.'

The doctor produced a copy of her latest blood test and showed them the results. 'As you can see,' continued the doctor, 'your platelet count should be between 150 and 450, but it's sitting on around 120, and your neutrophil count should range between 2 and 8, but it's reading around 1.7. What this means is that your immune system may find it difficult to cope if you, say, get a cold. Now, although the results are not dangerously low, I want Elizabeth to make sure that she's not placed in a situation where she comes into contact with someone or something that will jeopardise this. I also want Elizabeth to monitor her diet and minimise her intake of fatty or processed foods. Eat more leafy vegetables and vegetables that will help increase the platelets and neutrophil count such as beetroot and spinach. Red but lean meat is also good, even liver if you like it. Wash your hands thoroughly and more frequently, especially after handling anything. Don't handle any soil and stay away from animals.'

'You mean no more gardening or riding?' questioned Elizabeth.

'Absolutely not,' stated the doctor. 'Soil contains bacteria as do animals through their faeces, and they can lead to infections which your body may find difficult to attack. What I'd like is for Elizabeth to come in as soon as she can so we remove some of her bone marrow for examination.'

'What's caused this, Doc?' asked Charles.

'At this stage, I want to examine Elizabeth's bone marrow before I can determine a possible cause,' replied the doctor.

The next day, Charles and Elizabeth returned to the hospital for Elizabeth's bone marrow to be removed. Although it was a quick procedure, even with the local anaesthetic, it was quite painful.

When they returned to the doctor two days later, the diagnosis wasn't encouraging.

'What we believe Elizabeth has is myelodysplastic syndromes, or MDS for short,' said the doctor. 'What this means is that Elizabeth's bone marrow is not producing healthy blood cells, and the blood cells that she is producing are immature and weak. I'm hoping that by Elizabeth changing her diet and minimising her contact with germs and bacteria, the bone marrow will start producing healthy blood cells and her body start fighting infections. Now, Elizabeth, I'd like you to come in on a monthly basis and have blood tests done until we get this under control.'

'OK, Doc. What's caused this?' asked Charles again.

'MDS is very uncommon and something recently discovered,' replied the doctor. 'It appears to stem from the chemotherapy she had after treating her ovarian cancer. In a small number of patients, the chemotherapy affects the bone marrow. I'm sorry to say that MDS is considered a type of cancer. Unfortunately, it can't be treated with more chemotherapy. Look, we are getting ahead of ourselves at this stage. We can monitor her blood results and take action if it worsens.'

'But why can't we take action now rather than after she gets worse?' pleaded Charles. 'Isn't it better to help her now rather than later when her . . . platelet and neutrophil counts get too low?'

Elizabeth said nothing.

'There are two types of treatment we can try,' said the doctor. 'One is a blood transfusion, and the other—which is a more drastic option—is a bone marrow transplant. My concern is that the body may reject them or they may lower her immune system even more. I'll see if we have a close-enough match that we can try either one of these two options, but in the meantime, I'd like to see Elizabeth in a month's time after I have the results of her next blood test.'

Charles and Elizabeth returned home. James was withdrawn, and his mother sat with him, trying to lift his spirits.

'Mum, I'm worried about you. Are you going to . . . die?' asked James.

'Oh, Chudo, my sweet boy, my angel, of course I'm not going to die,' replied Elizabeth. 'I'm going to watch you grow up to be like your loving father.' She hugged him close and kissed his forehead.

Elizabeth's blood test results the following month showed that her platelet and neutrophil counts had dropped by another 20 per cent. The doctor hadn't found a suitable bone marrow donor, but he was prepared to give her a blood transfusion.

The following month, her blood test results indicated no further decline, but there was no improvement either. The doctor was concerned.

Over the course of the next month, Elizabeth began to feel lethargic and was constantly light-headed. She finally collapsed and had to be taken to the hospital by ambulance. 'We'll monitor her condition and give her a platelet transfusion,' said the doctor. 'Although it is a temporary solution, it may assist in improving her condition whilst I continue to try and find a bone marrow donor.'

Elizabeth stayed in hospital for a few days until she felt well enough to return home. In the meantime, Charles had decided to clean the house and minimise areas where Elizabeth would come into contact with germs and bacteria that might affect her immune system. He even gave away the horses and thoroughly cleaned the stables. Although James was devastated, he understood why his father was doing it.

Elizabeth returned home, appearing a lot better. She no longer had that pail complexion, but she did look frail. She was pampered by both Charles and James who were cooking all the meals for her. Even James was involved in the kitchen, taking after his father.

The garden, however, was neglected, with weeds starting to appear in the garden beds and vegetable garden. Some of the vegetables that should have been picked by now had begun to go to seed.

On a warm and sunny day, whilst Elizabeth sat on the back porch, drinking herbal tea that James had made for her, she had her husband and son on their hands and knees crawling around the garden beds and vegetable patches, pulling out all the weeds and removing all the now useless vegetables that were too old to eat.

Elizabeth's health was short-lived because within a couple of weeks, she began feeling lightheaded and started breaking out in cold sweats.

The next test results confirmed that her platelet and neutrophil counts had started dropping again. They were almost half below the minimum range.

'I still haven't been able to find a matching bone marrow donor, I'm afraid,' said the doctor. 'I've even tried to call in favours from hospitals I've helped, and I've extended my search to overseas. The thing is that being a bone marrow donor is something relatively new, and there aren't too many people on donor lists.'

'Do you think a bone marrow transplant would help?' questioned Charles.

'It would,' replied the doctor, 'but I don't know for how long. The body might accept the new bone marrow and start making healthy blood cells. I've spoken to countless of specialists in this field, both from the US and overseas, none of which had a positive solution. All they say is "you can try this" or "attempt that" but nothing definitive.'

'Can I be tested to see if I'm compatible?' asked Charles.

'There's no reason. Why not?' replied the doctor. 'But it's highly unlikely that you will be. I'll organise for you to be tested this afternoon if you like.' The doctor rang through to pathology, informing them that a Charles Shaw would be arriving shortly for a bone marrow extraction and analysis. 'You're all set,' concluded the doctor.

'What about Elizabeth's parents?' asked Charles. 'They would certainly be compatible. I'd be quite happy to fly them over and be tested.'

'They would have a better chance, I'll admit, as long as they're healthy,' agreed the doctor. 'They wouldn't have to come here to be tested though. They can be tested in one of the hospitals there as long as they had a pathology department. How old are your parents, Elizabeth?'

'My mother is in her late sixties, but she's very frail. My father is seventy-five, but he still works,' replied Elizabeth, trying to appear positive.

'Then we have a problem,' said the doctor. 'We've had no success when the donor has been over sixty, sixty-five. Is there anyone else?'

'I don't have any other relatives, I'm afraid,' said Elizabeth.

'What about James?' jumped in Charles.

'No! Absolutely not,' said Elizabeth. 'I don't want my son to be subjected to this ordeal.'

'But if there's a chance,' started Charles before Elizabeth jumped in.

'Charles, no. I won't have it,' she concluded.

Charles was distraught, but he had to abide by her wishes. The only hope there was, was for him to be a match or the doctor finding a miraculous donor.

Disappointingly, Charles's bone marrow results weren't a match.

Elizabeth's condition rapidly deteriorated, and she was admitted to the hospital by ambulance again. She was placed on a ventilator fed by oxygen. Her breathing was laboured, and she had a white and pasty complexion.

'I'm sorry, Charles,' said the doctor, 'but there's nothing more that we can do other than trying to keep her comfortable.'

Charles said nothing. He had been beaten down, and he didn't know how to fight anymore. James sat in one of the waiting room chairs, crying.

Elizabeth turned to Charles and said, 'Take me home, my love, one more time.'

She was driven home by ambulance. Charles and James stood on either side of the front door as she was wheeled in by the two paramedics. Elizabeth reached for James as she passed him, and he followed her through accompanied by his father.

The paramedics gently placed Elizabeth on the bed and reattached the ventilator around her nose and mouth, connected to an oxygen bottle sitting on the floor by the bed.

After the paramedics had left, Elizabeth asked to speak with James alone for a minute and Charles stepped out of the room.

'Come sit beside me, my little rabbit,' said Elizabeth.

James sat on the edge of the bed, facing her, and she took his hand.

'I'm sorry, Chudo, for not being strong enough, but your father loves you and will take very good care of you. Although I won't be here, I'll still be looking over you, making sure you're safe. God wants me with him before I wanted to go.'

James was looking down at their joined hands, crying. 'I love you, Mum. Please don't go.'

'Oh, Chudo, I'm sorry, but I have to,' Elizabeth replied. 'Just remember all the happy and wonderful times we've shared together. Be happy that our life has always been filled with love, and think of those times when you're feeling sad.'

Charles made sure that James ate his dinner, and although he himself didn't feel like eating, he forced himself to eat as well.

James said goodnight to his mother and gave his mother a big kiss and hug before going to bed.

Charles locked up the house before lying beside his wife. He looked into her eyes with tears running down his face.

'I'm sorry, my love, for being a burden,' she began, 'for leaving you with so many things undone.'

'You've never been a burden,' replied Charles with a tight throat. 'You're the one who's given me strength and courage. You've shown me love that I would never have imagined. My life was empty before I met you.'

James had moved into the spare bedroom next to his mother's room and lay on the bed so that he could be close to her. He could hear his father and mother talking, although he couldn't make out their words. His mother sounded calm, but his father's words came out in sobs.

'Oh dear,' said Elizabeth, 'it looks like it's time to go.' With that, she closed her eyes, and she was gone.

James could hear his father crying, but he couldn't hear his mother anymore. James placed his face into the pillow and began crying too.

Sometime later, Charles stepped out of the bedroom in search of his son. He found him in the spare bedroom, still crying. Charles went over and held him for what seemed like an eternity until both their sobs subsided.

'Do you want to say goodbye to your mum?' asked Charles.

'No,' said James, 'I don't want the last memory of her being like that.'

Chapter 12

The funeral was sombre, and only a small number of mourners attended, including Charles's work colleagues, close friends, and Dr Rowlings.

Charles looked across the gardens before the burial and saw a short stocky man with short-cropped grey hair and moustache walking towards the group. His suit was dark and well worn. The man stopped when he saw Charles, holding what appeared to be a beret in his hands in front of him. Although Charles had only seen this man in photos, he knew exactly who he was. Charles rushed over and hugged him as they cried in each other's shoulders, one for the loss of his only child and the other for his wife.

Charles had forgotten that he'd sent Elizabeth's parents a Russian-translated note about the passing of their daughter and money for plane tickets. Alexander only stayed for the service and returned home to his wife Irina that afternoon.

The house was quiet with only the two of them. Charles and James spent very little time together, each mourning in their own way. James spent most his time in his room, either reading or doing his homework. Charles spent all his time in the study, doing very little. He just looked at the photos they had taken together, all of which he had uploaded onto his computer or watched videos taken during their many trips.

The only time they spent any time together was during dinner which Charles forced himself to prepare. Charles showed no emotions and appeared to be always looking into the distance. He did things in pilot mode as if he no longer cared. The times that Charles did go to work, everyone kept clear of him because they didn't want to tell him how sorry they felt for him. Even Linda avoided him. Charles just sat in the office, gazing out the window.

With James's eighteenth birthday approaching, Charles's attitude appeared to change. He tried to joke with James to lift his mood. They went fishing or boating together and, since they no longer had the horses, went hiking behind the house.

Charles told James that he could use the large house for his eighteenth birthday party and invite all the friends he wanted. James was relieved that his father had finally come out of his melancholy state and treated him like a son again.

Charles and James went shopping together several days before the party and purchased streamers, balloons, and signs and, of course, ordered the birthday cake.

They decorated the entry room the night before the party, both giggling as they tried to blow up the balloons before hanging them up. It was the first time they had really laughed together.

The caterers arrived the morning of the party to set out tables and prepare the snacks to serve, whilst Charles went to collect the cake. Just before noon, the DJ arrived, and the party was ready to go.

The guests started arriving at one in the afternoon, filling up the parking spaces and most of the way along the drive.

The waiters walked around the room, offering snacks and various types of soft drinks to the guests whilst the 'now music' teenagers enjoyed played in the background all through the afternoon. James seemed to be happy as he walked around, talking to his friends and opening the presents they had brought. He was constantly surrounded by girls and not always the same ones, so Charles assumed that James must have been popular at school.

The cake was finally rolled in with eighteen burning candles, and everyone sang 'Happy Birthday' to James as he promptly blew the candles out.

Charles stepped forward and made a speech, thanking everyone for coming and hoping they were all enjoying themselves.

'James,' said his father, 'you've been the joy of my life ever since you were born, and I couldn't be more happy and proud of the man you've become. I know things have been hard for you lately, and I hope this small gift will show how much I love you.'

Charles handed James a small box wrapped and tied up in a bow. James looked at the box and gave it a shake. Nothing. It felt light in his hand. He pulled on the bow and lifted the lid. All he could see was tissue paper. He lifted the tissue paper and felt something inside. Placing the empty box on the table next to the cake, he unwrapped the paper and found a key with three letters stamped on the leather key ring: 'BMW'.

'Take a look outside,' said Charles.

Somehow, someone had put a car directly in front of the main door whilst everyone was singing 'Happy Birthday'.

It was a brand-new metallic blue BMW M4 convertible.

'Gee, thanks, Dad,' said James, and although he was eighteen and in front of his peers, he hugged his dad and kissed him on the cheek. James jumped into the driver's seat and loudly revved the engine whilst his young guests cheered and whistled.

The party continued for several more hours before the guests started leaving.

That night, Charles and James had a light dinner since they'd been snacking and drinking all afternoon before saying goodnight and going to bed.

It was Sunday morning, and the house was quiet when James got up. He went to his father's bedroom, but it looked like he'd already gotten up, so he went to see if he'd gone out. His father's car was still in the driveway, so he checked the kitchen. Nothing.

'Dad!' he yelled. Nothing. He checked the rest of the house. Nothing. James opened the secret door in the study and walked through to the big house and called his name again.

'DAD!' Nothing. He stepped outside and looked around whilst walking the perimeter of the house. He wasn't in the orchard or the vegetable garden. He continued round the back and proceeded to the small cottage. Nothing.

James was puzzled. *Maybe he's gone for a walk,* he thought. He started walking back to the house and checked the boat shed. Nothing. He opened the door to the stable . . . there he was.

Charles was hanging from one of the rafters with a noose around his neck. 'NO!' yelled James. He froze before running into the stable and tried to lift his father's lifeless body so that the strain was not on his neck, but his father was too heavy, and James knew it was too late.

James sat on the floor under his swaying father and cried.

He returned to the house and dialled 911.

When the ambulance and police arrived, they went to the back of the house whilst James stayed in the kitchen, sitting on the table with his hands clasped together, fingers overlapping in front of him.

One of the police officers returned and handed James a letter addressed to him they'd found on the floor next to his father. James set it on the table.

'What happens now?' asks James, expressionless.

'We'll take your dad back to the morgue and have him examined to determine the cause of death,' the officer replied.

'Clearly, he's hung himself,' retorted James.

'I understand, Son, but he needs to be examined to see if there are other factors, such as whether he had been drinking or taking drugs so that a formal cause is recorded,' continued the officer.

James felt nothing. He had no idea on what to do next. He waited until the ambulance and the police left before he opened the letter with contempt.

My son James,

I know you hate me for what I've done, and I don't blame you. After my parents died in a horrific accident, my loss was so great that it took me until I met your mother before I thought life was worth living again. She was the keystone that made my life whole. I loved your mother with all my heart and soul as I do you. Your mother was my soulmate and thought that we would live a long and happy life together, even after you had left and started your own life. When she passed away, I didn't feel that I could start again. I was completely crushed, and I had nothing left to give. I couldn't see a life ahead for me without her. I hope one day you'll understand and forgive me.

Although I know you're feeling the pain and loss of your mother and probably nothing for me, I believe you're strong enough to live a long and happy life. I've made sure you're looked after and there is enough for you to live comfortably. Please contact Tim Larson who holds my will, and he will guide you. I've known him for a long time, and he will help in any way he can. His phone number is in the cardholder in the study.

I hope you'll have the heart to forgive me because what I've done is not because of you. I love you with all my heart, and I know you have the courage to get over this terrible time that I've made for you.

Your loving father

James tore up the letter and threw it in the bin.

He walked to the study, sat in his father's chair, and searched through the business cards which were in alphabetical order. He found Tim Larson's card and dialled the office number appearing on it.

'Hello, Mr Larson. This is James Shaw,' said James.

'Oh, hello, James,' said Tim, surprised. 'What can I do for you?'

'I found my father dead in the stable this morning, and I read the letter my father left to ring you,' continued James with no emotion.

'Oh my god, I'm sorry to hear that. Please accept my deepest condolences. I've known your father for a long time, and I wouldn't have expected him to do something like this,' said Tim.

'Well, he did,' stated James. 'When can I come in to see you?'

'Ah, anytime this afternoon if you have the time,' replied Tim.

'I'll be over at two. Goodbye, Mr Larson,' concluded James and hung up the phone before Tim could reply.

James sat in Tim Larson's office, showing no expression whilst Tim read out the will. His father had left him everything, including the house his mother had built, his father's old house, and his father's company, along with a bank account holding nearly $6 million. There was, however, one exception—a small monthly payment of $5,000 payable to his mother's parents.

What the hell am I going to do with a designing firm? thought James.

'There's no stipulation on when you can access the money in the will or what you can do with the houses or company, so you can decide whatever you want at any time,' said Tim.

'I want to sell my father's old house because I certainly don't need two,' started James, 'but I have no idea on what to do with Shaw Design and Marketing.'

'I can help in selling the house for you,' replied Tim. 'And as for the company, it appears to be going quite well, so I suggest you don't do anything with it. Do you have any inclination in running it?'

'Not at all,' said James. 'I wouldn't know the first thing to do, and it's nothing I want to learn.'

'Then I suggest you allocate a CEO to run it and maybe create a board in the decision-making of the company. They can run the company and just pay you a percentage of the profits,' suggested Tim.

'Is that something you can do for me because I don't feel like facing anyone there?' asked James. 'And I wouldn't know what to say to them.'

'I believe I can arrange something,' replied Tim. 'I know someone who's had experience in these types of things if you want me to proceed.'

'I trust you, Mr Lawson. Please proceed,' continued James.

'All I need is your signature and date on each page of the will, and we're done,' concluded Tim. 'There is something else you need to consider though. What about your father's funeral?' he asked.

'I know I've asked a lot of you already, but can you arrange that too?' James asked.

'I can arrange that,' replied Tim. 'Do you have any preference on how . . . what type of service you want for him?'

'No, whatever you believe would be fitting,' said James.

After James signed the will and was given a copy, he left.

James stood outside Tim Larson's office, looking up and down the street. *'What the hell do I do now?'* mumbled James to himself.

He drove back to the house and prepared himself a meal.

James returned to school and avoided talking about his father to anyone.

His father was buried a few days later, and although Charles's colleagues and friends attended, James didn't go.

James finished high school. His grades had declined, but he had passed all his subjects. James had made no arrangements about going to university. He was going to have some time off before considering what he was going to do with his life.

Chapter 13

The phone rang. James sat in his favourite chair and let it ring. He thought it's probably someone who wanted to offer him a better phone deal, cheap life insurance, better mortgage rates, or funeral insurance. He has disconnected the answering machine so that they don't leave messages. The phone continued to ring. He knew that after around ten rings, they usually gave up and hung up. He turned to face the phone as it continued to ring. They seemed persistent.
It must be twenty rings by now, thought James. James stared at the phone, pleading for it to stop. Thirty rings. He leaned over and picked up the receiver. 'Hello?'

'Ah good, I'm glad you're home. Hi, James, this is Dr Rowlings. Just ringing up to see how you are since . . .' There was a long pause before the doctor continued, 'Since you were here last and to let you know that you are overdue for your routine check-up.'

I know what you were going to say, thought James, *since your mom died of cancer and your dad killed himself.* James knew he was being sarcastic. The doctor had looked after his mother during her long illness, and James had seen the doctor every six months since he was three to have blood tests done and make sure his mother's illness wasn't hereditary. The doctor had spent a lot of time at the house during the final stages of his mum's cancer, making sure she was comfortable and not in too much pain.

'I was in the bathroom,' lied James.

'No problem,' replied the doctor. 'I was wondering if you'd like to make an appointment to see me since it's been over twelve months since your last examination.'

'I don't know,' said James. 'I'm pretty busy at the moment, you know, with . . . things.'

'James,' said the doctor sternly, 'I promised your mother that I would look out for you, and it's important that we test you regularly. It's not going to take too long, so please say yes.'

'OK,' responded James. 'When can I come in?'

'Any time you like, the sooner the better. I'm sure I can fit you in whenever you can make it,' answered the doctor.

'I can make it tomorrow around three if that's all right,' said James.

'Perfect,' answered the doctor. 'See you then.'

James arrived at the doctor's office just after three. The waiting room was quite full. He approached the reception desk and introduced himself although he knew the receptionist Jane very well. Apart from being the receptionist, Jane was also the nurse who had taken James's blood for analysis for as long as he could remember.

'Thanks, James,' said the receptionist. 'I'll let the doctor know you're here. Please take a seat. Dr Rowlings won't be too long.'

Sure enough, within five minutes, Dr Rowlings strode out of this office and called James in.

James walked into the doctor's office and sat on one of the two patient chairs. Rather than the doctor sitting in his own chair, he turned the second patient chair to face James and sat a couple of feet away so that it didn't appear that he was encroaching on James's personal space.

'So how are you going, James?' started the doctor.

'You know, Doc . . . pretty lousy sometimes,' replied James.

'James,' responded the doctor gently, 'I'm here anytime you want or need to talk. You've got my mobile and home phone numbers so you can ring me anytime, day or night. I cared a lot for your mother, and I care the same for you, so don't be too shy to ring me, even just for a chat.'

James's eyes began to well up. He was leaning forward, with his elbows on his knees, looking at the floor. 'I can't take it anymore. I miss my mom . . . and dad, although I hate him for what he did. I've got no one, and I sometimes wonder . . . what's the point in life?'

'I know it's hard, Son,' said the doctor. 'I can't imagine how you're feeling right now. All I can tell you is that it does get easier. It's OK to grieve. It's healthy to grieve as long as you don't let it overpower you. I'll try and help you anyway I can. You don't have to do this alone. I'm here any time you need me. I'm quite happy to come over and spend some time with you in the evenings. We can even have dinner together. To tell you the truth, I'm not a bad cook.'

The doctor tried to lighten the mood, but James continued to look at the floor, wiping his tears with the back of his hand, continuously sniffing back the mucus that was welling up in his nose. The doctor leaned over his desk, picked up a box of tissues, and offered them to James. James plucked out one of the tissues and loudly blew his nose. He scrunched the tissue into a ball and plucked another tissue to wipe his eyes and scrunched that one up as well into his closed fist.

'I want you to be frank with me, James,' said the doctor. 'I'm not here to judge you. Have you had any bad thoughts?'

'When I'm not keeping my mind active, I do think sometimes that Dad was right in doing what he did. Then there won't be any more pain or sorrow or loss.' James was sobbing, and tears began streaming down his face again.

'Have you had thoughts of . . . suicide?' questioned the doctor.

'I have,' whimpered James, 'all the time.'

The doctor was becoming more concerned. 'Want kind of thoughts, James? How were you planning to do it?'

'You name it,' bawled James, looking at the doctor with tears running down his cheeks. 'I've thought about hanging myself, shooting myself, running a tube from the car exhaust into the car, driving headlong into a tree, drowning, electrocution—you name it, I've thought about it.'

'What's stopped you?' questioned the doctor.

'Because I'm gutless,' answered James. 'I'm afraid that if I do it wrong, then I'll still be here and maybe be a vegetable or, worse, still with my mind intact but not being able to do anything.'

'James,' said the doctor, 'what your father did was wrong. He took the easy way out and left you all alone. He should be here grieving with you about losing your mother. You should both be helping each other, supporting each other, loving each other so that the pain could be shared, and help each other accept the loss and move forward.

'Now there's a couple of things I'm going to suggest for you. One is that I would like to refer you to a support councillor. She is very good, and I've known her for a long time. She actually lives in Oak View, not far from where you are, so you wouldn't have to travel too far, and she works out of her home. She is a kind and caring person and has helped many people in your situation.

'The second thing I'd like to propose is to put you on some mild antidepressants. They will help stabilise your mood so that it doesn't get too low, as well as helping you sleep. The only thing with issuing antidepressants is that you will need to take a drug and alcohol test, something the government has decided to introduce so that they are not prescribed to those who will abuse them. Anyway, since you're going to have your normal blood test today, you'll just have to pee in a cup for me as well. I'll just write up the script so that Jane knows what I've asked for. Whilst you're having the tests done, I'll ring the councillor and see when she can see you. I think the sooner the better. Are you OK to see her tomorrow if I can get you in?'

'Sure,' replied James as the doctor wrote up the script.

'Great,' said the doctor. 'Give this to Jane, and I'll see you in a little while.'

As James re-entered the waiting room, he saw that there were very few people waiting to see the doctor. He couldn't understand how this could be since Dr Rowlings was the only doctor practicing here unless that had changed since he was here last.

'You got something for me, James?' asked the nurse. James handed Jane his script as they proceeded into another private room.

'What happened to the people waiting?' enquired James as he sat in his usual chair.

'I thought you might be in with Dr Rowlings for a while, so I've rescheduled some of their appointments,' replied Jane. 'Now let's see what he's written here,' continued Jane as she read the additional notes the doctor had made.

She looked puzzled. She picked up the phone and rang the doctor's extension. 'Hi, Dr Rowlings. I see here that you've asked for James to also have a drug and alcohol test. Do you want the test supervised or unsupervised?' There was a pause as she listened to the doctor's response, 'OK, no problem.'

Jane asked James to recite his full name, address, and date of birth as he had done countless times before as part of the verification process. She nodded and began placing the tourniquet around James's arm about four inches above his elbow.

'What does supervised and unsupervised mean?' asked James, as Jane tightened the tourniquet.

'Well,' replied Jane, 'all that means is that if it's a supervised test, I have to watch you pee into the cup, something that I don't like doing as I feel I'm intruding. This only happens when there is a dispute with someone's previous test results, and they want an independent analysis made. It's to show that the sample did come from the person being tested and not from someone else. Thank goodness, I've only had to see that a few times. It's uncomfortable for both me and the patient, especially if he's a male. Unsupervised means that I give you the empty cup and you bring it back full, without me following you.'

'What sort of test did the doctor ask for?' stuttered James.

'Unsupervised.' Jane giggled. James let out a sigh of relief.

Jane proceeded to retrieve several glass tubes, a needle, and a sachet containing the alcohol swab. Once everything was prepared, Jane put on a clean pair of disposable rubber gloves and disinfected the area where she would draw the blood from. Within a minute,

Jane had the needle in, the tubes full of James's blood, tourniquet off, and gauze over the puncture. To say she was efficient was an understatement. Whilst James applied pressure over the gauze, Jane filled in the details on the glass tubes full of his blood.

Jane removed her disposable rubber gloves and handed James a plastic cup with a lid, a sealable plastic bag, and a sachet. James looked at her with a puzzled look.

'I gather you haven't done this before,' said Jane. James shook his head.

'When you get to the toilet,' started Jane, 'unscrew the lid off the plastic cup and place it on the sink, near enough to get to whilst you are standing over the toilet. Remove the swab from the sachet and wipe the head of your willy to disinfect it. You start peeing in the toilet and, halfway through, stop and get the plastic cup. Pee into the cup until its half-full and stop. Try not to fill it to the top. Put the cup onto the sink without spilling it and finish your pee. Screw the cap back onto the cup. Make sure the lid is tight and on right. Put the cup into the plastic bag and seal it. Clean up and bring the cup back to me. That's it . . . easy.'

James looked like a rabbit caught in headlights. Jane put her hand behind James's back and ushered him to the office door. 'You'll do fine. Once you're there and ready to pee, you'll know what to do. Trust me.'

Five minutes later, James was back with the half-filled cup in the plastic bag which he handed to Jane. Jane removed the cup from the bag and placed a plastic seal over the cap and over the sides of the cup. 'This is to make sure the sample is not tampered with before it's examined,' explained Jane. 'All I need from you is your signature on this form, acknowledging that the sample is yours and that it was sealed in your presence.'

After James signed the form, Jane completed the paperwork and asked him to wait in the waiting room to see Dr Rowlings again.

When one of the doctor's patients came out of the doctor's office, the doctor waved James in.

'Thanks, Doc, for making it an unsupervised test,' said James. 'The last thing I wanted was for Jane looking at me peeing into that cup. Although I've known Jane for a long time, the only thing I've ever exposed to her has been my arm.'

The doctor let out a genuine laugh. 'You'll be surprised to know that Jane was in theatre when I delivered you. She was the one who cleaned you up, weighed you, and checked that you had all your fingers and toes and other things.' The doctor chuckled.

'Well,' replied James seriously, 'everything has grown since she saw me last.'

The doctor realised how young and vulnerable James was. No one so young should be in the situation he was in and face this alone. He wished that he could do more to help and support him.

The doctor became serious again. 'I've made contact with the councillor, and she can see you tomorrow morning at eleven. Here is her name, address, and phone number. I've told her about you, and she is very happy to help in any way she can. Just be yourself and be open with her. She'll understand and won't judge what you tell her. Everything will be held in strict confidence. Now these are the antidepressants I've prescribed for you.' The doctor handed James a box of thirty fifteen-milligram Mirtazapine tablets.

'These tablets are very mild,' continued the doctor, 'and will not make you drowsy. Take one tablet every night after dinner with a glass of water. They'll take a day or two to take effect, but you should feel calmer, and they will minimise your mood swings, and they will help you sleep. If you feel any bad side effects such as vomiting, diarrhoea, chills, or sweats, come and see me straight away. Don't make an appointment. Just come in. I don't expect that you'll have any side effects though.

'If everything goes well, I'd like to see you in around two weeks just to see how the tablets are working and how things are going with the councillor. Try and see her every week until you feel that you can manage things, and then you can extend the visits to every two or four weeks. You two can decide that after a few visits, but don't try and manage things on your own. We are here to help you, so don't push us away. Although you may think of me as a stranger, I've known you all your life and your mother for a lot longer. Please call me if you have any problems, no matter how big or small. I will always be here for you. Promise me that you won't do anything stupid and that you'll ask for help if you're getting bad thoughts that you can't handle.'

'I promise,' replied James.

'Great. I'll hold you to that promise. Please go and see the councillor tomorrow, and I'll see you in a couple of weeks,' concluded the doctor. 'Goodbye, James, and take care of yourself.'

Chapter 14

The next morning at eleven, James stood in front of a small well-kept manicured garden. He could smell the faint sweet scent of the flowers growing in the councillor's cottage garden. The house itself was of a wooden design, with a front porch, a small round metal table with two chairs of a similar design to one side, and more flowers hanging from the eves in hanging baskets. The place felt warm and welcoming. James walked to the front porch and pressed the button on the front door frame. He heard a faint chime from inside the house, followed by footsteps approaching the front door. The door opened.

'Hi, miss . . . Ah, Mrs Channing, I'm James,' started James.

'Actually, it is Ms Channing, but you can call me Margaret . . . Hello, James. It's nice to meet you. Dr Rowlings has told me so much about you. Please come in.' Margaret smiled as she held the door open and stepped to one side to let James in. Her smile was friendly and addictive, and James couldn't help smiling back. She was quite slender and tall, with dark raven hair tied back into a bun. He estimated her to be in her mid-forties, and although she didn't appear to be wearing any makeup, she was quite pretty. Her fine gold-framed glasses accentuated her eyes which were a pale blue.

James entered the lounge room, and although he could see the furnishings were quite old, they had been well kept. The room felt warm and conformable, and he could smell what appeared to be freshly baked cookies or cake wafting from the kitchen ahead.

'Please take a seat in either of the lounge chairs, and I'll be right back,' said Margaret. 'I've just baked some chocolate cookies, and I was just making myself a cup of tea. Would you like a drink, maybe a soda?'

'Tea would be just fine,' replied James. James remembered the countless times he had spent in the kitchen with his mother who had introduced him to tea at an early age. He remembered watching his mother make cake or biscuit batters and fillings for various Russian creations, and he enjoyed licking the beaters afterwards. The filling he liked the best was sour cream and caster sugar for one of his mother's famous multi-layered cakes.

James hadn't noticed that he had been staring across the room, remembering those enjoyable times with his mother. Tears were running down his cheeks when Margaret re-entered the room, holding a tray with tea and cookies. 'Oh dear, I'm sorry for leaving you alone in a strange house,' said Margaret as she placed the tray on the coffee table between the two lounge chairs and knelt in front of James, taking his hands in hers.

'That's all right,' replied James. 'I was just thinking of the times I had spent with my mom in the kitchen.'

'It's good to grieve. It's healthy to grieve,' said Margaret. 'The worst thing you can do is keep it bottled inside. You need to remember your parents and grieve for them. That's the only way that you will get through this, and I'll be here to help you every step of the way if you let me. Now before the tea gets cold, would you like cream and sugar?'

They took small steps that day during their first session, and over the coming weeks, James confided in Margaret, opening up with his feelings, crying uncontrollably sometimes, and laughing during others.

James returned to the doctor two weeks after his previous visit where he was given a clean bill of health with his blood test results and urine sample confirmed that he had no illicit drugs in his system or that he had been drinking. The doctor gave James a six-month repeat script for antidepressants and made an appointment to see him within the next six months.

Two months later, James arrived at Margaret's house for his fortnightly sessions and found two police cars and an ambulance in front of Margaret's house, sirens wailing and lights flashing. He rushed to the police tape surrounding the house where he was confronted by three police officers.

'What happened?' screeched James. 'Where's Margaret? Where is she?'

'I'm sorry, Son, but there's been an aggravated burglary. We can't let you through,' replied one of the police officers.

James was distraught. 'How's Margaret? Tell me where she is,' pleaded James. With that, he saw the front door to the house open. Two ambulance officers were pushing a gurney through the door and gently down the porch steps. The gurney held a long black plastic bag, fully sealed. James had seen the same type of plastic bag six months ago. His father had been in that one.

James ran back to the car, crying. He started the car, screeched a U-turn, and sped back the way he had come.

Somehow, James had managed to reach home without incident. He felt numb. He had no feeling on his face, and his eyes were dry. His hands were cold and clammy. He was shaking uncontrollably as if he had been exposed to the cold for too long, and his body was shutting down. He staggered into the house, walked to the liquor cabinet, and took out two bottles of unopened vodka, one in each hand.

James sat in his favourite chair, placed one of the bottles on the nearby coffee table, and opened the other. He drank the vodka as if it were water and drained half the bottle before resting it on his knee.

Why me? thought James. *What the fuck am I doing here?*

James's mother had been religious and had taken James to church every Sunday. He believed in God, or at least he thought he did. Now he wasn't too sure.

'If there is a god, then he sure isn't loving, caring, or forgiving. He's taken everyone I have loved in my life from me. Now I'm alone . . . again. Why would God make life so miserable for most of the people in this world until their death, just for a promise that there is life after death in his kingdom? What if that kingdom is just as miserable as the one we've left? Are we to suffer forever?

'Irrespective of whether you believe in creation or evolution, the end result is the same . . . you die, most of us in poverty or suffering or persecution or pain or hardship. It might be our own doing or the effect of others in our lives, whether directly or indirectly, to an individual or to a group or race or religion of peoples. You suffer and struggle for the whole of your life, and then you die. All your thoughts and knowledge and experiences and memories and pain and suffering die with you.'

With the first bottle finished, James started on the second.

'Even if you have loved ones or family or friends or people who have known you, whether you are one of the countless many nobodies who have had little or no impact on others, or one of the few somebodies with power and riches and influence, in the end . . . you die. You might be remembered by those you've influenced, those you've loved, your family, your friends, your neighbours, your colleagues, those you've harmed, those you've killed, those you've persecuted, those you've helped. How long will you be remembered for? One generation? Maybe two? In the end, few of us are remembered for any notable period. The majority of us, apart from a handful of people, are forgotten forever within fifty years after our death. You cease to be. So why do we struggle for the whole of our lives when the whole cycle is pointless?

'If I weren't here, I'd have no more feelings or thoughts or sadness or pain. There would be nothing. Only peace, silence. No one will remember me anyway. No one would care. The world doesn't give a shit. It's destroying itself anyway. How long will we survive before the world becomes toxic? People don't respect one another. All they want to do is kill one another. We pollute and destroy everything we touch. We try and better our surroundings at the expense of others and the environment. In the end, everyone loses.'

James is halfway through the second bottle. His mind is jumping from one option of ending his life to another. His courage is building as the alcohol is dwindling. He downed the remainder of the second bottle. 'Fuck it. Let's do it. Let's get it over with.'

Chapter 15

'Hello, Chudo.'

James looks around. The room is spinning. He tries to focus, but all he can see are shadows and darkness. Looking out the window, he notices that the world outside is dark and grey. Twilight has fallen. How long has he been sitting, drinking? James fumbles for the table lamp and knocks over one of the empty bottles of vodka before finding the light switch. The darkness recedes to the far corners of the room. He sits alone.

'Good evening, Chudo.'

'Who's there? Dr Rowlings?'

'No . . . just someone listening to your thoughts.'

'Who's there? Who are you?'

'Someone interested in what you've been thinking.'

James looks around the room. Nothing. 'Where are you?'

'I'm here.'

'Where? Who are you? What's your name?'

'Actually, I don't have a name. I'm just here.'

'This has to be a joke. If you're here, why can't I see you?'

'Ah, that's the question. Because . . . I don't have anything that you can see.'

'Seriously? This has to be a joke, but I can't imagine anyone I know who would do this.'

'It's no joke, Chudo, I was just interested in what you were thinking, and I thought we'd have a chat.'

'Why do you call me Chudo? How do you know my name? The only one who's ever called me that was my mom.'

***'I know. I like it better than James. At least it has meaning. I believe it means* miracle.'**

'Look, I may be drunk, but this makes no sense whatsoever, even to me. Are you trying to tell me that you're here but you're invisible? Like a ghost? This is not like the burning bush thing where Moses speaks to God on Mount Sinai?'

'Hardly. I'm not a ghost, and I'm certainly not God.'

'If I can't see you, prove to me that you're not someone hiding somewhere in here, making fun of me. Make something appear or disappear or levitate something, something.' James becomes frustrated.

'I can't do anything like that, but believe me, I'm not someone hiding in here, making fun of you. I promise.'

'You do know how sceptical that sounds? You expect me to believe someone has entered my house who is . . . I don't know. I DON'T KNOW!'

James gets out of the chair, walks to the bathroom, splashes his face with cold water, dries it with the hand towel, walks back into the lounge, and sit. James is in shock. His eyes are open wide, and he's looking around the room. He wasn't groggy and didn't feel drunk anymore.

'What the fuck was that? How did you do that?'

'You wanted me to show you something that I can do. Well, that's something, right?'

'I can't understand it. That was amazing. I had no control over what I was doing. OK, if you wanna talk, let's talk. I had nothing else planned anyway.'

'Hardly . . . I believe you were planning your . . . termination.'

'If you wanna call it that, yes. I've had enough of this life, and there's no point in me being here anymore.'

'Well, I have a proposal for you if you're interested.'

'Seriously, what can I do for you? I can't imagine anything that I could help you with.'

'I'm glad you asked. I'll try and explain why I'm here, but I'll have to start at the beginning so that you understand. Maybe we can come up with a plan to help me. ...Millennia ago, when universe was forming—'

'What? How old are you?'

'I don't know. "I've always been" is the only answer I can give you. Although time has no meaning for us, I'll use a timeline that you can relate to.'

'How many of you are there?'

'We number ten, and we are scattered throughout the universe. We gather together every few thousand years to describe what new discoveries we've encountered in out travels.

'Anyway, as I was explaining, when the universe was forming around fourteen billion of your earth years ago, we decided to go our separate ways and explore it. I came upon this planet around five billion years ago, and I thought it had potential for being something wondrous. I remember you thinking about the world as being either created or evolving. You are both right and wrong there. I found various elements around your planet that I encouraged to combine to form molecules which produced water. Over the next billion years, I continued to nurture these molecules which began to grow and divide and multiply, forming more intricate molecules, eventually developing into what you would call plants. I boasted about my achievement when we came together since all the others only spoke about what they had seen in their travels.

'Other molecules subdivided and combined with others to form simple organisms that were able to reproduce themselves. The increase in molecule variations began producing a myriad of plant and animal life, and a billion years ago, the planet was covered in vegetation and small animals. I was elated and proud to present the evolution of the planet to the others. Eventually, the animal species grew and formed their own communities, some of which were more or less dominant than others. One species, however, although not physically dominant than others, developed

skills beyond my expectation. It was able to think and learn and utilise what it found in its surroundings to protect itself, to feed itself, to shelter itself.

'I'm talking about human beings who, around one million years ago, began to show their increasing dominance, and I became concerned. I thought, however, that this was part of the evolution cycle and that other species would take their place as I had seen happen previously. Ten thousand years ago, however, it became obvious that humans were going to remain dominant, even though other animals were stronger and were more equipped to survive in their environment.

'Although humans have shown to be the most intelligent species on this planet, they are wasteful, destructive, heartless, and poisonous to the survival of this planet. They destroy their environment, kill off species for their own needs or pleasure, and even kill one another. The planet is at a tipping point that if humans continue to abuse it, all life will suffer and die. The destruction, pollution, and overpopulation man has created in such a short time frame appals me. I cannot believe that humans cannot see what they have done and continue to do to this once beautiful planet. I am ashamed on what I have created, and I no longer discuss its existence with the others. I can think of nothing I can do to make a change to this earth. All I can do is watch it destroy itself or just leave it be and never return. If I had the power, I would eradicate every human life on this planet.'

'Wow!' says James. 'I never really thought about how we're killing ourselves. So how long do you think we have?'

'I believe you have maybe a hundred years, two at most, before everything becomes so toxic to live in. The effects caused by humans to this planet will be irreversible not only to them but to all life.'

'You do know that I'm only eighteen years old, right? What can I do to make a difference? I'm nothing in the whole scheme of things, and I'm certainly not in a position to influence others to make a change.'

'Actually, you are the perfect person to help me. You're young enough not to have your own agenda and old and intelligent enough to make your own decisions. Your state of mind, although it's self-destructing, you won't be swayed by others to change the plan we decide to formulate.'

'Clearly then, you do have an idea on what you want to happen. If you're asking for my help, then you haven't given up on us.'

'I believe that the only people who can make a difference and change the direction you are going are the ones with power, the ones who have caused this catastrophe to continue.'

'I gather you mean the leaders of their countries, like presidents and prime ministers, and kings.'

'They are the ones with power who manage their resources and money. They are the ones who can influence change.'

'So what, you want me to convince them? You can do that. I don't believe they're going to listen to an eighteen year old boy.'

'The problem is that if I try and convince them, I wouldn't have the tolerance or the patience to listen to their excuses on why they can't or won't do it. I would just eliminate them.'

'So you can take people's lives. I thought you said that you don't have the power to eradicate humans?'

'I can . . . manipulate minds and get them to do things, but only on an individual basis. The more intricate the mind is, the more difficult it is to . . . control them. I can manipulate, say, a small group of rabbits because their thoughts are primitive, but human minds are more developed.'

'So where do I fit into this? What can I do?'

'I believe that you have the patience to talk and convince them to change.'

'Seriously . . . I can't just rock up at, say, the White House and say, "I want to speak to the president." At best, they'd tell me to go away. At worst, they'd shoot me for being a nut or put me in a mental asylum.'

'You wouldn't need to ask to see them. You'd just be there, not in person, like transporting yourself into their office. But your mind would be there, just like I'm here now.'

'You can do that? Make me do that? How?'

'I can make you be able to . . . transport your mind to where they are. You just think of whom you want to see, and your mind goes there.'

'Wow, that sounds amazing. So I can just think of being there, and I can talk to them through my mind.'

'Exactly. Your body would be here, but your mind travels to where they are.'

'Let's just say that's possible, but convincing one person isn't going to make a difference. I'd have to . . . convince other leaders so that there would be enough of them to pull enough of their resources and money for change to happen.'

'It is possible, and it is within my power to do so.'

'But I speak English and a little Italian and Russian. Many of these leaders speak languages that I wouldn't be possible to communicate with them.'

'Ah, that's where you're wrong. Communicating with your mind is not the same as speaking with them. You would be communicating with them through thought, which does not have a language as such. Whomever you communicate with will understand you, and you would understand them.'

'So how am I going to convince any of them to listen to me and do what I say? You know how ridiculous that sounds? I can't just say that I want them to stop destroying the world and help their fellow human beings. They'd just say no and tell me to go away.'

'Well, you would have to get them to listen to reason. This is where you may need to be ruthless as I believe that you can.'

'Like how, tell them that if they don't do this, the world is going to end? They're only going to laugh at me.'

'No. This is where being ruthless comes in. You will need to show them that if they don't listen to you, they are part of the cause and will be . . . eliminated and replaced with someone who will listen to you.'

'Empty threats aren't going to win them over. They'll probably laugh louder.'

'They wouldn't be empty threats, Chudo. You know how I made you walk into the bathroom and wash your face? Well, you can make them do anything through your mind to convince them that you are serious.'

'You mean you can give me that?'

'Exactly. You can make them sing and dance if you want, and they wouldn't be able to stop themselves.'

'But you can do that. You don't need me.'

'That's where you're wrong, Chudo. I wouldn't have the patience to reason with them. I'd just . . . eliminate them and leave. And I certainly wouldn't be able to try this with all the world leaders who would be needed to help your planet survive. I know you would have the patience to do so. You are creative and methodical like your father and have the compassion and love like your mother. Although you were in the process of extinguishing your life, I believe that you still care enough for this planet that you would try and save it. I don't believe that you would put up with any insubordination from these leaders after giving them compelling reasons for their help. I know I'm repeating myself, but I do believe that you have the patience to convince these leaders, either by getting them to see reason or forcing them to help.'

'I think you're overestimating my intelligence or my capabilities.'

'I don't believe I am, Chudo. I believe that you can help me. All I want is that you try for me.'

'Why not . . . So what happens now?'

'First of all, I need to explain what happens when your mind leaves your body. Although it will continue to breathe, it will have no protection, say, if there is a fire, and you won't know what's happening. If your body dies, you will cease to be, including your mind.'

'OK, so I need to make sure that my body is safe when I'm . . . travelling. I can do that.'

'Whomever you are communicating with will only hear the thoughts you relay to them, so it is important that you keep your thoughts under control. You must not divulge, say who you are or where you're from. Otherwise, they can find you.

'*The same applies to them. You will only know the thoughts that they relay to you. You won't know whether they are lying unless they are relaying these thoughts.*'

'Any other interesting pieces of information I should know about?'

'*Make sure that you have a clear picture in your mind on whom you want to . . . visit. Otherwise, you may wind up somewhere else. And when you want to return to your body, you just think of yourself.*'

'OK, so how do I get these magical powers? Will it hurt?'

'*You have them.*'

'What? How? When?'

'*It's a simple process . . . for me. It's not like you need to be operated on or I have to wave a magic wand. My thoughts have fine-tuned yours to allow your mind to travel.*'

'I don't feel anything. Are you sure it worked?'

'*Well, how about you try and travel somewhere? Think of someone's face.*'

'Hang on. Give me a moment. And it can be anyone, right?'

'*I would suggest for now to think of someone you know well.*'

'OK, got it. I'm thinking of Dr Rowlings.'

'*Ah, the doctor who treated your mother. Now sit back in your chair. Put your arms on the armrests and your head on the headrest. That's it. Now close your eyes. Good. Are you comfortable?*'

'Yes.'

'*Remember that once your mind leaves your body, your muscles will no longer support you. If you are using your muscles to keep you in a position, you may topple over if what you are sitting on is not fully supporting you. You can try doing this lying down if you wish.*'

James wriggles further into the chair and relaxes even more.

'No, I'm good.'

'*Now just concentrate on the doctor's face. Clear your mind of everything else. Concentrate on his face and go to him.*'

James feels as if he were floating. He opens his eyes, and he sees Dr Rowlings sitting at his office desk, head down, writing. It must be late evening, but the doctor is still at work.

James looks around the room. He has been in this room countless times—the doctor's medical certificates hanging in a row behind him, the examination table, the eye chart, large coloured pictures showing various parts of the human anatomy.

James looks back at the doctor who is still writing.

James forms words in his mind. 'Dr Rowlings?'

The doctor raises his head, looking in James's direction. 'James?'

James thinks of himself and starts to feel the pressure of the chair supporting his body. He's back in his house, still sitting in his chair.

'I forgot to mention, you are also able to hear when people are speaking.'

'You were there?'

'I had to make sure that you were safe and that you had travelled to the right place.'

'That was amazing. It was like being in a dream, only it felt real.'

'It was real. Your mind was actually there. So now that you know that you have . . . this power, are you willing to help me?'

'Why not? Just give me some time to think about whom I should visit and formulate what I'm going to say to them. The other thing I need to consider is how I'm going to protect myself, my body, when I'm . . . my mind is travelling.'

'How much time do you think you'll need?'

'Give me three months to sort things out.'

'I see what you're planning to do to protect yourself. I'll come back in three months and see how you're progressing.'

Silence. 'Hello,' says James. Nothing. He's alone. The being has left.

James showers and goes to bed, his mind still racing as he lays there in the dark until sleep finally comes.

Chapter 16

James wakes up the next morning, thinking on what happened the night before. Had it been a dream?

James walks into the kitchen and brews himself a cup of coffee, the same way his father had done, and prepares a couple of pieces of toast with honey. The phone rings.

'Hello?' says James.

'Hello, James. It's Dr Rowlings, ringing to see how you are. I heard about Margaret Channing when I was reading the paper this morning, and I was concerned about you,' the doctor replies.

'I'm fine, Doctor,' says James. 'I was there when the ambulance was taking Margaret away, and I took it quite hard. But I've had time to think about it, and I'm OK this morning. How anyone could do such a thing to a gentle woman like her is unbelievable. Life is unjust.'

Dr Rowlings is surprised on how well James was taking all of this, considering that he'd lost his parents recently and that Margaret had been counselling him because of his state of mind.

'You won't believe this,' continues the doctor, 'but I was in my office last night, and I swear that I heard you calling my name. I thought it was a premonition and that you were in trouble.'

'No, Doctor. I'm fine. Believe me,' replies James.

'Well, if you're not coping and you need help, you can come and see me. I'm sure that I can find you another counsellor if you still need to confide in someone,' says the doctor.

'I'm coping at the moment, Doc,' states James, 'but if I need help, you'll be the first person I'll call.'

'Good, and don't forget, I'm always here for you. Please ring me if you want to talk,' concludes the doctor. 'Goodbye, James.'

'See ya, Doc,' replies James and hangs up the phone.

Well, clearly, last night wasn't a dream. He had a lot of work ahead of him. James ruffles through his dad's business cards and finds the number of the design company they had used to build the house. He makes an appointment for one of them to come and visit him at the house.

'Now that I'm alone,' James says to the representative Tom from the design company when he arrives, 'and even though it's a wonderful house, I'm concerned about break-ins. There was an aggravated burglary in Oak View just the other day where a woman was murdered, and I want to protect myself. Are you able to design and build me a panic room?'

'Sure,' replies Tom. 'I remember your mum when I helped her design this house. She was one lovely lady, although she was tough. She knew exactly what she wanted, and I was impressed with the ideas she'd come up with. The house is amazing. I'm sorry that she passed away.'

'I am too,' says James. 'So what do you think about a panic room?'

'We're getting more and more enquiries about panic rooms lately,' says Tom, 'and we've built a few around the Los Angeles area. Do you have anything in mind, like how big, what you want in it, how much do you want to spend?'

'I was thinking of something that is self-contained,' replies James. 'Something that I could spend, say, up to a week, without the need to come out during that time. Something with sleeping quarters, a bath, and kitchen.'

'OK,' says Tom, puzzled. 'Do you want it above or below ground? Because if you want it below ground, it's going to be more expensive since we would need to excavate, and we're looking at, at least at two rooms, maybe three?'

'I would prefer it below ground, something that I can access from inside the house,' replies James. 'And another thing. I would like a security system installed, with motion sensors and closed-circuit television that I can view from both the study and inside the panic room.'

'Wow, you've thought of everything!' exclaims Tom. 'You certainly take after your mother. She was pretty thorough too.'

'Draw up the plans,' says James. 'Tell me how much it will cost and how long it will take to build.'

'I'll have the plans drawn up in a week,' concludes Tom, 'and we can decide on where we go from there. Considering it's your mother's house, I'm sure that I can make you a good deal.'

The following week, Tom returns with the plans, and after some minor alterations, they shake hands, and the deal is struck.

Over the next three months, whilst excavation began, James goes online, records details of all the world leaders he should visit and the expenditure of each country on their defence and nuclear capabilities, and saves the latest available picture of each leader, whether they are president, prime minister, king, or ruler.

The house looks like a construction site. From the front corner of the big house, all the way to the entrance to the small house, the area is being excavated to get to the underside of the house. Large support beams have been erected to support the house whilst they excavate to create the cavity of the panic room. The ambiguous driveway leading to the front entrance of the small house has been obliterated. There was now a gradual drop for the diggers to access the underside of the house and bring up the excess dirt they are removing. There is a constant stream on fully laden trucks removing the dirt from the property and the same number returning empty to be refilled again until the cavity is finally excavated.

For James to access the small house, rather than repeatedly going through the main entrance and using the hidden doorway between the two sections of the house, a dirt track has been created starting from the corner of the property and following the treeline to the front door of the small house.

Because of the tight deadline James has given to the design company, construction was from first light to sunset each day. The good thing was that since there were no nearby neighbours, construction continued seven days a week. The bad news was that construction continued seven days a week, and although the house was well insulated and soundproofed, James can hear the jackhammers constantly until he feels as if his teeth are rattling in his mouth.

When he wasn't researching world leaders or taking notes on how to approach each one, he usually got into his BMW and went for long drives or to the local theatre house to watch a movie.

Finally, the hammering under the house subsides, and the concrete pouring begins to form the one-foot-thick re-enforced walls of the panic room and access way. It was agreed to access to the panic room from behind the staircase in the main house between the bathroom and toilet. A concealed swinging door would lead to the stairway down to the re-enforced door of the panic room.

With the concrete walls in place, they backfill the driveway, and by the time they have finished relaying the path, it looks no different to how it had looked prior to the excavation.

The internal fitting of the panic room begins, including the installation of the security and surveillance systems. Five months after the commencement of construction, James is a proud owner of a panic room.

The stairs leading down to the panic room are basic concrete construction with a galvanised metal handrail, no frills or colour, and a series of lights along one of the walls guiding the way to the entry door which is two-inch-thick solid hardened steel. Entry is via a ten-digit PIN in a number pad set on one side of the door. The door itself would lock into position with one-inch metal spikes, two spikes top and bottom and four spikes through each side. If James forgets the PIN, he was neither getting in nor out.

The door opens into the largest room comprising of the lounge and kitchen areas equipped with sink, stove, and refrigerator. In one corner of the room is a desk and a bank of six monitors mounted to the wall above, showing views of the inside of the two houses, the entryways, and the perimeter of the houses, including the driveway. Each monitor displays four views.

To one side of the room, there is a door leading to the small sleeping quarters containing a double bed, cupboard space, and television. To the other side of the main room is another door which leads to the bath and toilet, although the bath is actually a shower.

If you didn't know it was a panic room, you would think you were in a small and well-maintained apartment, although the bank of monitors gave that away a little.

James is impressed on how well the designers had planned the layout and finished the inside, even though they had taken two months more than they had agreed to. He is surprised that the being that had visited him five months ago hadn't returned. James did remember telling him to give him three months to sort things out.

Chapter 17

James begins to worry that the being wouldn't return, but that night, whilst relaxing after dinner and no longer hearing loud noises coming from under the house, James has a visitor.

'Hello, Chudo. I like what you've done with the place.'

'I was wondering why you hadn't returned earlier.'

'I could see that you weren't ready, so I waited until you were . . . Or have you backed out of our deal? Are you ready?'

'I didn't think of it as striking a deal. I just agreed to help, and I haven't backed out. And yes, I'm as ready as I'll ever be. I've made a list of the top forty most powerful countries, found photos of their leaders, which of these countries have nuclear capabilities, and how much money they're worth. I've even made a list of the poorest countries.'

'Interesting way of looking at it. Your analytical mind at work, I see.'

'I had to start somewhere. I need to get those countries who have the most money and resources to agree for change as well as helping the poorer ones. Anyway, I've made some notes on how to approach these leaders and get them to agree.'

'You're being optimistic, but it's not going to be that simple. In the end, you will need to be forceful and show them what will happen if they don't agree.'

'What do you mean? How can I force them if they don't want to listen?'

'The only way that change is going to happen is by the cooperation of all, especially the most powerful nations, because without them, it's going to fail. You will need to be ruthless if they refuse. Whether you want to call it a threat, you will need to show them that they must agree. You have the power to control them, not physically but mentally. You need to use this to your advantage. Show them that their refusal is unacceptable.'

'I know what you're trying to tell me, but I don't know whether I have that type of resolve to impose such violence on them, to them.'

'Ah, that will be your greatest challenge because there will be many who won't believe you, who won't think that you can threaten them unless you show them. Hopefully, you'll only need to show the power you have over them for them to agree to comply.'

'Well, I've listed the leaders, and I'm going to start with the ones who possibly want change and want to help. Hopefully, I'll build up enough courage to confront the more aggressive leaders who will refuse because they fear they have the most to lose, who only care about themselves and the power they hold over their peoples.'

'I wish you all the best in your attempt, Chudo, but I must leave now. I've spent too much time on this planet.'

'What? Where are you going? When will you be back?'

'I have many wondrous places still to explore, and I'll be meeting with the others shortly to discuss what we've encountered in our travels. I don't want to go empty-handed, so to speak. I will be back in maybe five or ten years. By then, you would have failed miserably or hopefully started making changes that will save your planet. Goodbye Chudo, and the very best of luck to you.'

With that, the being was gone. James knows and feels that he's left. No point in asking whether he was still there. Actually, that was one question he hadn't asked the being—whether it has a gender. Oh well, he'd try and ask he or she when *it* returned . . . if James was still here, that is.

James has decided that he would first try and contact either the German chancellor Angela Merkel or the Canadian Prime Minister Justin Trudeau. They appear to be the ones most likely to listen to his extraordinary proposal and convince them to join his cause. He might even be able to get advice from them. Having seen them appear on the occasional TV news broadcast, they appeared to be genuine and compassionate people.

James has created an extensive spreadsheet covering everything from each country's leaders, their titles, their photos, whether they have nuclear capabilities and the number of nuclear missiles they might have, each country's worth in US dollars, their population, and their time zones relative to Los Angeles so that he can determine the most opportune time to visit them.

James locks up the house, sets the alarms, heads off to his bunker, and locks himself in. He reads through the notes he's made on how to approach his discussions with them and finally decides to approach the Canadian prime minister first. It's now midmorning, so it should be close to noon where the prime minister should be. James lays on the bed and closes his eyes, focusing on the prime minister's face.

There are crowds everywhere, and the Canadian prime minister is shaking hands with the people lining the street. The position of the sun on this bright sunny day indicates that it's mid to late afternoon, so it doesn't appear that the prime minister is in Canada. Clearly, it's not a good time to interrupt him. James stops focusing on the prime minister, and he's back in the panic room again.

OK, that didn't go as planned. Let's try the German chancellor, James thinks to himself. He checks the time it should be in Germany and realises it's around six in the evening there, not a good time. 'She's probably having dinner, and I don't think she'd be eating alone. *I think you should be planning this a little better, James,*' he tells himself.

James decides to take a walk in the woods behind the house to kill a little time and clear his head for a couple of hours before trying again. Although the sun is out, there's no warmth to it. The little breeze that is blowing makes it feel cooler than what it actually was. James puts on a warm jacket with a hood and heads out, hands deep in the jacket pockets to keep them warm. Even though he's been here countless times, there was always something new to discover. By the time James returns to the house, his nose feels cold, and his cheeks are tingling.

Back in the bunker again, James tries to contact the German chancellor. She's sitting casually on the large couch, with the light of the television reflecting off her face. She is alone. James didn't know what to expect, but he is surprised that leaders sometimes did ordinary things that us peasants do. James is nervous.

'*Hello, Chancellor*,' begins James.

Startled, the German chancellor reaches for the lamp and turns it on. 'What? Who's there? How did you get in here?' she replies.

'*Please don't be alarmed*,' continues James. '*I'm not here to hurt you. I just want to have a chat.*'

'Who are you? Why can't I see you? What do you want?'

'*I know this is going to sound strange, but I'm only here in spirit, so to speak. That's why you can't see me. I only want to talk and possibly get some advice.*'

'If this is a joke, it's in poor taste. Now show yourself before I call for help.'

'*Please don't. I only want to talk, I promise. This is the first time I've done this . . . well, actually the second, but the first time doesn't count. No, my third time. Forgot about when I was testing my ability. Sorry, I'm babbling on. Anyway, I am in the room with you but not physically, only my thought is.*'

'Rubbish, you're either in here or someone is using a speaker. Now show yourself.'

'*Believe me, there is no speaker. Only you can hear me. I was in the same position as you are, and I know I couldn't pinpoint the sound of the voice either. It was just in my head. If you still don't believe me, you can call someone into the room and ask them if they can hear anything whilst I still talk to you. Just don't alarm them. All I want to do is talk to you and ask for your help. You will be interested in what I have to say, even though it will sound fantastic, but I only have good intentions.*'

'OK, I'll listen. You have me intrigued.'

'I've been told that we have maybe one to two hundred years before our world becomes too toxic to live in, not only for us but also for all animal and plant life as well, that's if we don't blow ourselves up before them.'

'Although it may be true, who's come up with this theory?'

'The same one who's given me the power to communicate like this. I listened to them for a long time before I agreed to help with their cause. And before you jump to any conclusions, no, it wasn't God who spoke to me. I'm going to try and convince enough leaders to help reverse what they are doing to our world and help those peoples who are persecuted or living in poverty to improve their lives and be self-sufficient. I know this sounds impossible, but I believe that if I get enough of them to agree, we can do this.'

'Are you trying to tell me that you're going to convince people like that Trump and Putin and big countries like China and India to stop polluting this planet? Impossible!'

'I'm going to try. I'm going to try my hardest. All I'm asking is that you participate in the decision-making on what we need to do when the time comes.'

'I still can't see how you're going to convince any of them. They are arrogant people who are only looking after their own interests. They strut around like roosters showing off to the world, and they don't care about what other people have to say.'

'I believe I can convince them, and if they still don't want to help, I'll . . . be a little forceful.'

'If you are only a voice in a room, what can you do to them that will make them change their minds?'

'Ah, but that's not the only thing that I can do. Although I haven't tried it, I can also manipulate their movements. I can make them do things they can't control, even though they are aware.'

'Seriously?' The chancellor is giggling. 'I'm sorry. I was imagining you making Trump strut around like a rooster, with his arms flapping, or that Putin, or together.' She starts giggling louder. 'You can really do that?'

'If I have to, yes.'

'Prove it to me. Don't make me strut around, but make me do something that I'm not in control of.'

The chancellor twists, reaches over, and turns off the lamp before turning it back on again.

'OK, I'm convinced. I don't know how you did that, but it appears you can. So what now?'

'I've made a list of leaders whom I'm going to contact and get them to agree to hold a joint meeting to discuss how to help one another and the world. I'm going to get countries to disarm and dispose of their nuclear weapons, and I'm going to get them to use that money and resources to eliminate poverty, reduce pollution, and eradicate radical groups who are killing innocent people. Have I missed out on anything?'

'You know, there is going to be a lot of resistance from countries who have a lot to lose by giving up their toys of threat and destruction and spending their money on things that do not benefit them directly.'

'But it will benefit them. By being a clean and unified world, it's going to benefit everyone and everything on it.'

'It is a grand plan. I hope you pull it off. What do you need from me?'

'Nothing at the moment, but I will be back once I have the others' agreement to hold a meeting. Do you have any suggestions on where we can have it?'

'If you ask that question to any other representative, they will answer the same as me. It would be my honour to hold it here in Berlin.'

'I'll hold you to that. If that changes for some reason, I'll let you know. I'm hoping that I'll make contact with you again once I've contacted everyone else with a meeting date. One more thing that I nearly forgot. You do know that since you are on the list of countries I will be contacting, I will be asking for you to also contribute to this change with resources and money.'

'As long as the contribution is fair for each country and you don't leave us broke, then I agree. I wish you the best of luck in pulling this off. I will be very surprised if you do come back confirming that you've managed to convince everyone.'

'Goodbye, Chancellor, and see you soon . . . ah, talk to you soon. Sorry, I'm new at this.'

Chapter 18

James opens his eyes, elated. 'Yes, one down, thirty-nine leaders to go.' James remains on the bed, thinking of the mountainous challenge he has ahead of him. Although the discussions with Angela Merkel went well, he doesn't expect them to go as smoothly with all of them. James can begin with the countries who have the most to gain, but eventually, he will need to confront the leaders who have the most to lose. These will be the countries that he will need to rely on the most. They have the largest resources and amount of money needed to influence change.

James decides to have an early dinner before trying to contact the Canadian prime minister again.

Laying on the bed again, James closes his eyes and concentrates on the prime minister's face.

The room is dark, and he can barely see what appears to be a large bed with two forms on it, each facing away from each other. James assumes that the other person is the prime minister's wife.

'Prime Minister?' says James.

'Uh, who's there? What is it?' Trudeau asks.

'Please step outside, sir. There is something of importance I need to speak with you about.'

There is a rustle of blankets as the prime minister sits up in bed.

'Please step outside, sir.'

The prime minster, still groggy from being awakened from his sleep, obeys, stands, puts on a dressing gown and slippers, and walks out of the bedroom. He yawns, rubs his eyes, and looks around. He sees no one. 'Who's there?' he asks again.

'Please don't be alarmed. I would like to have a talk.'

'What?' The prime minister is fully awake now and looks around the room, startled. There's no one there.

'Is there somewhere where we can talk without waking anyone?'

'Who are you? Where are you?'

'I am here to ask for your help. This will sound strange, but I am not here. You can only hear me. Can we please talk somewhere in private? I will explain everything there.'

The prime minster reluctantly walks to the study, closes the door, and turns on the light. He squints until his eyes adjust to the harshness of the light.

'Where are you?'

'I am here, sir, but you cannot see me. I am here to ask for your help. Please don't be alarmed.'

The prime minister opens his eyes wider and swivels his body around the room, trying to pinpoint the direction of the voice he's hearing. He appears frightened.

'I know this is hard to understand because it took me some time to convince the German councillor as well. My intentions are good. I'm not here to hurt you. I only want your help and support.'

'You've spoken to Angela?'

'Yes, sir, only a few hours ago. I believe she understands what I'm trying to do, and she was willing to help. Please have a seat, and I'll try and explain everything, I promise.'

Reluctantly, the prime minister sits. 'This is crazy. I must be going insane.'

'Not at all, sir. I'm sure you are as sane as most people.'

'So why can't I see you?'

'I am only here in thought. My body is elsewhere. I was given this gift because I agreed to help someone.'

'And you think that I can help you help that someone? That sounds ridiculous.'

'I said the same thing to that someone, and the German chancellor said the same thing to me.'

'And how did she react?'

'She was as unbelieving and surprised as you are, sir, but after I explained what I was trying to do, she was willing to help. She doesn't believe that I can do it, but she has offered to hold the discussions in Berlin if I manage to get the leaders on my list to attend. She even laughed when I told her that I was intending to speak with leaders such as the presidents of America and Russia.'

'You actually got Angela to laugh?'

'Yes, sir. You see, other than me being able to communicate with others, the same way we are now, I can also control them. The chancellor was imagining me making Putin and Trump strut around like roosters and started giggling.'

'I can see how that would be funny. You can actually do that? How?'

'I can also manipulate people's movements. I can make them do things, and even though they are aware of what they're doing, they can't stop themselves from doing them. I can show you if you like.'

'That won't be necessary. I'll ring Angela in the morning and ask whether you have indeed, what, spoken, communicated with her.'

'I call it communicating, but I can hear you either through your thoughts or voice. I'm sure you'll have an interesting conversation with her.'

'So what do you want from me?'

'All I want is your agreement to participate in the discussions with the group of leaders who attend the meeting. The aim of the meeting is to come up with a plan on how to help one another and the world. I'm going to get countries to disarm and dispose of their nuclear weapons, and I'm going to get them to use that money and resources to eliminate poverty, reduce pollution, and eradicate radical groups who are killing innocent people, to help poor countries with little or no resources become self-reliant and achieve independence without being a burden on the diminishing

resources we have. Your contribution will also include a small percentage of your resources and money in helping this cause.'

'I have no objection in contributing to this challenging cause because we donate a lot of money and food to poor countries and refugees already. I sometimes wonder whether what we are donating is going to the right people or making a difference. I would even consider being part of a committee who is responsible for distributing these funds. But I'm getting ahead of myself. I don't even know whether you're going to be able to pull this off.'

'My aim is to try, and I have no intentions of giving up. I know I have a huge challenge ahead of me, especially with countries that believe they have a lot to lose and will refuse to participate. But I'll get them to see reason, one way or the other, because in the end, this will help everyone. I'll only be back once I have the agreement of all the leaders on my list. I'll then give the date and location of where the meeting will be held. In the meantime, it would be helpful if you spend some time in noting possible topics for discussion.'

'I look forward to hearing from you. I'll be surprised, but I hope you succeed.'

'Goodnight, Prime Minister, and I'm sorry I disturbed your sleep.'

'I'm glad we had this discussion, although I don't think I'll be able to get back to sleep now. My mind is working overtime with ideas.'

'A cup of hot chocolate milk will help. Goodnight, sir.'

With that, the prime minister is alone, and James is sitting up in bed.

Chapter 19

Buoyed by his success, James decides to tackle his list of countries with fervour. He groups his list of countries into time zones. He realises that most leaders would be busy most days, holding or attending meetings, meeting and greeting people including dignitaries, and would be pretty much surrounded by others, with very little time being alone. James decides that the best time to approach them would be in the middle of the night whilst they are sleeping.

Ticking off both Germany and Canada, James proceeds to contact the leaders of smaller countries and leaders who have little or no reason to refuse his proposal. Over the next six weeks, James contacts another twenty-nine leaders, getting them to agree to attend and participate in this inaugural meeting. James finds little or no resistance by these leaders who, in the end, were looking forward to being part of what they hoped would lead to peace and prosperity for all.

Apart from the list of twenty of the poorest countries James needs to contact and have them attend, since they were the countries that needed the help most, it left the nine countries with nuclear capabilities who would more than likely require the greatest effort to convince.

There were three leaders in particular that James was not looking forward to contacting, two of which had their own agendas in making the world miserable and being power hungry, and the other showing insolence and further destabilising peace. James knows that he would eventually need to confront the presidents of the USA and Russia and the so-called supreme leader of North Korea. James can't understand how a leader of a small country with a population of twenty-five million could be so disruptive and have such an impact on world markets.

James throws himself into the deep end and finally choses the president of Russia to contact first. With the time difference, Russia was around ten hours ahead, give or take an hour, depending on which season it was. James decides to have an early dinner and prepares himself to contact Putin.

Laying in his bed in the bunker, James feels anxious and nervous, probably the most nervous he'd ever felt. He knows this is going to be a difficult encounter. James closes his eyes and focuses his mind on Putin's face.

The bedroom is dark, and James can only see the silhouette of one body in the big king-sized bed.

'Mr President?'

Nothing.

'Mr President, please wake up. I wish to speak with you.'

There is movement on the bed as a hand reaches for the lamp on the bedside table. The light shows the president face down, and he begins to roll over to a sitting position, looking around the room. The president doesn't appear to be surprised.

'What is it?' The president looks around the room. 'What? Who's there? Who said that?'

'Please don't be alarmed sir. I'm only here to talk with you.'

James feels that the president is about to yell and silences him. Putin's eyes widen in shock or surprise.

'Please don't attempt to yell out. As I said, I'm only here to talk with you. I know you can't see me because I'm only here in thought, but believe me, I am here.'

Putin nods. James let him speak.

'I don't know how you're doing this, but I don't think it's right to continue this conversation in my bedchamber. Can we continue this in my office?'

'Certainly sir. Lead the way.'

The president slides his feet over the edge of the bed and stands. All he's wearing are light blue boxer shorts. He slips on a burgundy dressing gown and heads for the bedroom door.

Putin starts walking down the hall as James follows. James notices two guards standing on either side of the bedroom door. They stand at attention as Putin walks past. Putin looks behind him in surprise as neither of the two guards make any motion other than looking in his direction and salute.

You little sneak, thinks James. *You thought that the guards would see me and jump me. Wrong, buddy.*

Putin opens the door to his office, steps inside before closing it again, and sits behind his gaudy desk. He looks around the empty room.

'I would like your advice and assistance on an important matter.'

The president is startled in hearing the voice again without seeing anyone in the room.

'I don't know how you're doing this, but I can't see how I can help you.' The president leans back in his chair, appearing casual. James knows that this is a front.

'I believe you can, sir. You are one of the most intelligent and powerful leaders of the world, and with your support and assistance, we can make this world a better place for everyone and everything on it.'

'Those are big words from a voice coming from nowhere. Who are you to think that I would help you in your glorious quest?'

'I am someone who knows where this world is heading—to its destruction—which you and others like you are turning it into.'

'Come now, you expect me to believe that you know where this world is heading. Tell me who you are to make these accusations and assumptions.'

'I am someone who cares, although I didn't care so much until I was, let's just say, enlightened. I have given my commitment to try and change this world before it destroys itself.'

'You are delusional to think that you know what's right for this world. You, whoever you are, won't and can't make me do your bidding. You are nothing!' The president is yelling, trying to entice James. It's working.

'Mr President, firstly, I am going to try my hardest to convince leaders to join a group and discuss what actions are required to improve the life of everyone living on it, without destroying the environment we are rapidly polluting. Secondly, I'm going to do it with or without your help. I am here to convince you to be part of the solution, one way or the other.'

'Are you threatening me, you little shit? Tell me who you are rather than hiding in the shadows. Tell me. TELL ME!'

Without thinking, James's mind form the words 'James Shaw' before he forces them from his thoughts. James looks at the president who only has anger in his eyes. The only thoughts James feels from the president are of anger and hatred.

'I knew this wasn't going to go well, but I didn't expect this amount of hatred or resistance. I am going to give you one final chance to help in this cause because in the end, you would be helping not only countries you don't care about but also your own people, your family, your future family, and yourself. In the end, we all benefit. I don't care whether you want to take credit for the change because I certainly don't, as long as you genuinely want to help.'

'There is nothing you have said to convince me to help you. And I believe there is nothing you can do to change that.'

'That's where you're wrong, sir. Although I don't want to do it, I can tell you many ways on how I can force you to agree. The thing is that I want you to agree willingly without my threat hanging over your head. But if I have to, I will. Remember when you first heard me and I stopped you from calling out to your guards? I can make you stop breathing until you suffocate. I can

also control your movements. I can make you jump off a building, stick your head under water until you drown, shoot yourself with your own pistol. So what's your pleasure? Do you want to die, or do you want to help?'

'Nonsense! I didn't call out because I was in shock. That's all. You can do nothing to me to make me change my mind.'

The president is sitting at his desk, looking across the room at nothing. His eyes widen. He's no longer breathing. He tries to take a breath, but no air passes through his nostrils. He opens his mouth, but his diaphragm refuses to contract or expand. His eyes begin to lose focus. His peripheral vision starts to darken as the darkness deepens. The president raises his hands above his head, waving furiously.

Air rushes into his lungs through his mouth. It rushes in so fast that the president doubles over and starts to cough uncontrollably. After several more breaths, the president looks up.

'OK, OK, I understand. I will help your cause, I promise. What do you want me to do?'

'There will be a meeting, shortly comprising around sixty leaders. I will tell you the time and place the meeting will take place. You will need to bring an interpreter if you need one as there will be leaders from many countries speaking many languages. Each leader will have their own interpreter who can translate their words into English. Your translator will be doing the same as well as translating English into Russian for you to understand.

I would like you to participate and contribute to the meeting positively. Being one of our great leaders, I'm hoping that you will volunteer to be one of the main chairpersons as I believe your word would encourage others to support change and possibly be part of the committee. I want you to come up with ideas on how we can help poor countries with little or no resources become self-reliant and achieve independence without being a burden on the diminishing resources we have, how we can eradicate violence and extremists, how we can help the environment heal by stopping the destruction of forests and wildlife and using cleaner energy.'

'That is a very impressive and challenging list.'

'It is, and it can be achieved. With your help, and the help of every country, we can do this. There are a couple of more things I'm afraid, but remember, everyone will contribute and contribute fairly. You will provide resources and money which will be held in a trust fund to be used as the committee decides. This last item concerns you and the other eight countries with nuclear capabilities. I want you to think about how you intend to efficiently disarm and destroy all your nuclear weapons. Remember, however, that I will be asking the same of all other countries with nuclear capabilities to do the same, including the USA, China, the UK, France, India, Israel, Pakistan, and North Korea. The money that these countries will not be using on nuclear weapons will go into the trust fund as well.'

'You are demanding too much. By imposing the destruction of nuclear weapons, you will leave us defenceless if there . . . is a need to use them.'

'I don't believe so because if we work in unison and show everyone that we intend to help one another become a peaceful, supportive, and productive peoples, then there will be no need of this type of destructive force.'

'I disagree, but if you can convince the other countries to destroy their weapons, then my country will do the same.'

'I will, and I can, including the USA. Think about what I've asked, and I will return once I have the agreement from all the other leaders. Do you have any questions, sir?'

'No, but I have much to think about.'

'Then I will say goodnight, Mr President.'

James opens his eyes and takes a deep, staggered breath. He is mentally drained but is relieved that he's finally convinced possibly the most difficult leader he would face to help in his cause.

James leaves the panic room and makes himself a cup of hot chocolate before having an early night. He knows that he has a few more difficult confrontations ahead.

Chapter 20

The next morning, James checks his list and marks off the Russian president. He has eight leaders left, apart from those from the poor countries.

James decides to leave the US president until he's spoken with the seven remaining leaders with nuclear weapons.

Although difficult, James manages to convince the leaders of the United Kingdom, France, China, India, Israel, Pakistan, and North Korea to join the group. Some of the leaders such as the Pakistani president and the supreme leader of North Korea needed more convincing than the others, but the same technique used on Putin make them see reason. Once they knew that James had more control over them than they expected, they appeared willing to participate.

The other leaders were surprised that James had convinced the Russian president and were intrigued on how he had pulled it off. They even said that they were looking forward to seeing the Russian president speak at the meeting and that he had agreed to disarm his country for the good of the world.

A week after speaking with Putin, James is ready to confront the American president. Not knowing where the president would be residing, James waits until late evening before contacting him.

James follows his usual routine and closes his eyes.

The room he's in is totally dark. The curtains so fully cover the windows that no light enters the room.

'Mr President, Mr President, sir. May I speak with you?'

James hears the rustle of sheets.

'Mr President, I wish to speak with you.'

'What? Who's there?' The bedside light comes on. The president is alone. James wonders where the president's wife is. He throws the covers from around himself and jumps out of bed, looking around. He's wearing a white singlet and boxer shorts. His hair is tussled from the pillow.

'Mr President, I wish to speak with you on an important matter.'

'Who's there? Where are you? Come out from where you're hiding before I call my security.' The president uses his fingers to straighten his hair, trying to look presentable.

'I'm here, sir, but you can't see me. Please don't be alarmed. I'll explain everything, I promise. Please don't call out to anyone.'

'Who's put you up to this? Where are you hiding? Tell me now, or I'll call my secret service agents.'

'Please don't do that, sir. I promise I'll explain everything. I'm only here to ask for your help and advice.'

'Who the hell are you to ask for my help? Get out. Get out now!'

'Mr President, I'm only here to talk with you. I've been through this enough times that I just want you to listen and understand what I'm saying.'

'What the fuck are you talking about? Come out. Show yourself.'

'Mr President, I'm only here in thought, not in person.'

'That's ridiculous. Are you some nut trying to kill me? How did you get in?'

James is frustrated and doesn't want to continue this line of conversation as it's getting them nowhere.

'Please sit down, sir.'

Unwillingly, the president moves over the bed bench in front of the bed and sits.

'What? How did you do that?'

'It's one of the many things that I can do, sir. Now please listen to what I have to say, and try and keep an open mind.'

'I don't know who you are, and I have no intention of hearing what you have to say.'

'Ah, but you will.'

The president tries to object, but no words leave his mouth. His eyes widen in shock and surprise.

'I am here to ask for your help. I've spoken with other leaders, and I've got their agreement to help with the problems the world is facing. I've spoken with the most influential leaders of countries who can help in this cause, including Russia, China, India, Canada, and Japan, totalling around forty countries.'

James lets the president speak.

'Are you trying to tell me that that you've spoken with these leaders and managed to convince them, including Putin?'

'Absolutely, sir. They have all agreed to help, granted that some of them were difficult to convince. But in the end, they have, including Putin.'

'If you've managed to convince Putin, I'm all ears.'

'Thank you, sir. As I said, please be open-minded because what I have to say is true. The world is becoming so toxic that we have maybe one to two hundred years before we destroy the environment we live in to the extent that it will no longer be able to sustain animal or plant life, including humans. We're wasting resources, and what we continue to do is unsustainable.

'I've asked all the major leaders of the world to attend a meeting to discuss options to restore our environment and to help poor countries become self-reliant and achieve independence without being a burden on the diminishing resources we have, how we can eradicate violence and extremists, how we can help the environment heal by stopping the destruction of forests and wildlife, and using cleaner energy.

'With the input and help of major countries, I believe that it is achievable. Now I know that you've been resistant to change because you believe that other countries would renege on their promises or take advantage by plundering weaker countries, but this will not happen. Everyone will agree and contribute fairly both financially and physically. Everyone will offer their resources subject to what is agreed by the group.

'As I said to Putin, with your help and the help of every country, we can do this. There are a couple more things I'm afraid, but remember, everyone will contribute and contribute fairly. You will provide resources and money which will be held in a trust fund to be used as the committee agrees. This last item concerns you and the other eight countries with nuclear capabilities. I want you to think about how you intend to efficiently disarm and destroy all your nuclear weapons. Remember, however, that I have asked the same of all other countries with nuclear capabilities to do the same, including Russia, China, the UK, France, India, Israel, Pakistan, and North Korea. The money that these countries will not be using on nuclear weapons will go into the trust fund as well.

'Being one of our great leaders, sir, I believe that with your agreement, it will encourage other countries to support and contribute willingly. Remember, however, that I require your genuine commitment and not to use this to your personal advantage or the advantage of the USA alone.'

'So you expect me to bow down to your vision of how the world should be to the detriment of the United States?'

James feels as if he's been reciting the same hymn over and over, and he's getting sick of it.

'Mr President, I don't want to threaten you. I want your genuine commitment and support. I want you to understand that this change will benefit everyone on this planet for its future survival. If you don't want to help, then I can force you to. I would rather have your help willingly because I don't want to waste my time, keeping an eye on someone whom I cannot trust. So what's it going to be?'

'If you've managed to convince the others that this cause is worthy and they are willing to commit to change, then I will agree as well, as long as you can guarantee that no country will take advantage of this because we will not be in any position to defend ourselves should they have hidden weapons to threaten us with.'

'Believe me sir, that if a leader of any country lies to me, I will show them no mercy.'

'Then you have my word. The United States will help in any way that you believe we should.'

'No, sir, the way the group agrees everyone should help. You will have an equal voice and have as much say as any other member. It will be a group decision. That is why I want all leaders to be true to their word and participate willingly for the benefit of everyone, sir.'

'You're very polite, calling me *sir* all the time.'

'Yes, sir. My parents taught me to respect people.'

'So you're . . .'

'Yes, sir, I am human just like you.'

'Well, your parents have taught you well. They must be proud.'

'They were . . . are, sir.'

'Ah, I see. I understand. I assume you're not going to tell me who you are then?'

'No, sir, I'd rather keep that to myself.'

'Your age?'

'No, sir, but I'm probably younger than you think I might be.'

'Can I ask where you're from then?'

'No, I'd rather keep that to myself as well, sir. I will tell you, however, that I am a red, white, and blue American just like you though.'

'Then I trust you even more.'

'Thank you, sir. There is one more thing though. Once you decide on how you are going to disarm and destroy America's nuclear weapons, I don't want you do anything else until after the meeting with the other leaders is held.'

'You certainly come straight to the point, don't you? I'll have a meeting with my joint chiefs of staff and discuss it with them whilst I wait for you to return.'

'I've had the same discussion countless times now, and I'm glad that I've covered everyone on my list. If there is nothing else, sir, I will say goodnight. I will contact you shortly with a meeting date and location. Goodnight, Mr President.'

James opens his eyes with relief. The mountain had been finally conquered. All that is left is to invite the leaders of the poor countries to attend the meeting as their input and agreement is just as important as those countries that were offering help. James could see another mountain looming ahead.

James leaves that thought to ponder tomorrow. He is tired and needs to rest his mind and body before he moves to climbing the next mountain.

Chapter 21

James is awakened from his sleep by the low but high-pitched sound of the alarm. He has set the alarms system to omit a low sound when the external sensors detect movement outside and a screeching high-pitched sound when the door and window sensors are triggered.

He looks at the bedside clock which displays fluorescent numbers: 2:20 a.m. He's only been asleep for just over an hour after speaking with the US president. James slips on his dressing gown and rushes to the study. He doesn't turn on the lights, informing anyone that the occupants of the house are awake. He turns on the monitors which instantly come to life.

The bank of monitors display scenes from both the inside and the outside of the house. One of the night-vision cameras is displaying a scene of a dark car driving slowly up his driveway with its lights off in shades of grey and black. He can't make out the colour of the car or how many occupants it contains.

James switches off the monitors and the alarm, and goes through the hidden door through to the big house, making sure that he closes the door behind him. His cold feet slap on the cold marble floor heading towards the spiral staircase. James hears the sound of tyres crunching over the scoria at the front of the house. James's heart is trying to beat through his chest as he locates the hidden door behind the stairway. He pushes through the door and closes it behind him. The bank of lights come on automatically as they sense movement. The bright lights temporarily blind him until his eyes adjust. James rushes down the stairs, holding onto the handrail. He feels the hardness and coarseness of the concrete stairs leading down to the main door of the panic room. He thinks that he should have put on some slippers as the skin on his tender feet start feeling the cold and rough floor.

James enters the ten-digit PIN on the entry panel. The panel displays an error message. James's panic increases. Has he forgotten the PIN? He takes a deep breath and tries the PIN again. He hears the door pins retract, and the door opens.

He closes the door behind him, rushes to the bank of panels, and turns them on. He sees four men dressed in suits approaching the big house; one of them is carrying what appears to be a leather carpetbag. Two of the men are heading for the front door and the other two are moving to either side of the house. One of the two men approaching the front door and carrying the bag tries to peer through the frosty glass panels on the door and notices the doorbell which doubles as a camera. James freezes the screen and looks closely at the man. He doesn't appear to be American, but he doesn't appear to be Asian or black either. His hair is cut short as if he were in the military, and furrows appear on his forehead.

The other man grabs the collar of his jacket and slips in his other hand, pulling out a pouch. Within seconds, the front door is opened. No alarm sounds. James has disconnected it. The two men pull out two small torches and turned them on, scanning the room. The man with the free hand also pulls out what appears to be a gun with a silencer attached.

The two men outside continue to circle the house on either side. Eventually, James knows that they will find the front door to the small house.

The two men inside the house slowly move from room to room, searching. Finding nothing, including the secret door and passage leading to the panic room, they move on upstairs, their flashlights moving from side to side and reflecting off the walls. There are no cameras installed upstairs so James can't tell what they are doing. James moves his attention to the two men outside. One of them has found the other entryway, the other now at the back of the house, travelling past the stable and boathouse. The first man at the small house entry has stopped and lights a cigarette whilst he waits for the other. The other continues around the house and approaches the front entry where his partner waits for him. He joins him in a cigarette.

The two men in the big house have finished their excursion upstairs and start coming down again. They stand in the centre of the room, talking. A few moments later, the man with the bag opens it and hands some small square boxes to the other. James can't tell what they are. The two men move to either side of the room and place these boxes in each corner of the room before continuing to the rooms beyond.

James observes each man crouch down, place the box on the floor, and adjust something attached to it. He notices that each box begins omitting a small flashing light as the men get up and move to another area to set another box. All James can assume is that these boxes are actually bombs set to blow, either by a timer or by a remote control. He'd seen enough spy movies, including James Bond, where bombs are set to blow buildings to smithereens.

James panics. Clearly, these guys aren't going to leave quietly if they find nothing. They are planning to blow the place up, and although James knows that the panic room will withstand the blast, or blasts, he won't have a place to live in if the house is levelled to the ground. It will also be difficult to explain to the authorities and house insurance company on why someone would want to blow up his house. He briefly considered the possibility of living in the panic room if these criminals aren't stopped and he can't save his home. James shakes his head, 'wake up stupid.'

The two men who have left James the small square and blinking surprises move outside and proceed together along the right side of the house, which will quickly lead them to the other two men who are waiting at the small entrance.

'Do something,' James tells himself. James can't think. He watches the bank of screens. 'Do something now, or there'll be nothing left, nothing to remind you of Mom or Dad.'

He continues to watch the screens. The first two men have turned the corner of the big house and are now heading towards the other two men who are still waiting.

James moves to the bedroom and lays on the bed, facing the ceiling. He closes his eyes and tries to slow his respiration and heartbeat. His mind continues to race, a vision of the house going up in a ball of flames.

He takes deep breaths and tries to visualise the man he had seen on the monitor. Short hair, furrowed forehead, short hair, furrowed forehead.

All of a sudden, James is following the two men heading towards their colleagues who are still smoking in front of the small house. *Now what?* James thinks. He can only communicate with one of these thugs at a time. What can he tell them? What can he do to scare them off?

The four men come together and say something to one another. They appear to be speaking Russian, and although his mother had taught James a little Russian when he was young, he only made out the occasional word. Nothing that he could determine their intent, apart from making the house go boom.

The four men begin turning towards the house, with the man carrying the carpetbag containing the explosives leading. 'DO SOMETHING NOW, FOR CHRIST'S SAKE!' James is yelling to himself.

The first man starts going up the three steps leading to the front door landing. He stops on the second step, turns, drops his bag, reaches into his jacket, pulls out his gun, and shoots the other three in the chest. They are in shock as they see their comrade shoot them, and they have no time to retaliate. They fall back. The first man steps forward and shoots them again, this time in the head before dropping the gun.

His eyes are wide open, and he's shaking. He tries to look around, but he can't move.

'Who are you?' questions James, the first time James communicates with him.

The man says nothing. **'WHO ARE YOU?'** storms James, now showing his anger. James didn't believe he had it in him, but now he was angry and infuriated.

'I am no one,' replies the man.

'That I can believe. Now the big question—and I expect an answer, or you will be lying next to your comrades—who sent you?'

'Ah, ah, ah, I can't tell you or I will be . . . eliminated,' replies the man.

The man's eyes widen again. He can't breathe. He's trying to inhale, but his chest won't expand. He panics. His eyes are moving left to right, and he's starting to shake again. Thirty seconds . . . forty-five . . . the man's eyes begin to flutter. James let the man's body take a breath. The man falls to his hands and knees, breathing in and then coughing. He takes another breath.

'Tell me who sent you . . . NOW.'

'It was . . . it was Putin. It was Putin,' pleads the man.

'Does anyone else know I'm here? And tell me the truth or else . . .'

'No, No. Putin gave my group your name, and we searched for everyone called James Shaw in the US,' replies the man.

'How many did you find?' enquires James, trying to appear casual so as not to alarm him.

'We found thirty-two with the same name,' replies the man.

'And how many have you visited?'

'You are number five,' confirms the man.

'You were lucky then. What did you do to the first four?' asks James in a quiet voice.

'We . . . ah . . . we killed them,' nervously says the man.

James says nothing more. The man leans forward, picks up his gun, and shoots himself through the temple before falling over.

James returns to his body and opens his eyes. He's damp with sweat. 'Well, it appears I can be ruthless,' he says to himself. He walks over to the bank of monitors and scans the outside of the house for any movement. Nothing. He sits there for several minutes, focusing on the blinking boxes. Are they on a timer? He couldn't sit there all night, waiting, so he leaves the panic room and gingerly climbs the concrete steps to the door leading to the main room of the house. He waits several seconds before building up enough courage to open the door and slowly heads to the nearest box. He finds no timer. A small antenna is protruding from the box. It must be a receiver so that the box can be activated remotely. James gives out a sigh of relief.

He gathers up the boxes and places them carefully near the front door. He then proceeds upstairs in search of other boxes that might have been placed there. He is thorough, searching each room, wardrobes, under the beds. Nothing.

James goes through the secret door leading to the small house and changes into some old clothes and sneakers before returning to the big house.

He gingerly picks up the small boxes, opens the front door, and proceeds to the car—a Dodge Durango with a large carry space in the back. The car is unlocked, and the keys are in the ignition. Thankfully, James doesn't have to search the four men for the car keys.

He places the boxes carefully in the back-seat foot area before getting into the driver's seat. He drives to where the four men are laying. He manhandles each man into the back carry space, making sure that he collects their guns, torches, and bags. Two of the guys were nearly twice James's body weight and could have easily played Line-backers for the Los Angeles Rams. Although trying to be careful, his hands and clothes are quickly covered in the dead men's blood. '*You won't be wearing these clothes again,*' James tells himself.

James wipes his hands on his old windcheater before driving the car into the stable and covering the bodies so that they can't be easily seen if someone notices the car. James has to decide on how he is going to get rid of it and the bodies.

James returns to the driveway where the men have been shot and examines the ground. There are several areas where blood is visible and still wet. He connects the garden hose to the sprinkler, places the sprinkler in the centre of the bloodstain area, and turns it on. James leaves it on whilst he checks the house to see if anything has been left behind. The house is clean. He returns to where the water sprinkler is doing its job to wash away the blood and lets it soak into the soil. He leaves the sprinkler on before going back into the house. James is surprised how calm he's been, considering what has taken place that night.

James let the sprinkler run all night, and when he wakes from a restless sleep the next morning, he finds the ground is completely water-soaked and the bloodstains are no longer visible. He, however, notices small sparkling points in the scoria; they appear to be bullet shells. He thinks back to the previous night and remembers that a total of seven shots had been fired and proceeds to search for the seven shells. Thankfully, he finds all seven shells and places them in the Dodge as well.

Chapter 22

Surprisingly, James is hungry enough to have breakfast, and whilst he's eating toast and drinking coffee, he goes onto the Internet and scans newspapers using keywords such as 'murder' and 'Shaw'.

Three articles appear, containing these keywords. There have been two murders in Washington two days apart a week ago. One was a Jimmy Shaw who had been shot in the head in his apartment. The other was a James Shaw who had also been found shot through the head. There was another Jimmy Shaw who had been found shot in the head, three days ago in Oregon. There was, however, no news about the fourth murder. Either it had taken place within the past day or so, or the police were keeping it quiet. Clearly though, James could see a pattern emerging. These four thugs had started their murder spree, beginning on the west coast and moving towards the east, progressively finding and killing every James Shaw on their list.

James is angry that this Russian dictator was willing to kill innocent human beings at will. He sits at the kitchen bench whilst he thinks of his plan on how to dispose of the bodies. He can't just ring the police and ask them to remove them from his property for trespassing, although he was legally permitted to kill anyone who intended harm to him. He is sure that the police would have a few questions for James to answer, and he had no plausible excuse to explain how an eighteen-year-old boy had managed to shoot and kill four professional killers. The police would also finally link them to the other murders which had taken place over the past week.

He then thinks that if these four killers were travelling along the west coast, they would possibly be staying low between each kill before travelling to the next destination. James didn't remember seeing any change of clothes in the Dodge, and unless the murderers were intending to wear the same clothes until all the Shaw's on their list were disposed of, they would have left them somewhere. He imagines these thugs walking into a drycleaner, wearing only their singlets, boxer shorts, shoes, and a gun and gun holder strapped around their chest and arm, carrying their suits and asking for an express service to clean them.

James has no choice but to search these guys and see if he can find some form of motel key or something that tells him where they are staying.

He walks to the stable and opens the tailgate of the Dodge. There is a faint smell of urine and faeces. Clearly, one or more of them had emptied their bowels. James had read somewhere that bodies do that after they die. This was going to be more difficult than he thought.

He removes the cover off the bodies and begins to search the pockets of the first one. Nothing. He pushes the body to one side to access the second. The foul odour intensified, so James began breathing through his mouth before the stench made him bring up his breakfast. He thankfully finds a key attached to a plastic key ring on the second. He imagined removing all the soiled bodies from the car so that he could examine them.

James looks at the key ring. *Mussel Shoals Motel and Caravan Park*. The key itself is stamped with the number 9. James knows of the place as he had driven past there a few times. For what he remembered, it was an old and rundown place with cheap accommodation for tourists passing through. He knew he had to go there to see if there was anything of interest the thugs had left behind, or something that might implicate that they had or were coming to his house.

As the sun sets, James drives his BMW along Santa Ana Road back towards Ventura and turns right along a narrow winding dirt road towards Lake Casitas. He had come this way with his father when he was younger, searching for good fishing spots. There was a secluded area along this arm of the lake where the water was deep blue. The final twenty yards to the lake's edge had a steep slope where his father had launched the boat from many times. The water here was deep, and the fishing had been good. When James reaches the clearing before the slope, he finds no other cars. He drives the BMW to the edge of the clearing, away from the slope, and parks the car. He gets out. The darkness is almost complete, and James can barely distinguish between the trees and sky above.

'Idiot,' James chastises himself. He's forgotten to bring a torch with him. '*These minor things will get you into trouble if you don't start using your grey matter, stupid,*' James reprimands himself. James reaches into the front pocket of his jeans and pulls out his mobile phone. He turns on the light function and scans the path he's come from and starts walking in that direction.

Eventually, he reaches Santa Ana Road and turns off the light function on his phone. Using the shoulder on the road, he starts heading back towards the house. He estimates that he has between three to four miles walking ahead of him. James tries to walk as close to the treeline, taking care not to trip on any exposed tree roots or rocks and break a leg as the road was poorly lit by street lamps, so that he's not as noticeable to traffic travelling along the road.

James finally arrives home, breathing heavily as it was uphill all the way. It's just on ten in the evening. He goes inside, has a drink of water, and grabs a plastic bag containing the bloodstained clothes he'd worn the previous night, before heading towards the Dodge which is still holding the four covered dead bodies. James throws the plastic bag in the back-seat foot area before starting the car and heading towards the Mussel Shoals Hotel. When he arrives at the car park of the hotel, James drives, slowing along the motel rooms until he sees the door marked with the number 9 and parks the car in front, reversing into the car space.

He casually steps out of the car and walks to the door, giving the impression to anyone who notices him that he is staying there.

James gives a quick glance to either side before inserting the key and enters the hotel room. James draws the curtains and turns on the light. The room has a musty smell, and the decor hadn't been changed since the mid-sixties. The furniture is worn, with cigarette burns on most of the chairs and all over the carpet. How anyone would want to stay here was baffling.

The room doubles as both a bedroom containing a double and single bed, and a lounge. A smaller room ahead is another bedroom containing two single beds. To the right is the bathroom.

James begins to search in the cupboards, under the beds, and in the drawers and pulls out everything that belongs to the men. He even checks between the bed mattresses to see if anything is hidden there. He places everything on the double bed, including the contents of the bathroom. James examines what he's retrieved from the two rooms and quickly searches the suitcases for anything of interest. Apart from clothes, he finds spare boxes of bullets, the men's passports with the Russian insignia on the covers, and a long list of addresses. Clearly, it shows the addresses of every James Shaw they had identified and planned to execute if they were allowed to continue their sightseeing trip across the United States. James doesn't think he needs to keep any of it.

He places everything in the four suitcases, not caring to fold any of the clothes before throwing them in as well. These suitcases will never be unpacked again, he hopes. James places the four suitcases close to the front door before checking the rooms one final time. Once he's satisfied, he heads back to the front door.

James knows he had to be quick, but he must maintain a casual appearance when he steps out the door. He steps outside, carrying two of the suitcases, and walks to the Dodge. He opens the car door behind the driver's seat, throws the two suitcases in, and briskly walks back to the room. He retrieves the final two suitcases, closes and locks the front door to the room, and throws these two suitcases in with the first. James gets into the driver's seat, starts the car, and heads out of the car park. His pulse is racing, but looking in the rear-view mirror, he sees no one. James tries to relax. He travels back to Santa Ana Road, making sure he's not speeding or swerving all over the road. The last thing he needs is to be pulled over by a police car. '*Licence and registration,*' James could hear the police officer saying, '*and by the way, can we check what you've got in the back?*' He shakes his head and concentrates on the task ahead.

James arrives at the narrow dirt road he had travelled earlier and turns right towards the lake. He slowly makes his way until he reaches the clearing where his BMW is parked. No one. Good. James faces the Dodge towards the lake just before the slope and slightly lowers the windows on all four doors before getting out. He pats himself down to make sure he has all his belongings and has nothing belonging to the men. James finds the hotel room key in his pocket and throws that into the car.

He leans into the car and tries to move the gearshift from park to neutral. It won't more. He realises that he needed to press the brake pedal before he can move the gearshift. He gets back in with the driver's side door open, puts one foot on the brake pedal, and moves the gearshift to neutral. James briskly steps out and closes the car door. The car remains stubbornly stationary. He moves to the back of the car and pushes on the tailgate. After a small resistance, the car lurches forward and slowly rolls down towards the lake.

James has his fingers crossed as he sees the car pick up speed and hit the water. After the initial impact with the water, the car levels out and begins floating across the surface, its momentum moving it further into the lake. It continues to float. James panics. *Those car doors must have bloody good seals*, he thinks. The car finally tilts back and starts its journey down. The car appears to have floated around fifty yards before beginning to sink. The water reaches the level of the partially opened windows, and James can hear the bubbles as the air in the car is replaced with the water rushing in. It disappears from view, although James can still see and hear bubbles rising to the surface. He watches for a few more minutes until he can't hear any more bubbles popping on the surface before getting into his BMW and heading home. James finally sits in his reclining chair, mentally and physically drained.

<h1 style="text-align:center">Chapter 23</h1>

The next morning, James makes himself breakfast before heading to the panic room. '*Time to confront the Russian president again,*' he mumbles to himself. James locks himself in, lays on the bed, and closes his eyes.

He sees the president sitting behind his ornate desk, talking to a couple of soldiers who are standing at attention on the other side of the desk. The president appears to be discussing some type of strategy but can't understand exactly what. James waits, not exposing his presence. He has to be firm with this guy without showing emotion because the president has clearly deceived James during their previous discussions where the president had agreed to cooperate. The two soldiers salute and leave the room as the president resumes writing something.

'*You FUCK,*' starts James. So much for not showing his emotions.

The president looks up. James silences him before he starts to speak. The president's eyes widen, and he appears frightened.

'*You promised me that you would help and encourage the other leaders to fix this world that you are all destroying,*' continues James with a little more control. '*Instead, you send your henchmen to come and kill me. They even killed innocent people trying to find me.*'

'I don't know what you mean.'

'*Bullshit! Your little furrowed forehead friend told me exactly who was behind this.*'

'Sasha? What have you done to him?'

'The same thing he tried to do to me, the same thing he did to innocent people. But not before he shot his three comrades. He shot them at point blank in their chests and heads before shooting himself in the head.'

There is a hint of anger in the president's face although James can't read his mind.

'I don't care whether you want to help or not. I don't give a shit, but I'll give you three possibilities on how this will go down. I can make you a puppet so that you appear a fool in front of everyone. I kill you now and encourage your replacement to help, or you do this willingly. Which is your pleasure?'

'I'm not going to be made a fool of, and I'm not going to help you.'

'Fine!'

The president opens the right-hand top drawer of his desk, finds nothing, and opens the drawer below. He reaches inside, pulls out a PSM pistol, and holds it to his head. The president's eyes widen. He can feel his index finger beginning to press the trigger.

'Wait, stop,' pleads the president.

James let the president rest the gun on his desk.

'OK, I promise I will help you.'

'I am completely baffled as to why you are totally against helping change the world for the good of mankind. I understand that the majority of your people love and worship you, but everyone else hates your guts. Others think you're an arrogant tyrant, a liar, and a lowlife. Wouldn't you rather be remembered as the greatest saviour of the world? A leader with the foresight and the passion to help his fellow man? I don't care whether you take credit for the contribution you will make in helping the world but as long as you do it for the right reasons and not take advantage or manipulate those who are vulnerable and are trying to help.'

'Yes, I understand what you are saying.'

'I hope I can believe you because we will have no further discussions. If you lie to me again, I will not give you another

chance to plead for forgiveness. You will cease to be. You may consider this a threat, but I call it giving advice. Agree willingly, contribute positively, participate completely, and help change the world, and humankind will live a long and peaceful life, including your family, for generations to come.'

'I still don't understand why you are doing this. What's in it for you?'

'Nothing, nothing at all. I'm not in this for fame or gratitude, and I don't want to be mentioned outside the group. I've had a happy life, but I've also experienced great sorrow, so much sorrow that I wanted to end my life. The majority of the people on this planet know nothing but sorrow and hardship until they die. On the other hand, very few of them enjoy wealth and power and sometimes greed to the detriment of the poor and the environment. But no more. I want those people like you, with wealth and power, to contribute and help everyone and everything on this planet for its long-term survival and happiness. You may think that I'm a fool, but I know what's coming even though you don't believe it. The destruction of this planet will not come in our lifetime, but it's not that far away. In two, three, or maybe four generations, we will have contributed to our own destruction to the point where change will not make a difference. We need to start changing now before it's too late.'

'I give you my word that I will help willingly. I promise.'

'Good, I'm glad. I want to trust you because you are one of the few people who will encourage others to follow, who has the tenacity to take this important responsibility on and help change this world. Now I have a few more errands to finish, but I should be back shortly to tell you the place and date of the meeting. See you soon, Mr President.'

***

James sets about contacting the leaders of the twenty poorest countries on his list, such as Uganda, Afghanistan, Ethiopia,

Rwanda, and Mozambique. Although they are all sceptical of his proposal at first, unbelieving that it's possible, they looked forward to participating and contributing to this great event. Within two weeks, he has their agreements. Time to organise the meeting date, but there was one last thing he has to do.

James goes to a department store and purchases a nondescript prepaid mobile phone and pays for a one-year access. He then proceeds to an electronic store and enquires about options to stop anyone from tracking his phone. The geeky salesperson is very knowledgeable and proceeds to show James on how to change the various setting on his phone to prevent tracking. In addition, the salesperson sells James a Faraday pouch to carry the phone in that completely blocks all Wi-Fi, GPS, and RFID signals.

James has a late breakfast, and by noon, he is in his usual place, laying on the bed in the bunker. James closes his eyes.

'Good evening, Chancellor.'

It is nine in the evening. The German chancellor is relaxing on the couch, watching a movie, and eating popcorn. James is still surprised that an important woman such as Angela Merkel acts like normal people.

'Ah hello.' The Chancellor turns off the TV screen and puts the popcorn down.

'It still surprises me that an important person like you acts like us normal people.'

'Are you implying that I'm not a normal person?' she responds jokingly. 'Yes, we have to present ourselves professionally when we're conducting formal duties and in the presence of others, but at home, we are as normal as anyone. Well, most of us are anyway. So I assume by your return that you've either failed miserably or you've had success.'

'I'm happy to report the latter. I've contacted everyone on my list, and they have all agreed to meet at a designated place and time. I'm here to discuss when and where that will be. Does your offer still stand about having the meeting here in Berlin?'

'Absolutely. I'm surprised that you've managed to get everyone to agree. I wasn't expecting it.'

'I hit a few roadblocks along the way, actually one big one, but that's been sorted now, so we're good to go. This is where I will need your help because I've never been to Germany, so I don't know where we can hold the meeting or where all the leaders and their interpreters can stay.'

'The German Bundestag in the Reichstag building, which is our parliament, is large enough to hold up to 700 people, so it should easily accommodate everyone. There is also an excellent hotel no more than 500 metres from the Reichstag building called Hotel Adlon Kempinski where the visitors can stay. Once we agree on a date to hold the meeting, I will have both the hotel and Bundestag made available. Being so close together, it will be much easier to police and prevent access by anyone other than out guests.'

'We need this to go smoothly because I don't believe we'll have a second chance, and we want everyone to feel safe and secure.'

'Absolutely. There will be no one else staying at the hotel, and all the staff there will be replaced by my people who will be thoroughly screened and held to complete silence. There will be soldiers stationed on each level of the hotel, two for every guest, and there will be an exclusion zone of 500 metres surrounding the hotel, the route our guests will take to the Reichstag building, and around Bundestag itself.'

'I see you've been making plans on how to tackle this.'

'I think what you are attempting will be momentous and inspirational if you pull it off. I consider it an honour being permitted to hold this meeting for all our future.'

'OK, now we have to decide on a date. If I give myself one month to contact everyone, then we can hold the meeting on the twenty-ninth of September. We should also consider starting the meeting in the morning so that we'll have time to discuss the purpose of the meeting, have everyone speak on behalf of their countries, and formulate an agreed plan.'

'I think you're being optimistic if you think we can do that all in one day. I wouldn't be surprised if it takes two to three days, even longer, considering there will be sixty leaders in attendance.'

'Not having done this before, I'll take your advice. I'll tell them all that they should allow up to five days to be present and that they should arrive no later than the day before the meeting commences. If you don't mind, I'll have each leader contact you after I've spoken with them so that they can inform you of when they will be arriving and the number of people they will bring.'

'Certainly. I need to know that information so that I can plan for their arrival and allocate rooms for them. I would, however, suggest that they limit the number of their entourage. Otherwise, there may be insufficient rooms for all of them in the hotel. If there are too many people, I will have to find another hotel to house them, making security more difficult.'

'Then I'll tell them that they should limit the people they intend to bring to no more than two as they will only be allocated two rooms. Does the hotel have 120 rooms?'

'Yes, it does. We'll have thirty rooms to spare should we need to use them.'

'OK, so let's plan the meeting and discuss an agenda.'

The German chancellor walks to her study, sits behind her desk, and pulls out a large writing pad from one of her desk drawers.

'Let's begin,' she says.

Over the next few hours, the chancellor listens, takes notes, and contributes on how the meeting should be structured. And after compromising on specific points, the agenda is finally set.

'I wish to thank you for all your help and contribution in making this happen. In my wildest dreams, I didn't think I'd pull this off.'

'What you are attempting to do should be commended. I am honoured that you've chosen me to help you turn your vision into fruition. I only hope that I don't let you down and that it culminates into a unified world.'

'I have every faith in you, Chancellor. All I've done is prepared the soil and planted the seeds. We'll soon know whether the soil is rich enough for the seeds to grow and whether those seeds become weeds or flowers.'

'A very fitting way to put it.'

'Thanks again, Chancellor. Goodnight. What's left of it, and I'll see you in a month.'

Chapter 24

Over the next two weeks, James revisits all the leaders, four to five leaders a day . . . or night, depending on time zones. He prepares a standard speech to relay to them so that he can cover it as efficiently as possible and minimise the time he spends explaining what they need to know.

'The meeting will be held in Berlin, Germany, and will commence at 10 a.m. on the twenty-ninth of September. You will need to arrive in Berlin the day before the meeting. You will be allocated two rooms in the hotel, so please limit your staff to no more than two people as they will be sharing the second room.

'If you need an interpreter, they will be one of the two people you are permitted to bring. Once you've organised your flight plan, please contact the German chancellor and relay the time you will be arriving and the number of staff that you will bring. She is expecting your call. All security and protection will be provided by the German chancellor. Please trust her as I do. She is taking every precaution to ensure your safety. Do not be alarmed with all the security present because they are there for your protection.

'If you have any dietary or other special requirements, please let the chancellor know, and she will arrange it. Please prepare any notes or speech you wish to make as every leader will be heard. I wish that you make a positive contribution because every contribution will achieve a stronger agreement.'

For those countries with nuclear capabilities, he added, *'As part of your speech, you will detail the time you will require to disarm all your nuclear weapons and the time you will require to destroy them. The disposal of these weapons should be done as efficiently and as quickly as possible as it will show the others that you are committed to this cause.'*

James is surprised that all the leaders agree willingly to his proposal, although some require convincing that they don't need to bring their own security.

James is sleeping odd hours, and his body is beginning to object. With his intermitted and erratic sleeping, some days he feels like a zombie, his head full of cotton wool. He's neglected eating regularly, and he has lost a considerable amount of weight.

With all his hard work completed, well, until the meeting takes place anyway, James spends the last two weeks getting back into some form of routine. He goes shopping and stocks up on food, both for the house and for the bunker. He starts cooking his own meals again rather than just scooping the contents of cans without bothering to heat them up. James even goes to see Dr Rowlings for his routine blood test. Apart from minor malnutrition, the doctor gives James a clean bill of health, with James promising to eat regularly.

Chapter 25

Four young men in their mid-twenties land in Zagreb, Croatia, on a flight from Syria carrying small bags containing only a change of clothes. They are clean-shaven and have short military-cut hair. Once they pass through customs, they take a taxi to a mechanics workshop where they've been expected. A non-descript Land Rover has been prepared for them, containing bags of warm clothing, hiking gear, and four sets of skis mounted to the roof racks.

They've given themselves two days to travel the 700 miles to Berlin and arrive by 28 September. They pass several checkpoints where their vehicle is thoroughly searched, and they are questioned on their destination. 'We're going to try skiing the slopes of Roskilde in Denmark, and if we have no luck there, we'll try the women in Copenhagen,' says one of the four men jokingly, with the other three men laughing loudly in unison.

Although the Land Rover is searched inside and out, including the under chassis, nothing is found. None of the checkpoint officers bother to check more thoroughly, thinking these four young men were either planning to mount the ski slopes in Denmark or the women there, and sent them on their way.

All the checkpoints these clean-cut young men pass through fail to discover the 200 pounds of C-4 hidden in the door cavities. So full are these door cavities that the window mechanisms have been removed and the windows are inoperable.

***

On the day before the meeting, as the leaders arrive at the Berlin Tegel Airport, there is a constant stream of limousines, police cars, and motorbikes transporting the leaders to the Hotel Adlon Kempinski, with the German chancellor greeting every one of them as they land.

One of the airport runways has been commandeered to accept only the leaders' planes, bypassing airport security and efficiently whisking them away. The fastest route along Saatwinkler Damm is protected by armed guards along its full length, with marksmen positioned on rooftops along the way.

The well-rehearsed hotel staff greet the leaders upon their arrival, and everything goes like clockwork. The guests are settled into their hotel rooms, and two army personnel are positioned outside every door.

***

The four men arrive in Berlin mid-morning on 28 September where they rent a cheap room in a hotel near the airport and walk to the airport where they rent a car, leaving the Land Rover in the hotel car park. They cruise around the airport and follow the route along the adjoining roads that the leaders are ferried along to Hotel Adlon Kempinski. They are stopped several times by the military police and their car inspected. Finding nothing and accepting the reason for their visit to sightsee attractions around Berlin, they are allowed to proceed.

Once the four men have determined that all the leaders are staying in the same hotel, they proceed with the next part of their plan. They park the rental car near the hotel and proceed on foot, strolling through the streets surrounding the hotel until they are approached by two armed army personnel who see them loitering in the doorway of a clothing store which has decided to remain closed because of the exclusion zone the army has in place. The street is quiet, with the only noise coming from the four men who appear to be jokingly pushing one another around. Before the two army personnel are able to question the four men on why they are in the area, the four men pounce. Two of them seize the army personnel, restricting their arms, whilst the other two grab hold of their heads from behind and break their necks.

So quickly and efficiently is their action that the two army personnel have no time to either call out for help or fire their rifles. The dead army personnel are shoved against the door of the clothing store and placed into a sitting position. Two of the men sit on the dead men's laps, making it appear from a distance that they are just two people sitting.

The other two men rush off to retrieve their rental car, and within minutes, they have the two dead army men in the trunk of the car. They proceed to the hotel where they are staying, collect their Land Rover, and drive both vehicles to the outskirts of Berlin. They stop on a quiet dirt road, park behind a grove of trees that could not be seen from the road, and begin to remove the clothing from the two army personnel. The bodies are thrown into the grove, and pulling off some of the lower branches from the trees, the bodies are covered.

They place the clothes, guns, and hats neatly into the trunk of the rental car and proceed to disassemble the door panels on the Land Rover to remove the C-4. The C-4 is distributed among the four bags the men used to carry their spare clothes in and place them in the trunk of the rental. After refitting the door panels on the Range Rover, they drive both cars back to their hotel.

By mid-afternoon, the men are back in their hotel room with the army personnel clothes and bags of C-4. One of the men places the C-4 blocks from the first bag on the table and begins inserting detonators in each, wiring them together in sequence, and finally attaching the initiating mechanism attached to a digital timer. The timer is off. He carefully places the wired C-4 with a timer back into the first bag and proceeds to do the same with the remaining three bags of C-4.

With the C-4 prepared and placed in the wardrobe of their hotel room, they go in search of dinner. It will be some time before the next part of their plan can proceed.

***

There is chatter and laughter in the dining room of the Hotel Adlon Kempinski that evening as the leaders greet one another, some of them sitting together to share the evening meal before finally turning in for the night.

At the makeshift security command centre positioned between the hotel and parliament, as shifts conclude and new ones begin, police officers, army, and other security personnel, including the hotel personnel, are required to sign in and sign out. The army officer in charge, however, notices that two of his men have failed to sign out. Their shift had ended more than two hours ago, and they had yet to return. The officer in charge knows these men quite well, and he doesn't believe that they would have forgotten to sign out after concluding their shift. He checks their details in his logbook and dials their home phone numbers. The men's wives confirm that their husbands have not returned home.

The officer dials the number of the German chancellor. 'I'm sorry to disturb you, Chancellor, but we may have a problem, maybe a serious one. Two of my men have failed to sign off after their shift, and they have not returned home. Their shift ended at twenty hundred hours, and they are overdue by more than two hours.'

'Increase security in and around the hotel,' replies the chancellor, 'and find out whether all our guests have arrived and are still there. Do this as discreetly and as quickly as possible.'

'Yes, Chancellor. I'll let you know within the hour,' concludes the officer before hanging up.

The officer in charge summons his subordinates and instructs them to search in and around the hotel where the guests are staying as well as the Reichstag building where the meeting would be held in the morning, and to report back to him in forty-five minutes if they find anything suspicious.

The officer then rushes to the hotel and instructs the concierge to conduct a verification that all the guests are present and accounted for.

The concierge finds the dining room empty as all the leaders would have returned to their hotel rooms. He returns to the reception desk, turns on his Ultra High Frequency (UHF) handheld radio, and adjusts the frequency so that he can communicate with all the security officers stationed outside each of the hotel bedrooms at once. He instructs each of them to check that each guest is in their room, to physically sight them before confirming that they are there, including the guests' entourage.

As each security officer responds, the concierge marks off each of the guests from his list. They are all accounted for, and the concierge notifies the officer in change that all the guests are in their rooms.

As promised and within the hour, the officer in charge rings the German chancellor and informs her that they have found nothing unusual either around the hotel or in the Reichstag Building and that all the guests were accounted for.

The German chancellor instructs the officer in charge to double the security and begin searching for the two missing men.

The chancellor is worried and concerned that something may be about to happen even though nothing has been found to contradict that. She opens her notebook and rings the number given to her.

James is taking a walk behind the house after having some lunch when his mobile phone rings. It rings for the first time. His heart starts to beat faster as he removes the phone from his belt.

'Hello?' answers James.

'I don't know how to begin, but I think we have a problem,' says the German chancellor with a slightly shrill voice.

'Why? What's happened?'

'Two of the security personnel have gone missing and have not returned to check out after their shift ended. We've contacted their homes, and they are not there either. The officer in charge knows them well, and he believes this is unusual for them. We've checked around the hotel and parliament and found nothing unusual. We've checked all the guests, and they appear to be all here. I don't know what else to do other than keep searching and increase security everywhere.'

'I don't know how I can help unless you can tell me who is behind this. I can only do something if you tell me who they are. I suggest that you keep a close eye on the hotel to start with, because if something is going to happen, it will be there. Tomorrow morning, if you find nothing, you can shift your security around the Reichstag building. If someone is going do something, it will happen soon. Whoever is behind this will know that they have a short amount of time to carry out what they plan to do. Please use whatever means you have to protect everyone. Let me know if there is further news.'

'I thought that maybe you could . . . do something. Use your power to search for . . . find out what's happening.'

'I'm sorry, but what I have doesn't work that way. Wait a minute. There is something that I might be able to do. Do you have or can you get photos of the missing men?'

'I can't see why not. What do you need them for?'

'If I know what they look like, I should be able to find them.'

'I'll have their photos available promptly then. I'll hear from you soon.'

James rushes back to the house and heads for the panic room.

The German chancellor rings the officer in charge and asks him to bring photos of the missing men to her office promptly. Before he can ask why, she hangs up.

The officer searches though his folder and finds photos of the missing men attached to their files detailing their service history. He removes them from the folder and heads for the chancellor's offices.

'I'm here. Did you get the photos?' asks James.

'I'm waiting for the officer in charge to bring them. He should be here momentarily,' replies the German chancellor.

There's a knock on her door, and she calls out, 'ENTER.'

The officer in charge enters the room and hands the two files to the chancellor. 'Why do you need their files?' enquires the officer in charge.

'One moment,' replies the chancellor as she holds the files out in front of herself and looks at the two photos.

'Are they acceptable?' the chancellor asks.

'Excuse me?' says the officer in charge, thinking that she's asked him the question.

'One moment,' repeats the chancellor.

James scans the photos.

'I think so. I just have to see how I'm going to do this.'

James visualises one of the two men, but nothing happens. He has to think. Why isn't it working? He tries again. Nothing. Maybe he can't transport his mind when he's already somewhere else. James opens his eyes in the bunker, closes them, and visualises the man again.

James is in an open space, outdoors. It's dark. There's a light breeze blowing through the trees. The only light is coming from the half-crescent moon. He looks down and sees what appears to be broken branches placed in a pile in the centre of the grove of trees. He assumes that this is where the two men are. James moves out to a clearing and looks for any landmarks. He sees the bright lights of Berlin in the distance, maybe ten to twenty miles away. Assuming that he has his bearings correct, Berlin is northwest of his position. He continues to look around, trying to find some landmark, but there's nothing of any significance. Then he sees the dark surface of what appears to be a lake, with the small waves reflecting the moon light.

'I've found them,' he says to the chancellor.

'Where? Are they all right?' the chancellor asks.

'Excuse me, Chancellor, but I don't know you're asking,' replies the officer in charge.

'I'm sorry, but please be silent. I'll explain shortly,' she tells the officer in charge.

'They are about ten to twenty miles southeast of here, somewhere near a lake. I didn't see them, but I believe they are in a grove of trees under a pile of fresh tree branches, so I assume they're dead.'

'Oh dear,' says the chancellor. 'Officer, do you know the lake southeast of here around fifteen miles away?'

'Yes, Chancellor,' replies the officer. 'It is called Great Müggelsee.'

'I'm sorry to say that you will find the two men near there. They are in a grove of trees under a pile of fresh tree branches,' she repeats.

'But how can you know this? You've only just seen the photos of the men, and you can tell me where they are?' questions the officer sceptically.

'Let's just say that I know someone who can,' replies the chancellor. 'Would you like to meet him? But we need to be quick because if these men are dead, then we have someone who is trying to kill our guests that we need to find, and find quickly. Please don't be frightened. I was in the same position as you are a few months ago, not believing, but the organisation of bringing these leaders together is due to who you are about to hear now.'

'Hello,' says James. *'What the chancellor has said is true, but she helped a lot in what we've accomplished so far.'*

'What? Who says that?' replies the officer.

'As the chancellor said, I am the one who found your men. I have been given the power to find people by just looking at their photos and visit people though my mind.'

James relays the image of the area where he's found the two men to the officer in charge. The officer's eyes widen as the image appears in his mind.

'I know it's difficult to understand, and maybe we can discuss this further when we're not in so much hurry. So please listen to your chancellor and help find these murderers, because we don't know whether there is one of more of them and what they are planning.'

'I'll look forward to having that discussion,' replies the officer.

'I assume you've heard our friend,' says the chancellor.

'What, you didn't hear him?' asks the officer.

'No. It appears that he can only communicate with one person at a time,' concludes the chancellor.

'I'll follow the officer around,' says James to the chancellor. **'But unless I know who this killer is or who they are, I won't be much help.'**

The officer in charge returns to the command centre and is updated on the search. Nothing had been found, and nothing appears to be out of place. The officer instructs two of his men to head off to the area around Great Müggelsee and to search around tree groves. He tells them to concentrate their efforts around the southwest side of the lake. He doesn't want to expend too many men as they were needed here. When this was all over and if nothing is found, he'd send more men to search the area.

The officer in charge maintains constant communication with the men in and around the hotel, but everything appears peaceful and quiet.

Around two in the morning, two army officers are cruising around the hotel in a Land Rover, acknowledging the army and security guards as they drive by, and start heading towards the underground hotel car park. They salute the guards on either side of the car park entry ramp as they proceed down to the lower floor.

As the two army officers reach the lower car park, they park the Land Rover, get out, and scan the area. There are a small number of cars scattered around the parking area, possibly belonging to the hotel staff, since none of the guests have arrived in their own cars. They select four cars closest to the outer walls, one in each corner of the car park, and jimmy the doors open before accessing the trunks.

The two men dressed as army officers return to the Land Rover and retrieve the four heavy bags containing the C-4. They each place one of the bags in the trunks of two of the cars they had opened, undo the bag zipper, access the digital timer, and set the countdown to fifteen minutes. After closing the trunk and relocking the car doors, they proceed to the remaining two cars and repeat the procedure.

With each bag containing fifty pounds of C-4, even though it would explode in a closed trunk, there would be so much explosive power that the foundations of the hotel would be totally destroyed, causing the fifteen-storey hotel to come crashing down.

The two so-called army officers leave the Land Rover in the car park and take the hotel elevator to the lobby and exit in that direction, so they won't be confronted by the same security personnel twice.

They walk to the bank of lifts in the car park and press the upwards arrow.

The guards standing outside the car park entry continue to look down the ramp, expecting the Land Rover to return within a few minutes since there was little to see down below. After five minutes however, they become concerned for the officers who have gone below as they might have encountered trouble.

The guards briskly walk down the ramp, and when they turn the corner to the lower level, they see the Land Rover parked in one of the parking bays, empty. They scan each car and use their flashlights to see inside the front and back seats. Nothing. They suspect something was wrong.

One of the officers presses the call button on his UHF radio pinned to his shoulder, informing security in the hotel lobby and outside the hotel to keep an eye out for two guards who would have come from either the elevators or stairwell.

By this time, the two so-called army officers have exited the elevator in the lobby and are casually proceeding to the front doors, trying not to make eye contact with anyone. They hear the radios around them come alive, but not knowing the German language, they don't know what is being said.

As the two army officers continue walking to the front doors, all the guards surround them, levelling their rifles and pistols in their direction, telling them to stop. The imposter army officers comply as two of the guards walk behind them, pointing their pistols to the back of their heads. As the two imposters attempt to draw their weapons yelling 'Allahu Akbar', they are both shot through the head by the guards standing behind them.

After confirming the officers are both dead, one of the guards speaks to the officer in charge using his UHF radio, telling him what has taken place.

'Search them and see if they have anything unusual, and get as many men down to the car park and search every car. Search them thoroughly,' barks the officer in charge. 'I'll be right there.'

The officer in charge sprints from the command centre and heads for the lower car park. When he arrives, the guards are smashing car door windows and searching the car interiors. They find nothing.

'Open the trunks!' yells the officer in charge. 'Make sure you check everywhere.'

One of the guards lifts the trunk lid of the car he's standing next to and started yelling, 'Here, sir! Here, here!'

The officer in charge runs over to the open trunk and sees the bag. He gingerly opens the zipper and is confronted by blocks of something and a digital timer counting down.

4:37

4:36

4:35

'Search every car now. Make sure you check every one of them. NOW!' the officer yells as he turned back to the bag.

He opens the zipper fully and places his hand in the bag, feeling around the timer. He holds his breath. He knows that if the timer is attached to an initiating mechanism, it will detonate if the timer is stopped. Then they would be in big trouble. If they had more time, they would be able to evacuate the hotel. He hears more guards yelling that they've also found something. He focuses on the bag.

3:45

3:44

3:43

He turns the timer over and gives a visible sigh of relief. He presses the off button on the timer, and the screen goes blank. Nothing happens.

He turns to the guards yelling and runs to the nearest one. A similar bag is sitting in the trunk. He opens the zip, quickly checks the timer . . .

2:58

2:57

2:56

He confirms that the timer configuration is the same as the first before pressing the off button.

He sprints to the next one, checks the timer . . .

2:12

2:11

2:10

He confirms the configuration and presses the off button.

He sprints to the next officer yelling, checks the timer . . .

1:31

1:30

1:29

He confirms the configuration and presses the off button.

'Are there any more? Have you checked all the cars?' he screeches to everyone.

'Clear, sir. No, sir. All clear, sir,' each respond. The officer in charge looks around the car park. All the cars have their trunks open. Even the Land Rover has all the doors and tailgate open. The guards are looking in his direction, waiting for instructions.

'Get these bags out of here and secure them,' he orders. 'The rest of you, sweep the grounds and make sure it's all clear. Notify the guards patrolling the streets to keep an eye out for anyone suspicious. Stop any car and interrogate them thoroughly. If these guys were planning to walk out on foot, then they must have accomplices nearby waiting for them. I want them found, and try to keep them alive if you can. I want to have words with them. Oh, and one last thing. Tell the staff who've parked here that their cars may be slightly damaged, but they'll be compensated.'

'Yes, sir,' they all salute and start following his instructions.

The officer in charge starts walking back to the command centre to notify the German chancellor.

'You've done well,' commends James.

'You were watching?' asks the officer.

'I was watching and was very impressed by your actions. I am in your debt that you've managed to save the people I have asked

here. I'd hate to think what would have happened if we'd been too late or missed this terrorist act altogether.'

'I think the whole world would despise up until the end of time.'

'That's not as far away as you think.'

'What? What do you mean?'

'That's the main reason we're having this meeting. We're causing our own destruction, and we are the only ones who can fix it.'

'Then I am in your debt if you manage to succeed.'

The officer in charge updates the German chancellor on what has taken place. She is physically shaken but relieved that the attempt had been thwarted.

'Make sure that there's no sign of what's transpired here tonight,' instructs the chancellor. 'We don't need any of our guests to know, and back down on attending the meeting.'

'Rest assured, Chancellor,' replies the officer. 'I know why we're holding this meeting, and every one of them will be there even if I have to carry them there myself.'

'I assume you've been speaking with our friend then,' says the chancellor.

'Yes, Chancellor,' responds the officer, 'and I'm glad that you chose our country to hold this important meeting.'

'I only offered,' says the chancellor. 'Our friend accepted. When this is all over, we will need to investigate how these terrorists found out about the meeting. It appears that we have an informant in our midst, or from somewhere else. Anyway, goodnight and thank you for your success.'

The patrolling armed forces find the fake army officers' accomplices within an hour, parked half a mile from the hotel. But once they are discovered, they shoot each other, yelling 'Allahu Akbar'.

Thankfully, the rest of the night is quiet. The two dead army officers are discovered the next morning just where James had indicated.

Chapter 26

After breakfast that morning, as a group surrounded by armed police, the leaders and their staff walk from the hotel to the Reichstag building where the meeting will take place. Initially, the German chancellor had planned to transport them by bus, but being a warm and sunny morning and because of the events of the previous night, she decides to change her plans.

The leaders are led into a huge chamber and seated around the lower level, facing the podium where the German chancellor stands alone. Each leader has their own microphone placed on the table in front of them or in front of their interpreter if they were using one.

'Hello, Chancellor. Is everyone here?' asks James.

'Ah, good morning. I wasn't sure whether you were coming after having a late night last night. Yes, everyone is here,' replies the German chancellor.

'I wouldn't miss this for the world. I hope everything goes well.'

'So do I.' With that, she addresses the group. She taps the microphone in front of her to make sure it was working, and everyone looks in her direction.

'Good morning,' the German chancellor begins. 'I extend you all a warm welcome, both on behalf of myself and the German people. I am proud to be part of this unprecedented coming together of leaders for the good of mankind, and I would like to personally thank our mutual friend who has astonishingly been able to make this happen.'

She pauses as the translators relay her words to their leaders. In unison, they are cheering and clapping, all of them appearing sincerely grateful that they are part of this as well.

'We have a lot to cover,' the chancellor continues, 'and although there is an agenda, no time frame has been set to cover what we need to discuss. Firstly, however, we need to discuss the rules on what each of us needs to abide by. There is a copy of the agenda and rules printed in your native language in front of you. We can amend these rules if required once we proceed with discussions.'

The chancellor waits as all the leaders pick up their copy of the rules and agenda before continuing.

She begins reading the agenda:

'Every member of the group will have the same rights and have an equal voice in the decision-making of the group.

'The group will agree to elect one member to be the main speaker of the group.

'Each country will select one person to be part of a joint committee.

'The committee will be independent and oversee the actions the group agrees on.

'The committee will have unrestricted access to countries where actions are taking place and report back on the progress being made.

'Each country will contribute one percent of their gross domestic product per year, which will be held in trust and used on actions agreed by the group.

'Each country will contribute 10 per cent of their armed forces to be used by the group in assisting in the decisions made by the group requiring their deployment.

'No one country will benefit, take advantage, or otherwise abuse to the detriment of others, including their own people. This also means that they cannot raise taxes to pay for their contribution to the trust. The money will come out of the government funds.

'Countries with nuclear weapons will detail their efficient time frame to dismantle and destroy these weapons. No other country will take advantage of their disarmament or consider developing their own weapons.

'No country will attack or intimidate any other country.

'The group will assist any country which is not part of the group, should the group agree that they need assistance.

'Countries will abide by the decision made by the group, which may directly or indirectly affect them.

'We will, as a group, decide on the best options to stop and reverse the man-made pollution of our world.

'We will replace polluting power-generating plants with renewable, clean options, whether they be wind, solar, hydro, or nuclear or a combination of all.

'We will stop or restrict the reliance to fossil fuels which are contributing to pollution.

'We will stop the destruction of forests caused by us and help regeneration of these forests.

'We will stop and prevent the extinction of animals caused by us.

'We will stop the persecution and killing of innocent peoples by radical groups.

'We will help countries to become self-reliant so that they are no longer a burden on the diminishing resources we have by providing them with the means to do so. By introducing new technologies, we will help with fertilising arid lands so that they can grow their own food. We will help with irrigation and water by digging wells, by building dams or desalination plants, or by laying pipelines.

'Our aim as a group is to co-exist peacefully with all life on this planet without destroying it. We are the species who are causing the destruction of this planet, and we are the only species who can change this for the benefit of everyone and everything living on it.'

The chancellor pauses, calming her emotions before continuing. There is silence in the chamber as she takes a few deep breaths.

The leader of North Korea stands to his feet, holding the agenda and rules in his raised hand, and says something in Korean.

After several moments, once it has been translated into English by his interpreter, the group cheer and clap.

'Where do I sign?' he'd said.

The first order of business is for the group to elect their speaker. The German chancellor is voted unopposed as they agree that since their mutual friend has confided in her, she is the ideal candidate.

The remainder of the day and into early evening, the leader of each country speaks in turn about what they would contribute to the group, resources, money, and other help they are willing to offer.

The two most powerful leaders from the USA and Russia detail how long it would take for them to disarm and destroy all their nuclear weapons, both agreeing to do this within six months. The other seven countries with nuclear weapons agree to do this within the same time frame.

The following three days consist of discussions, some of which are heated arguments on how to tackle pollution, poverty, hunger, prosecution. But in the end, they all reach agreement. James listens to the discussions and is pleased on how they are proceeding.

Countries unite in solving some of the problems associated with what has been agreed to, volunteering some of their best people to come up with solutions and plans. Other countries agree to investigate options to create efficient equipment to replace old technology which is causing pollution.

They consider environment-friendly options, cheap and efficient housing, infrastructure, irrigation, farming, food crops, and the most efficient way of using land both infertile and arid, as well as reforestation. The list appears to be endless, but every leader contributes positively to the discussions.

The American and Russian presidents agree to work in partnership on ways to fight terrorism and clear affected areas where radicals are killing innocent people and destroying communities.

By the fifth day, the group has agreed and covered every item on the list they have created, allocating responsibilities, the time frames required to complete each item from beginning to end, the resources and equipment required, the allocation of money, and the deployment of personnel. Each country offers more than what has been requested of them.

The German chancellor stands on the podium and addresses the group before concluding this inaugural meeting.

'I thank you all for your contribution, and I hope that what we've agreed on comes to fruition. The responsibility now lies with every one of us to make this happen. We are the guardians and protectors of this blue planet, and it is our responsibility to take care of it, not only for ourselves but also for future generations to come, for our children and their children, for every living thing on it.

'We have all been given tasks to do, so please proceed with urgency and belief. We will reconvene in six months' time to see how we are progressing. If, for any reason, you need some help or assistance or have some concern, please contact me. If you need help from our mutual friend, you can contact him through me.'

The chancellor stops for a moment, listening to James speak to her before she continues.

'Our mutual friend thanks you all for being here and hopes we have success. I wish all of us the very best of luck, and I hope you all have a safe journey home. See you all again soon.'

Everyone cheers and claps loudly for what seems like an eternity before they begin shaking one another's hands and reluctantly leave the chamber.

Chapter 27

Once the world leaders return home, they each hold news conferences, detailing what has taken place during the past week and how they are jointly going to improve the lives of everyone and everything living on their planet.

The leaders promise that they would govern for the benefit of everyone and invite those with experience and knowledge to contribute in solving many of the problems being encountered throughout the world—from famine to drought, pollution, overpopulation, and persecution—and encourage the wealthy to contribute to the trust fund being created to make these changes.

Many are sceptical as they have heard this countless times before. What has previously been promised was found to be too difficult to do, or there wasn't enough money or resources, or there wasn't a solution that could be agreed to, and they eventually disappeared, never to be heard from again.

Progress commences in earnest as the world leaders assigned to specific tasks joined with their counterparts to come up with plans and solutions in tackling what they had volunteered for:

- Working on reforestation
- Deciding on clean-energy options to replace polluting equipment and processes
- Eradicating famine
- Farming and reclaiming arid land

- Bringing fresh drinking water to dry and arid areas for both people and farming
- Designing and building housing for the displaced and the poor
- Designing new farming techniques and crops to grow
- Eradicating radical groups
- Protecting animals nearing extinction and providing them with protected land where they can multiply
- Considering various options of increasing animal numbers through incubation and artificial insemination
- Within the first month, each of the forty countries with the exception of one has transferred their agreed share of money into the trust fund totalling nearly $2 trillion to be used to fund the tasks agreed on by the group.

As the word spreads of this wondrous change, people become less sceptical, and other countries volunteer their services and contribute to the ever-growing trust fund. People with experience in their field, from medicine to agriculture, volunteer their services free of charge. Companies throughout the world offer to design and build machinery, equipment, and housing and offered food, timber, steel, medicines for little or no money. Even ordinary people approach their governments, volunteering their services in any way they can.

The countries with nuclear weapons begin removing these weapons from aircrafts and ships and storage facilities, and begin transporting them to specific sites to be disassembled and destroyed, with the exception of one.

The independent committee responsible for overseeing the disassembly and destruction of nuclear weapons decide to visit North Korea during the second month of being elected since North Korea has also failed to transfer their agreed share of money into the trust.

When the committee, however, attempts to request clearance from the North Korean government, they are refused entry.

The committee contacts the elected speaker of the group, the German chancellor, informing her of this abnormality.

After the German chancellor informs James of this discrepancy, James decides to pay the so-called supreme leader of North Korea a visit. James waits until mid-morning to visit the supreme leader as it would be early morning in North Korea, and he should find him asleep.

Sure enough, Kim Jong-un is fast asleep as James can hear him snoring. James tries the direct approach as he is sick and tired of convincing this individual who has previously agreed to his proposal and even wanted to sign the rules agreed to at the inaugural meeting in Berlin.

James controls the supreme leader's mind and makes him get out of bed, preventing him from speaking. James leads him out onto the palace balcony, five storeys above. In the cloudless night sky, the partial moon shows that the North Korean leader is only wearing white boxer shorts.

James can see the concerned look in the leader's eyes as they are open wide and are darting around the balcony.

'So tell me, Supreme Leader of North Korea, why have you refused entry to the committee members, and why haven't you transferred your agreed share to the trust fund?'

'Because I've changed my mind,' says the leader with frightened eyes.

'So when you said that you would help in making the world prosperous and peaceful the last time I was here, and wanting to sign the rules as if it were a contract during the meeting . . . it was all a lie?'

'Yes, because I felt threatened and I was caught up in the whole world peace thing.'

'Are you telling me that you don't intend to disarm and destroy your nuclear weapons then?'

'They're mine, and I'm going to keep them and use them how I want.'

'You know that I can't let you be the only country with nuclear capabilities, especially when all the other countries have agreed to dispose of their own. I'm not going to allow you to keep them and threaten other countries whenever you feel like it.'

'Well, you can't make me or threaten me. I'm not going to agree to your demands.'

'Firstly, they're not my demands. They are the rules agreed to by all the members, you being one of them. It will lead to humankind helping one another for the long-term survival of everyone and everything living on this planet. I'm not going to allow one individual to jeopardise what we've started.'

The supreme leader attempted to reply, but James silenced him.

'Secondly, about whether I can or can't make you, we've been through this before. If you are willing to participate willingly, genuinely, and fairly, it will make everyone's job much easier, including mine. If you refuse, you know what I can do. If you don't want to contribute and participate, then I'll convince your successor. I don't care either way because I'm tired of repeating myself over and over. So I'll ask you again, are you going to follow the guidelines set in the committee rules?'

'You can't make me, you can't make me,' repeated the supreme leader like a spoilt brat.

'Fine, so be it.'

Kin Jong-un starts walking to the railing surrounding the balcony and scrambles to the top. The white marble railing is wider than the supreme leader's bare feet, so it comfortably accommodates him.

The light breeze ruffles the supreme leader's boxer shorts, and he stands, facing the huge area where crowds of his people had stood countless times, cheering him. Kin Jong-un looks down to the concrete floor below with panic in his eyes, unmoving.

The guards patrolling the grounds around the palace have noticed their leader standing on the railing and are yelling at him to get back. James assumes that some of them are coming up to see why their leader is standing there.

'Although I'm not a professional in these things, I believe that we're high enough, that you landing head first onto the concrete below will kill you. Are you ready to try for a perfect landing?'

James lets the leader speak.

'Stop. What are you doing? You're trying to kill me. Stop.'

'That's exactly my point. I can make you, and I'm giving you the chance to agree willingly to abide by the rules agreed to by the committee.'

'OK, I promise, I promise. I'll agree to the rules. I agree to disarm my weapons. I'll let anyone in to confirm that I'm doing it. I'll pay the money. I'll pay it straight away.'

'See, that wasn't so difficult to say, something that a concerned and understanding person with power and influence wouldn't need to be threatened with.'

James lets the supreme leader scramble down from the balcony ledge on his own before he continues.

'But if I hear that you have again changed your mind and have failed to comply with what you have agreed to, I'm not going to give you another chance to explain yourself. You're just going to get on that ledge and make a forward dive straight to the ground below, and I'll wait for your successor to be elected, and I'll speak with them. Maybe they'll have better sense. Do I make myself clear?'

'Perfectly, and I promise not to change my mind again.'

'Excellent. I'll hold you to that promise. It looks like your guards are arriving, so I'll leave you to explain why you were taking a midnight stroll on your balcony. Goodnight, Supreme Leader, and I hope that I don't need to return.'

Chapter 28

The German chancellor is having a meeting with her advisors when one of her aids knocks on the boardroom door.

'Yes, what is it?' the chancellor asks.

'Sorry to disturb you, Chancellor,' replies the aid, 'but you have an urgent phone call from the Russian president.'

She adjourns the meeting and rushes to her office. She lifts the receiver and instructs the aid to put the phone call through.

'Hello, Vladimir. What can I help you with?' the chancellor asks.

'We have a problem, a very serious problem,' responds the Russian president. 'We've had a break in, in our so-called secure facility where our nuclear rockets were being dismantled. It appears that six of the warheads have somehow been stolen.'

'What?' the chancellor asks. 'How did this happen? How long ago?'

'I was informed a month ago,' responds the president, 'and I thought that we could track down the culprits ourselves without involving anyone. We've searched everywhere possible. We've placed roadblocks around the district, searched every vehicle coming in and out the area. We've even been checking every plane and ship leaving, but we've had no success.'

'Where were you holding these warheads that you've managed to lose?' questions the chancellor.

'We have transported all of our weapons to a special military base in Naryan-Mar around 700 miles northeast of St. Petersburg, near the Barents Sea,' replies the Russian president. 'We believed that being a remote area, we would be able to better manage the dismantling and destruction of these weapons. We had around-the-clock military security surrounding the facility. The two access roads in and out of the facility are heavily guarded, and every vehicle entering and leaving the facility is thoroughly searched. It's impossible that anyone managed to leave the base without being seen.'

'Clearly, they did, and they have,' states the chancellor. 'Surely, there must be something you've found out. Do you know what time of the day or night this robbery took place? Have you questioned the people stationed there? Have you checked for any other possible way they may have managed to remove these weapons from the facility? Are you sure the warheads are missing?'

'I am positive,' insists the Russian president. 'The progress of work and a count of the weapons are checked every morning. We've interro . . . ah, questioned everyone who was there over that twenty-four-hour period. Not one of them has seen or was involved in this theft, I am certain. We've checked the CCTV footage of all the vehicles entering and leaving the facility. There was nothing out of the ordinary. I saw the footage myself. Every single vehicle was thoroughly searched.'

'Could they have gone through some other part of the base?' suggests the chancellor. 'Maybe through a fence and not through the gates?'

'Impossible,' states the president. 'It is a double fence made of hardened chain link steel, with the outer fence electrified. There are guard dogs between the two fences and guards positioned every fifty metres both inside and outside the fence. If anyone tried to get through, day or night, the dogs would have alerted the guards, or the guards would have heard the noise. I myself have walked the perimeter of the fence. There is no break in the chain link fences, and the dogs are all accounted for. I am at a loss.'

'Could they have used helicopters to lift them out?' asks the chancellor.

'No, impossible,' counters the president. 'The helicopters would have been heard.'

'Well, you've missed something,' says the chancellor, frustrated. 'If they haven't gone through or over, then they must have found some other way. Have you got blueprints of the facility? Maybe it will show something that you've overlooked.'

'Thank you for your advice, Chancellor,' replies the Russian president. 'I will investigate this possibility. I'll contact you again if there is any news. Goodbye, Chancellor.'

The German chancellor is concerned. Whoever has possession of these warheads could cause chaos.

The Russian president is on the phone, barking orders, instructing his military leaders to search for blueprints of the Naryan-Mar military base. He paces in his office, hands clasped behind his back, thinking of what he might have overlooked. He continues pacing. The phone rings.

'Yes, what have you found out?' asks the president.

'We've located the blueprints,' replies the officer on the other end of the line nervously. He might have drawn the short straw to ring the Russian president. 'They are at the military archive building in St. Petersburg. They will be here within the hour. They are being flown in by helicopter.'

Fifty minutes later, the blueprints are unrolled on the president's table. The Russian president and his four military advisors start scouring though the several sheets of design drawings which appear to have been created centuries ago. They are brittle, and the edges frayed.

'Here, here, sir,' says one of his advisors enthusiastically, pointing to a section on the plan.

The president looks closely to where his advisor is pointing to. It was a tunnel, a tunnel leading from the main building in the centre of the complex and exiting around 400 metres past the fence line.

The president slams his open hand on the table in anger. 'Why didn't anyone know about this tunnel? Why wasn't anyone aware it was there?'

'I'm . . . I'm sorry, Mr President,' stammers one of the advisors. 'If the tunnel is still there, it was possibly covered up a long time ago, well before our time. And if anyone knows about this tunnel, they would have had to either access these blueprints or been part of the old Soviet Union.'

'Well then, find out which one it is!' yells the president. 'Check and see who's accessed these blueprints, say, in the past six months, and make a list of all living military personnel who were in the Soviet Union. NOW.'

With quick salutes, the four advisors rush out of the room, relieved to be out of there.

<h1 style="text-align:center">Chapter 29</h1>

The six nuclear warheads have since travelled on a cargo ship owned by the Indian Antiquities Company west along the Barents Sea, hugging the coastline of Sweden and Norway, south towards the North Atlantic Ocean and into a small port in Guyana, South America, called New Amsterdam. The six wooden crates are labelled 'Antiques – Fragile'. The crates have been unloaded along with the rest of the small cargo the ship is carrying and transported by truck—well, three trucks in fact—to a dilapidated building on the outskirts of town.

Although the building housing the warheads is old and rundown, the high walls surrounding the building have recently undergone repairs. The twelve-foot-high walls made of hollow concrete blocks have had the mortar replaced in several places where the wall was found loose, and shiny barbed wire has been strung along the top, including the top of the double metal gates. Clearly, the six men guarding this precious cargo do not want uninvited visitors. They are waiting for further instructions.

***

The Russian president is standing in the huge building housing the nuclear warheads in the Naryan-Mar military base surrounded by his senior army officers.

'Search the area for anything that resembles an access to a tunnel,' barks the president. The huge area is full of rockets in various states of disassembly. The warheads that have been removed from their rockets have been placed on wooden pallets in the centre of the room, each tagged as being recorded for disposal. There are six empty pallets thrown haphazardly to one side. The floor of the building is a combination of concrete and two-inch-thick large rectangle metal plates. The metal plates would have been used to support heavy machinery for stability so that when they were being operated, they would not crack the concrete floor.

Each of these metal plates is secured to the concrete floor with large bolts at each of the four corners. The officers begin the search of the building. One of the largest thick metal plates measuring twelve feet by twenty feet is found missing the securing bolts. The metal plate would have weighed over five tons.

'Move that bloody thing out of the way now,' orders the president.

Positioning the overhead crane over the metal plate, the officers attach the lifting bolts to each corner of the plate, lowering the chained hooks and attaching them to the lifting bolts.

The officers proceed to search for the handheld remote control that operates the crane, but it can't be found. Usually, the controller is either placed under the crane's position or returned to its holder for easy access, but it's nowhere to be found.

The officers have to revert to manually operating the crane using a block and tackle. Two of them are needed to lift the large and heavy metal plate, taking them five minutes to lift the metal plate a foot off the ground.

Using a torch, one of the officers gets on his hands and knees and focuses the beam of light under the metal plate. 'There's no floor under there. It's hollow,' he declares.

Rather than continuing to lift the plate further, the officers takes hold of the chained hooks supporting the metal plate and slowly swings it out of the way, fully exposing the cavity below.

On one side of this cavity are steps leading to the darkness below. As they cautiously descend into the darkness, they find a light switch on one of the walls. They flick the switch, and surprisingly, lights come on below.

Standing in the chamber, they see the crane's remote control thrown in the corner of the room. The room itself is empty, but it continues along a passage high and wide enough for a small truck to travel through. The lights continue along the passage, although some of the light bulbs had long blown, so it is poorly lit.

'Those cunning bastards,' says one of the officers. 'So that's why we couldn't find the remote control, and the metal plate was missing the hold down bolts. After lifting the metal plate, they took the warheads and lowered the plate back into position.'

The president and officers proceed along the half-mile long tunnel, noting the fresh tyre tracks on the dirt floor until they reach a double metal door. The door is shut and can't be opened.

They retreat back through the tunnel and drive jeeps to where the tunnel should have ended. The scrub surrounding the tunnel entrance has been cleared, and several faint tyre tracks are seen, starting from the entrance to the tunnel and continuing into the distance. The tunnel door itself has a new chain and padlock fitted. To one side of the path, they find the original lock and chain which has been cut, possibly using a metal grinder.

'Don't touch anything,' instructs the president. 'Have someone check the chains and locks for fingerprints as well as the remote control to the crane, and someone follow those tracks to see if they lead anywhere. Also, check the entry logs to the base. Someone would have come through the gates, and it looks like they didn't leave the same way. Let me know when you've found something, and make it quick.'

The following day, one of the officers relays what they've uncovered to the Russian president. 'We weren't able to lift any significant prints off the chains, locks, or remote. We followed the tyre track, but they lead to the road used to travel to and from the base. After that, it was impossible to determine which direction they had taken. As for the personnel entering and leaving the base, we found one abnormality. There was one technician whom we discovered entered the base twice but only left once.'

'What the hell does that mean?' yells the president.

'On the day we believe the warheads were taken,' replies the officer, 'the technician was signed in and was again signed in the next morning before being signed out that afternoon. It was assumed that someone had missed signing him out the first time.'

'You're joking, surely?' questions the president. 'So what have you been able to find out about this . . . technician?'

The officer appears nervous. 'We have no records of him.'

'WHAT?' yells the president. 'What do you mean you have no records of him?'

'We believe he was using forged documents,' stammers the officer. 'His name doesn't appear anywhere.'

'This is totally unacceptable,' shrieks the president. 'What sort of incompetent people are working for me? I'm holding you and everyone else involved responsible. If you don't find this so-called technician immediately, you and everyone else will spend the rest of your lives in prison. Now get out of my sight.'

The officer salutes and quickly leaves the president's office.

Chapter 30

One of the six men guarding the nuclear warheads in Guyana receives a phone call, asking him to proceed with preparing them as instructed.

The men begin unpacking the crates containing large plastic moulds, bags of plaster, and equipment.

The moulds are in two halves. The top half is a profile of an Egyptian pharaoh, and the bottom half is of the base the pharaoh would sit on. Each half consists of an outer shell and inner core which produces a hollow cast with a finished cast thickness of around two inches.

The plaster is mixed with water until a consistency of pancake batter is produced. Beginning with the shell of the pharaoh, the shell is placed on a support cradle upside down, and the plaster mix is poured into the outer shell until the mould is half-full. The inner core is inserted into the mould until it's flush with the top of the mould and the excess plaster overflows.

The top half of the mould now full of plaster remains on the cradle so that it doesn't tip over and allowed to harden. With the top section of the cast made, the men prepare more plaster so that the base cast can be produced. The cavity of the base is half-filled, and the core inserted.

Since there is only one set of moulds, the men wait until the following day to remove the first set of casts before making the second mould. After seven days, they have the number of casts required to house the six warheads.

***

It's now been several days since the German chancellor spoke with the Russian president. She needs to find out what the president had discovered. She calls him.

'Hello, Vladimir. Any news about the warheads?' she asks him.

'I'm working with incompetents,' replies the Russian president. 'We've confirmed that the warheads were smuggled through an old, unused tunnel under the military base. We know when they were taken. We know how they were taken. But we don't know who took them and where they've taken them to.'

'So you don't know what they look like or how many of them there were?' the chancellor asks.

'We know that one of them entered the base using fake credentials,' confirms the president, 'which my men failed to discover, but we don't know how many men were used to transport the weapons out.'

'Have you checked to see if your CCTV footage captured the man entering the base?' questions the chancellor.

'I did,' replies the president, 'but we don't use high-definition cameras, and the position of those cameras doesn't provide a clear image of him unfortunately.'

'Damn,' continues the chancellor. 'If you had a picture of the man, our mutual friend might be able to track him down.'

'He can do that?' asks the president. 'How do you know?'

'Let's just say that I found out about it prior to the first meeting we had in Berlin,' replies the chancellor without going into detail. Changing the subject so that she doesn't have to tell him that they were nearly blown up, she continues, 'So what's your next plan?'

'We're checking all ships that have arrived and left from nearby ports around the time the warheads were stolen and their destination,' the president replies, 'but I'm afraid that's going to be fruitless unless there's a miracle, and I don't believe in those. I don't know what other options I have, unless you do.'

'The warheads have now been missing for what, five weeks?' counters the chancellor. 'They could be anywhere in the world by now. All I can do is inform the other leaders to keep an eye out for anything suspicious, anyone carrying something that may be a bomb. But that's going to be more difficult than finding a needle in a haystack. With a haystack, however, you have a specific area to search. You just sit there bending every piece of straw until you prick your finger. The world, on the other hand, the search would be endless, and I don't think we have that much time. I'm certain something will happen, and soon. I'm surprised we haven't heard anything yet. Keep searching whilst I inform the others. Good luck, Mr President.'

***

The six moulds are made and are being cleaned and dressed to remove any excess plaster. In addition, the men line the inside of the bases with a thin sheet on malleable lead. The bottom lip on the top mould fits snugly into the base, and once together, it looks like a one-piece sculpture of a pharaoh with the body of a lion and the head of a human resting on a pedestal, similar to the Sphinx of Giza in Egypt.

The sculpture that has been prepared is supposed to depict the pharaoh Hatshepsut wearing a *nemes* headcloth and royal beard.

The man who received the instructions to proceed with preparing the moulds seven days earlier dials the same number. 'We have prepared the moulds, sir.'

'Complete the preparation and repackage the items,' the man on the other end orders.

'Understood,' he replies.

The six men wrestle with the first warhead as it weighed nearly 300 pounds. They carefully remove it from the crate and rest it on the support cradle on its side to access the digital display board on the underside of the base. The warhead is shaped like a cone with a base diameter of twelve inches and a length of around thirty-two inches.

The panel is unscrewed from the base, and the positive and negative terminals are connected to the battery before re-screwing the panel to the base.

The man presses the 'ON' button on the panel, and the digital display comes to life. As the panel computer goes through its start-up functions, the twelve-digit number starts counting down from nines to eights until the display is showing all zeroes. The man sets the panel to 'test mode' and retrieves the remote control, a handheld device that looks similar to a mobile phone.

By pressing the 'Test' and 'Display' buttons on the display board simultaneously, a unique twelve-digit number appears, which the man enters in the remote control. The man presses the 'Enter' button on the remote control, and the display board light begins to flash, confirming that the two devices are now synchronised.

With the synchronisation and test completed, the first warhead is strapped to the support cradle and lowered into the first plaster base.

A second support cradle is retrieved, and a second warhead prepared and synchronised, and then a third, until all six warheads have been set, synchronised and lowered into their individual bases.

The man presses the 'Enter' key on the remote control, confirming that all six warheads are responsive before turning off the remote control. The next part of the procedure would be extremely deadly and final to both the six men and the whole of New Amsterdam area should the 'Enter' button on the remote be pressed, because he hasn't been informed of the disarming procedure. The privilege of pressing the 'Enter' button will be left to the man whom they work for and who organised the warheads to be stolen in the first place.

Once the man presses the 'ARM' button on each control panel, a 'READY' signal is displayed. The man sets the countdown timers on the warhead display panels to commence at sixty minutes before the six bases are filled with polystyrene pellets and lightly compacted to prevent the cradles from moving during their journey to their final destination. That destination is not yet known to the men.

The top sections of the casts are glued into position, and the excess glue removed. The final process is to fully paint each of the casts with gold paint. Once the paint is dry, the eyes on the pharaoh, the alternate stripes of her head cloth, and the hieroglyphic symbols around the base are painted black.

The men place one of the completed sculptures in a clear area of the building, erect a temporary backdrop behind it, and take several photographs at different angles, ensuring that only the sculpture and backdrop are visible.

Each plaster sculpture is then placed on the base of the crate the warheads had arrived in and strapped down. The sides of the crates are screwed back into position, and the crates filled with larger polystyrene balls. The lids are finally screwed into position, and the six packages are ready for delivery.

Again, the man dials the number on his phone. 'Your order is ready for delivery, sir. I'll send you the photos of your order by email to make sure you are satisfied.'

'Excellent,' replies the man on the other end. 'I'll notify you shortly on where to make the deliveries.'

Chapter 31

A tall, well-dressed, slender man carrying a black briefcase enters the Bank of America Plaza in Dallas. He approaches the front desk and asks to see their manager. Several minutes later, the manager arrives, and the man introduces himself as the curator representing the Indian Antiquities Company. 'I know this is highly unusual, but my employer based in Mumbai is displaying his vast collection of Egyptian antiques and artefacts at the Bellagio in Las Vegas in six months' time.'

'I see,' replies the manager. 'And how can I be of service?'

'I have been asked to see if we could display a replica of the Hatshepsut sphinx in your foyer advertising the exhibition,' says the curator. He reaches into his briefcase and produces a photograph of the sphinx for the manager to see.

'What an interesting . . . artefact, did you say?' asks the manager. 'And he has this in his collection?'

'Oh yes, sir,' replies the curator enthusiastically. 'His collection is very large and priceless. He wants to show his collection to the world before he passes away. He is in his eighties and intends to donate it to the Egyptian museum. He's even happy to pay you to display it.'

'You are right,' says the manager. 'It is highly unusual. Well, I can't see why we can't put it on display here. We have plenty of floor space as you can see, and it would even brighten up the place,' he says as he waved his arms around him.

'Oh, thank you, sir!' exclaims the curator. 'My employer will be pleased. We will deliver it within two weeks.' He reaches into his jacket pocket and hands the manager his business card. 'If you have any questions or concerns, you can reach me on the number on the card at any time.'

The curator, with a smile, shakes the manager's hand and leaves.

The curator has been given a list of ten towers in priority order scattered around America to visit. The next tower on his list is the Wells Fargo Plaza in Houston.

His lines are so well rehearsed and appeared genuine that none of the first six destinations on his list refuse his proposal.

***

James's mobile phone rings. He removes it from its holder and answers it. *'Hello.'*

'I seem to ring you every time we have a serious problem, and I'm sorry to say we have another one,' says the German chancellor. 'It appears that six nuclear warheads have been stolen from a Russian facility that was dismantling them.'

'Are you sure they were stolen? Because I have a reason not to fully trust the Russian president.'

'I believe he is telling the truth. There'd be no reason for him to ring me otherwise. He seemed concerned and angry, and he's trying to find out how someone got into their facility which appears to have been secure.'

'Clearly, it was an inside job. Otherwise, they wouldn't have known where the rockets were being dismantled.'

'I agree, but unless the president can confirm who it was, I know you can't help. I thought you should know just in case something happens. Maybe you can think of something. I'll contact you again once I hear anything further. Goodbye.'

'Goodbye, Chancellor.'

***

One of the men nursing the deadly packages receives a phone call he has been expecting.

'We are ready to accept your order. I am sending you the bills of lading to be attached to each of the six packages. A cargo ship is arriving tomorrow morning to collect the order,' says the man on the other end of the line.

'Yes, sir. Understood,' replies the nursemaid.

Once the phone call ends, the man retrieves his laptop, connects the printer, downloads the bills of lading, and prints off two sets.

He inserts a copy of each bill in a clear plastic envelope and staples it to the outside of each crate, each showing a different final destination. The man places the second full set of bills in a single envelope to hand over to the cargo ship collecting the crates.

The cargo ship the *Santa Rosa* arrives at New Amsterdam the following morning, and the loading of the six crates goes smoothly, with the six men accompanying their cargo.

'Nice to see you again, Viktor,' says the captain to one of the six men.

'Not as glad as I am,' replies Viktor. 'I'll be glad to get back to civilisation again. Being cooped up in this hot shithole for nearly a month was starting to drive me crazy.'

'I think you were crazy long before you came here.' The captain chuckles. They both laugh.

'Well, I hope our boss knows what he's doing,' continues the captain, 'because if we get caught, I don't think we're going to see the inside of a jail cell or have a trial, for that matter. On the other hand, if we don't get caught, we're going to be set for life. I don't have to steer this rust bucket around anymore.'

'So far, he's thought of everything,' replies Viktor. 'He's a very smart man. I've been scanning the online news channels for the past month, and there's been nothing mentioned about'—he looks around to make sure they are not being overheard—'about what's happened.'

'Don't worry.' The captain chuckles. 'Everyone on this ship is part of my crew, and they all know what's going on. Our boss has a lot of people on his payroll, so I hope that he's asking enough to pay everyone.'

The *Santa Rosa* arrives at the Port of Miami where the cargo is unloaded. Although there are a lot of crates on the wharf, Viktor imagines his six crates gleaming with a spotlight above, telling everyone that they were full of bombs.

On the contrary, they looked like any other crates with markings on the outside panels displaying where they had come from or whom they belong to. The only difference was that his crates had 'Indian Antiquities Company' stencilled on them, with a rearing elephant standing on its hind legs underneath the lettering.

As the crates pass through customs and undergo scanning by the Port of Miami authorities, Viktor and the captain are called into where the crates are passing through the X-ray machine.

The customs officer questions Viktor on the contents of the crates as their scanner could not penetrate parts of the crates.

'The crates contain replicas of a sphinx,' confirms Viktor. 'It is supposed to depict the pharaoh Hatshepsut that my boss has in his collection which he is displaying in Las Vegas.'

'What are they made of?' asks the customs officer.

'They are plaster casts of the original,' replies Viktor.

'If it's only plaster,' questions the customs officer, 'why can't I see through them?'

Viktor tries to appear casual and relaxed as he replies. 'The bloody things weigh four hundred pounds each. I should know. I had to bloody manhandle the things into their crates.' Viktor tries to make a joke of his explanation. 'Anyway, the bases have been re-enforced with metal so that they don't crack. The last thing we want is for them to break before they're put on display advertising the exhibition in Las Vegas. I can send you some free tickets if you're interested in seeing the exhibition.'

'Thanks for the offer,' replies the customs officer, 'but the last place I want to go to is Las Vegas. Last time I was there, I was lucky to return with the shirt on my back.'

With that, Viktor knows that he'd broken the ice with the officer. They all laugh.

'Well, if you change your mind,' continues Viktor, 'let me know, and I'll send you some tickets. Are there any other questions?'

'No, that's all,' confirms the customs officer. 'I better get back to my scanning because I've got a lot of cargo to get through before my shift ends.'

And that was it. Several hours later, the crates are loaded onto a truck heading for the Miami airport accompanied by the six men. Each of the men buying an aeroplane ticket to the same destination their assigned crate is flying to—one to Dallas, one to Houston, one to Los Angeles, one to Atlanta, one to Chicago, and Viktor to New York City.

Once landing at their designated destinations, the six men find themselves accommodation and wait for the crates to be delivered to the assigned storage facilities. As each man waits to receive confirmation of the crates' arrival, they contact their counterparts who would be assisting in the unloading the replica of the Hatshepsut sphinx in the foyer of the building that has agreed to display it.

Viktor is one of the men who waits, and once he receives the phone call that the crate has arrived, he proceeds to the warehouse and meets up with the three men who would be required to handle such a heavy object. After donning overalls with the insignia of the transport company the truck belongs to and securing their fragile cargo in the back, the four men squeeze into the front compartment of the truck and proceed with the sphinx to its final destination.

Arriving at the Chrysler Building in New York, Viktor introduces himself to the manager. Using the hydraulic ramp on the truck, the crate is lowered to the ground, and the other three men begin to remove the sides of the crate to access the sphinx. Once they agree on where the sphinx will be placed, the double glass doors of the building are opened. Two six-inch-wide cloth straps are placed under the pedestal of the sphinx so that it can be carried into the building. Each man holds the end of the strap looped around their shoulder so that their hands are free to steady the sphinx as they manoeuvre it through the doors and to the agreed position.

'That looks pretty heavy,' says the manager.

'You're not wrong there,' replies Viktor as he strains to maintain control of the strap he's holding. Once the sphinx is lowered into position and the straps are removed, he continues his explanation. 'The base is solid plaster, and the plaster on the top is over two inches thick. The last thing we want is someone deciding to carry it away, because even though it not priceless like the original, it did cost a lot of money to make. The other reason is that it should be robust enough not to break if it's accidentally hit because we've only produced six of them.'

'I see,' says the manager. 'Rest assured it won't be stolen as we have security monitoring the place day and night.'

After wiping the surface of the sphinx of any dirt and bits of polystyrene, they place a wooden tripod next to the sphinx and sit a large plaque advertising the Egyptian exhibition in Las Vegas in six months' time. Surprisingly, the plaque doesn't specify an actual date the exhibition will start, or how long it will go for.

'It's odd that you don't say when the exhibition commences,' questions the manager as he becomes suspicious. The manager approaches the sphinx and closely examines the outside. He taps the sphinx with the second knuckle of his index finger in several places. It sounds solid.

'I know.' Viktor sighs, trying to distract the manager. 'The Indian Antiquities Company is still having discussions with your government. You can't believe the amount of red tape there is when trying to bring in such a large and priceless collection into the country. You need to show that everything is insured, and for how much and what it contains. You even need to detail the materials used for the packing. The questions are endless. Sometimes you feel like a dog jumping through hoops.'

'That's our government for you,' replies the manager.

'Anyway, once this is sorted,' continues Viktor, 'we'll come back and update the plaque. As you can see, we've even included a website on the plaque you can access, which is updated regularly. Not only will it contain the exhibition dates, but you can also order admission tickets from there as well.'

A website has indeed been created, although it would never be updated.

'Sounds fascinating,' comments the manager. 'I might take some time off and go there myself to see the exhibition.'

'You won't be disappointed,' concludes Viktor before shaking the manager's hand and leaving.

Once back at the warehouse, Viktor removes his overalls and makes a phone call. 'The delivery has been made, sir. I'm ready to see you.'

Viktor drives south along the New Jersey Turnpike and turns off at the Newark Liberty International Airport. He arrives at a warehouse surrounded by a chain-link fence where a man is sitting on a wooden crate, smoking a cigarette. The man looks up and casually walks over to the car.

'Hello, Viktor. I assume everything went well,' says the man.

'Like clockwork,' Viktor replies. 'The boss in?'

'Got here five minutes ago,' confirms the man. 'Gimme a sec. I'll let you in.'

The man unlocks the gates and opens them. After Viktor drives through, he closes them again and returns to his makeshift chair, lighting another cigarette.

Viktor drives to the side of the building and parks in front of a door marked 'Office' next to a beat-up old Buick. *Must be running out of money,* thinks Viktor with a chuckle.

He walks through the door without knocking and sees his boss facing in the other direction, leaning over a sink and filling up a glass jug to make percolated coffee. Viktor doesn't interrupt him as he pours coffee granules in the filter pouch, closes the lid, and turns it on. The man turns around, pretending to be surprised.

Viktor has known this man pretty much all his life. Alexander Chenkov and his father had fought together in the army of the Soviet Union before coming to America in the late seventies. There must have been some falling out soon after because Alexander wanted to start a construction company with the little money they had, but Viktor's father refused because he didn't want to take that gamble.

What made it worse was that his father struggled all his life working as a welder and boilermaker until he died of cancer a few years ago, whereas Alexander's vision came true, and he became a multimillionaire within ten years. Viktor's father not only resented Alexander for not offering him a position in his construction company later, but also hated himself for not taking the gamble in the first place. After Viktor's father died, Alexander approached Viktor and asked whether he would be interested in joining him in a new and exciting venture. Little did he know that it would involve handling nuclear weapons and threatening the world with them.

'Viktor, my friend, how are you?' Alexander asks.

'Better for seeing you again,' replies Viktor. 'Any news on how the others are going?'

'Four of our little surprises have been delivered, including yours,' confirms Alexander. 'I'm still waiting to hear back from the other two.'

'I'm worried about all this, you know. If we're found out, all this will be for nothing,' says Viktor.

'Nonsense,' retorts Alexander. 'Unless those buffoons drop one of the bloody things, nothing can go wrong. By the way, I assume you have something for me.'

'Ah yes,' confirms Viktor. 'I forgot.'

Viktor reaches into his inside jacket pocket and hands Alexander the remote control.

'So this is the little baby that controls our . . . other little babies,' says Alexander. 'So you've tested them before they were boxed up?'

'Yep, they all lit up like Christmas trees when I pressed the button,' responds Viktor. 'Remember, you have sixty minutes after pressing the button before they go boom, and the only way to disarm them is by entering the ten-digit number on the remote control. I've attached the activation number to the back of the remote because you need to enter that in first before the deactivation number.'

Alexander turns over the remote and removes the adhesive tape containing the number before sticking the remote in his pocket.

'We're not going to need it,' sneers Alexander. 'They'll give us what we want, you'll see.'

Viktor sees the half-crazed look in Alexander's eyes. He wonders for the first time whether Alexander is deranged, and what they are doing is wrong.

'So what now?' questions Viktor.

'Now we state our demands,' replies Alexander. 'I've planned this down to the finest detail. It's taken me years, and it's finally come to fruition. I couldn't believe my ears when I heard that Putin was disarming all his weapons. I thought that was going to be the hardest part of my plan, trying to acquire nuclear weapons, but he handed them over gift-wrapped. It was like taking candy from a baby. And now everyone is going to pay, and pay big.'

'You're not really going to detonate those warheads, are you?' questions Viktor.

'Of course not,' replies Alexander. 'But they are certainly the big reason they can't refuse my demands. Anyway, I'm ready to telecast our demands. The video's been recorded, and it will soon be broadcasted through every major television network in the United States.'

'And how are you planning to do that?' continues Viktor. 'There's no way that networks are going to let you televise anything like that.'

'That's where you're wrong,' contradicts Alexander. 'It's amazing what you can do when you know the right people and pay them enough money. We're going to break into their satellite links and just televise our little video, and they can't do anything about it until it's too late. By then, everyone will have seen the video, and social media will make it spread like wildfire throughout the world. Once you see the video tonight, notify all the others and get out of the United States as quickly as possible. We'll all meet at our designated rendezvous within the next twenty-four hours and watch the fireworks.'

Chapter 32

Alexander is right. At six in the evening that night, a silhouette of a man appears on all television channels from ABC, CBS, NBC, CNN, and Fox. His voice has been digitalised so that it is not recognisable.

'This message is for the American president and involves everyone living in the United States. What I am about to say is true, and if my demands are not met, there will be catastrophic consequences the world has not seen before. For too long, America has meddled in the affairs of other countries, which they have no reason to dictate what these countries can and cannot do. They send troops into these countries, kill their leaders, impose their ideology and twisted ideas, and plunder their resources. This will stop immediately. I have placed nuclear devices in many of your capital cities under my control, which I will detonate if my demands are not met. The US president will deposit $1 trillion into a nominated account within forty-eight hours. Failure to do so will result in the detonation of these weapons. The president is aware that nuclear warheads are missing, and I am in possession of these warheads. I repeat, you have forty-eight hours to meet my demands or die.'

James is making dinner when he hears the broadcast and watches the television screen to see if he can make out the face of the man speaking. He can see no visible features other than the outline of a man who is making these demands. James turns off the stove and heads for the bunker.

James's mind is in the American president's office where the president is surrounded by large number of people, some appearing to be military advisors. It is chaotic with people talking over one another. The president sits, elbows on the table and his hands over his head.

'We can't just sit and wait to see whether this madman is telling the truth or not,' says one of the advisors. 'We need to strike now. We need to find out where the video was sent from.'

'We've tried to do that, sir,' replies another, 'but the message has been bounced from satellite to satellite, and we're getting multiple locations on where it may have originated from, and when I say multiple, I'm saying thousands. There's no way to know whether any of these locations are correct.'

'What about the text message we received giving us the account number we're supposed to deposit the money into?' asks the president. 'And how the hell did they know where to send this message to?'

'They didn't, sir,' replies another advisor. 'They just sent a general message to everyone within a certain range. This means that whoever sent the message must have been in the area when they sent it. Everyone with a mobile phone in that area would have received the same message.'

'Can we trace who sent the message?' questions the president. 'Can we see who was in the area at the time? Can we check any CCTV footage and see who may have sent it? Can we do anything?'

'We've got every available person checking footage, sir, not only from our cameras but also from any other camera in the area,' responds the advisor. 'But we have no way of tracking where the message came from or where the phone that sent it is now.'

'So we're relying on finding that person through camera footage,' says the president as his voice became louder. 'What if the guy sent the message from a closed van or truck or casually strolling along like anyone else?'

There is silence in the room. James continues to listen without introducing himself to the president.

'What about the video?' continues the president? 'Can we analyse it to see if we can make out the face or the voice?'

'We're on that as we speak, sir,' replies one of the advisors, 'but it's going to take some time.'

'We don't have time!' yells the president. 'Assuming this maniac isn't lying, we've got less than forty-eight hours to give him what he wants before those things blow up in our faces.'

Again, silence fills the room.

'What about the warheads themselves?' continues the president. 'What are they?'

'We've been in contact with the Russian president, sir,' replies one of the military advisors, 'and he's given us the complete specifications of these nuclear warheads. They are R-36M2 warheads, each with a yield of twenty megatons.'

'Christ,' mutters the president. 'And what sort of damage can they do?'

'It all depends on where they are detonated from, sir,' says the advisor. 'But since they are only the warheads and not in rockets, and assuming they are in cities surrounded by large buildings, the blast radius could be as little as five miles and a thermal pulse of maybe forty miles.'

'Only five miles,' counters the president. 'Do you know how many people would be within that five-mile radius? And we've got six of them. We could have millions of casualties, not to mention how many more would be exposed to radiation. How can we track these fuckers?'

'If the warheads are armed,' confirms the advisor, 'they'll be omitting a frequency which we can track, sir. We now have that frequency, but we would need to be within a mile of their location to receive their signal, less if they are surrounded by concrete or protected in some way.'

'Protected how?' asks the president.

'Well, sir,' replies the advisor, 'there are certain metals such as lead which can reduce the range of the signal the warheads omit.'

'So what you're trying to tell me is that we'd need to drive down every fucking street in the United States, carrying receivers to locate these bombs?' asks the president. 'That would take years. What about using our jets to fly low over buildings? Would that work?'

'Possibly not, sir,' says the advisor. 'Assuming these warheads are somewhere inside buildings, possibly in the lowest levels, the signal would not reach that high.'

'Do we have any other options?' enquires the president.

After several seconds of silence, each advisor nervously responds with a 'No, sir'.

'What an intelligent and helpful bunch of people I have working for me,' concludes the president. 'I suggest you have every available person, with whatever means possible, go out there and search for these bombs by foot, by car, by plane, even on their hands and knees if they have to. Now go and let me know when you have something. Remember that we have less than forty-eight hours.'

In unison, the advisors say, 'Yes, sir,' salute, and quickly exit the president's office.

'Hello, Mr President,' says James. **'I see you're not having any luck in tracking down these bombs.'**

Startled, the President realises who's speaking. 'I assume you've heard the conversation we've been having. They're all a bunch of incompetents.'

'Whoever is behind this appears to have spent a lot of time planning every move he's made so far. It looks like he's been able to hide his tracks to make it difficult to find him or the bombs, for that matter.'

'He hasn't given us much time to find him either, assuming all this isn't just a nightmare. I've got no doubt though that he isn't bluffing. He must be pretty cunning, managing to smuggle these bombs into the country and threatening us with them. If I could believe that he wouldn't detonate the bombs after I transfer the money, I would, but I don't think that's going to be the end of it. Nothing's going to stop him detonating the bombs anyway unless we find him or the bombs first.'

'I'm sorry I can't be of help, sir. I'm disappointed that there are people out there taking advantage of what we're trying to do to help one another improve our lives and the health of our planet.'

'I don't blame you for what's happened because clearly, this person has been planning this for a lot longer than we've been planning to save the world. He would have eventually been able to get his hands on weapons anyway. We've just helped manage to push his schedule forward. On a positive note, I've had countless phone calls from the leaders who attended the meeting in Germany offering help and support. I didn't believe that would ever have been possible.'

'What do you mean, sir?'

'America is hated by a lot of countries, some of it caused by our own doing, but mainly, it is because we've been used to try and rid countries of insurgents, agreed to by the United Nations, who were killing innocent people and obliterating communities. We were the ones who had the guts to put our hands up to try and make this happen, spending billions of our dollars, deploying thousands of military personnel and equipment, and losing countless of lives in the process. Even our own people hate us for getting involved. Sorry for venting my anger, but it frustrates me that America is thought that way. Anyway, we have more pressing matters to deal with right now. A lot of the countries are sending over teams of specialists and equipment to help us try and find these bombs.'

'If you can find out who this person is, sir, then I'll be able to find him for you, but I need to know what he looks like.'

'I've got teams of people examining the video, scanning through CCTV footage, searching where this message has come from, and scouring the streets. I hope we have some luck in finding this guy because we're certainly going to need it.'

'If you have any news, sir, please contact me as soon as you do through the German chancellor. Good luck, sir.'

The CCTV footages from the White House and surrounding businesses who were using close-circuit television find no obvious activities that lead to locating who has sent the text message.

Although there were vans and trucks in the area at the time the message was sent, none led to any leads to follow. The message could even have been sent by someone linked to the White House itself or someone working in one of the nearby businesses.

As for tracking down who or where the video had been sent from, this also failed to achieve any positive leads.

The video itself is scrutinised using various programmes to enhance the image of the silhouette man, but the image remains unchanged, apart from the shade of grey it appeared.

The digitalised voice of the silhouette man is converted into an audio file and is scrutinised using countless filters and effects from numerous programmes. Several hours later, the team responsible for analysing the audio believe they've finally succeeded. The ominous voice had a heavy, raspy Russian accent. Now they have to decide what to do with this information.

One of the team members gets on the phone. The president is lying in bed, looking at the ceiling. He bolts upright in bed and answers the phone. 'Yes, what is it?' he asks.

'Mr President,' says the team member, 'sorry to ring you so late, sir, but we believe that we've been able to decipher the voice from the video. It appears to be Russian, sir.'

'Are you sure it has been accurately converted?' questions the president.

'Yes, sir, we believe it has,' the team member responds.

'Let me make a phone call,' replies the president, 'and I'll come back to you with instructions.'

The American president dials the direct number to the Kremlin.

'Hello, Vladimir,' starts the American president. 'For what it's worth, we've been able to decipher the voice on the demand video we received earlier this evening. It appears to be Russian.'

'Are you certain?' asks the Russian president.

'My team believes so, yes,' replies the American president. 'Is there any way that you can determine whom the voice belongs to?'

'My senior people and I have been watching the video,' says the Russian president, 'and we believe that whoever stole these nuclear warheads has some form of military background. We've also been trying to, how you say, convert the voice, without success. If you can send me the voice file, I'll gather as many senior army officers who are still . . . ah . . . living and see if any of them can put a face or name to the voice. I know it's a longshot, but I'll do whatever I can to help. I am . . . disappointed that we failed to prevent these warheads from being taken from right under our noses and put your country in danger.'

'I hope you have success, Vladimir,' continues the American president, 'because we're running out of time, and fast. Depending on where these warheads have been placed, we could be facing thousands, even millions of casualties and countless more from the aftereffects.'

'I understand,' replies the Russian president, 'and I'm sorry that our incompetence has put America in danger. If there is anything that I can do in the meantime, please let me know. Please send me the voice file, and I'll make sure that I have as many senior military personnel available to help.'

Although the Russian president appears to show genuine remorse, thinks the American president, *the people whom this is going to affect are Americans.*

The American president gets back on the phone and instructs his team to forward the converted voice recording to the Russian president.

Chapter 33

It is early evening in Moscow by the time the Russian president has been able to locate and assemble as many of the current and previous military leaders as possible. A table has been placed in the centre of the large room where a laptop connected to large speakers has been positioned. The president is the only one sitting, with all the military leaders standing around the table.

'We believe that the voice on this recording is the perpetrator who is responsible for stealing the six nuclear warheads from the Naryan-Mar military base, and who is now threatening to detonate them,' states the president. 'I want you to listen to the voice and see if you recognise it. I want every possible name you can think of, of the person who might be on this recording, no matter how probable or improbable it may be, and no matter how recent or how long ago you may have heard this voice. After I play the recording, you will give me the names of the persons you believe the voice may belong to. I will continue to play the recoding until you can think of no other possibilities. We have just over twenty-four hours to find this man before his threat turns to catastrophic reality.'

The voice on the recording begins and echoes throughout the room as the military leaders listen intently. At the end of the first play, possible names are noted down by the president. One of the military leaders steps forward, interrupting the others.

'I know that voice! I know that voice!' he yells. He pushes through the others until he reached the table. The president looks up and sees an army officer dressed in his old Soviet Union military uniform. The man appears frail and looks as if he got dressed specifically for this occasion. The president estimates that this old man must be in his eighties. The old man leans forward and places his bony hands on the table, possibly to support himself. The president looks at the hands and can see that each joint is swollen and his fingers are curved, possibly because of arthritis.

'Are you certain?' asks the president.

'Yes, sir,' replies the old man. 'He served under me in the sixties before he received an honorary discharge after a mortar explosion shattered his throat in a military conflict with Czechoslovakia in 1968. That's why he sounds like that. His name is, let me think, ah yes. It is Alexander Chenkov.'

'Do you know where he is?' questions the president.

'No, sir,' replies the old man. 'After Alexander received his honorary discharge, he went back home to his wife in Omsk. Although I tried to keep in touch with him, he was angry that the Russian government didn't provide any support or money for him or his family, and he wanted no contact with anyone associated with the army or government. Actually, no, there was someone he remained friends with who also served under me. His name was Nikolai Dubcek. I have no idea where his is now or whether he's still alive.'

'Although I believe what you're saying,' continues the president, 'I'm going to play the recording a few more times just to make sure no one else recognises the voice.'

Apart from Alexander Chenkov's name, six others are raised as possible names of the voice on the recording. Eventually, these other six names are dismissed because of either being confirmed as being deceased or still living in Russia.

The next thing that is done is to find a current photo of this Alexander Chenkov. Any military photo would be close to fifty years old, and Alexander would have changed and aged considerably.

Using the World Wide Web, however, considering Alexander Chenkov has not been silent all this time, countless photos and images of him are scattered all over the Internet, shaking hands with dignitaries and standing in front of buildings or cutting ribbons on bridges his company has constructed. Clearly, Alexander Chenkov is shown to be a successful businessman living in America and owning a multimillion-dollar construction company called Chenkov Constructions.

Using his millions, Chenkov has managed to steal the nuclear warheads and orchestrate the blackmailing of America to give him what he wants—a trillion dollars. 'You're not going to get away with this,' mutters Putin.

The American president's phone rings. It's nearly two o'clock in the afternoon. He's sitting in the Oval Office, going through the same notes he's read the night before. 'Hello, yes, what is it?' he asks.

'It's Vladimir. I have good news. We've found him,' replies the Russian president.

'So where, where is he?' questions the American president.

'He is living in America. His name is Alexander Chenkov, and he owns a large construction company based in Huston,' replies the Russian president. 'I'm sending you several recent images of him we've been able to download from the Internet as well as a link to his company's website. I don't know whether there's enough time, but I'm sending some of my very best people to help you track him down.'

'Don't,' says the American president. 'We don't want to spook him because he might have people checking who's coming into the country. We'll do some discreet checks to see where he is. I'll keep you updated if we need help.'

When an FBI agent makes a phone call to Chenkov Constructions, however, pretending to be a rich businessman wanting an office building built, Chenkov's personal secretary reports that Mr Chenkov is not available as he is on an overseas business trip, but refusing to say where Alexander Chenkov has travelled to. The secretary either isn't willing to provide that information or didn't know. The agent assumes the latter as she appears to be annoyed that Chenkov has not informed her.

The next action taken by the FBI is to scour all flights leaving the USA over the past forty-eight hours in search of Alexander Chenkov. The initial search, selecting the major airports, quickly returns a positive result confirming that Chenkov has flown out of John F. Kennedy International Airport, heading for Sydney, Australia, yesterday at around eight in the evening. Clearly, he wants to be as far away from any bomb blast as possible. The FBI agent also discovers that apart from Chenkov, there is another Russian by the name of Viktor Dubcek who is also on the same flight. Although not unusual, the agent records the second man's details anyway. Based on the fight duration, Chenkov will be landing at Sydney Airport about now. Once he clears customs, he could go anywhere he wants, even take another flight to another part of the country.

'Mr President,' says the FBI agent, 'we've tracked Chenkov to Sydney, Australia. It also appears that he may be flying there with another Russian by the name of Viktor Dubcek. I'm surprised that he was so easy to find.'

'Clearly, he thought that he's covered his tracks well enough and wasn't expecting to be associated with the missing warheads,' replies the American president. 'Of all the places to go to, Christ, that country's a basket case. They change their prime ministers more often than I have hot dinners. Oh well, don't make contact with the Australian authorities until I get back to you.'

'But, sir,' says the FBI agent, 'we don't have much time. Chenkov could be clearing customs as we speak.'

'Don't you think I know that?' yells the president. 'I'm well aware of how much time we have. Just wait for my phone call.' The president slams the phone down before giving the FBI agent a chance to reply.

'Hello, Angela,' says the American president.

'What's the latest?' asks the German chancellor.

'We've found the bastard who stole the nuclear weapons,' replies the president. 'I need you to contact our friend urgently and ask him to see . . . I mean, to speak with me. I need his help.'

'Right away,' confirms the chancellor.

***

'Hello, Mr President,' says James. **'I hope you've had some luck.'**

'If you want to call it that,' replies the American president, 'yes, we have. He's in Sydney, Australia, and we've got several photos of him.'

'Can you show me, sir?'

The president opens his laptop and brings up an email received from the Russian president.

'I see him.'

'Can you find where this arsehole is and let me know?'

'I can certainly do that.'

'Don't communicate with him or let him know you're there. Just confirm where he is. I can then coordinate with the Australian authorities in detaining him and hopefully encouraging him to stop this madness.'

'I will, sir. I'll get back to you as quickly as I can.'

Chapter 34

Time is running out, and there is now less than twenty-four hours before the money needs to be transferred or America would go boom.

James is in what appeared to be a large apartment building overlooking a city he doesn't recognise. The view from the room is breath-taking, with two of the walls being glass from floor to ceiling. In the distance, James can see a vast lake or possibly a harbour because further away, he can see what appears to be the ocean. To the left where the harbour narrows, James can see a huge bridge spanning the harbour, and on the foreshore to the right is a strange large white building that appears to be made of several massive boats, with the bow of the boats pointing straight up.

Two men are sitting at a large white round table covered with various plates of food, close to one of the windows overlooking the city. *It must be either lunch or dinner*, James thinks. James scans the room and sees a wall clock confirming that it is just past one in the afternoon. The two men are laughing and talking as they stab at the delicacies on the plates of food with their forks and shovelling them into their mouths.

James recognises the older man from the photo shown to him by the American president. The other man, possibly twenty to thirty years younger, James has not seen before.

Not wanting to pry their minds, James tries to listen to the conversation. The language is Russian, and he only recognises a few intermittent words, something about lots of money and America.

Although James is almost certain that these were the men the president is looking for, he needs to try and pry one of their minds to be sure. He chose the younger man.

Viktor becomes rigid and stops talking. He looks around but sees nothing out of the ordinary. He turns back to Alexander, and they continue their conversation.

'What's the matter?' asks Alexander.

'Nothing,' replies Viktor, 'I just felt strange for a moment.'

James can now understand their conversation.

'So,' continues Alexander, 'as I was saying, I'll keep checking the bank account to see when that dog deposits the money, and we'll all be set. I'll transfer the money to the team and you, of course, and you can all go wherever you want because it can't be traced, and live a long and happy life.'

'I understand that,' replies Viktor, 'but what if the president refuses to pay?'

'We've been through this before,' says Alexander with a sigh. 'They have no choice. They know the warheads are missing, and I've told them that we have them. They have no other option but to give us what we've asked for, or America will be blown off the face of the earth, well, most of it will.'

'I still don't like it,' questions Viktor. 'If they still refuse to give us the money and call our bluff, you can't just blow them up.'

'Viktor, Viktor, Viktor.' Alexander chuckles sarcastically. 'That's where you're wrong. Remember, we have nothing to lose, but they do. If they are so stubborn, then I'll have to show them that I'm not joking.'

'What do you mean?' asks Viktor.

'The remote can detonate the bombs together,' replies Alexander, 'but I can also programme it to detonate just one, granted that it's not an ideal way of convincing them, but if they leave us no choice, they'll know we're not joking.'

'But you'll be killing thousands if not millions of innocent people,' pleads Viktor. 'Surely, you're not that ruthless.'

'Firstly,' continues Alexander, 'no one in this world is innocent. And secondly, I haven't come this far and spent so much of my time and money to just forget everything I've planned and walk away without getting what I want.'

Trying to lighten the mood, Alexander adds, 'Anyway, you are only speculating what that American dog will or won't do. Believe me, he wouldn't jeopardise the murder of his own people. You'll see, he'll pay up.'

'I'm just concerned that this will all go wrong,' concludes Viktor.

'Let me worry about everything,' says Alexander. 'Anyway, any news on where the others are?'

'Actually,' replies Viktor, 'they all arrived before we did. They flew out after delivering the packages. Clearly, they had every faith in you getting your message on the television. They're all in their rooms downstairs, trying to recover from their long flights by sleeping their jetlag off.'

'Idiots,' states Alexander. 'Don't they know that the worst thing to do after flying for twenty odd hours is sleeping? They'll be wide-awake at midnight. Anyway, we've got quite a few things to discuss, so we'll wake them up for dinner and keep them awake until it's the right time for bed.'

'I'm not feeling that wide-awake either,' says Viktor. 'I wouldn't mind getting a few hours' sleep myself.'

'Not a good idea,' replies Alexander. 'Go and splash some cold water on your face.'

James has heard enough to know that these are the right men. He scans the room and finds the welcome letter from the hotel on the bedside table, thanking Mr Chenkov for selecting their hotel and wishing him an enjoyable stay. Time to let the American president know where they are hiding.

***

'I've found them, sir,' states James to the American president.

'Thank God you found them,' replies the president. 'Where are they?'

'Alexander Chenkov is staying at the Meriton World Tower in Sydney, Australia, room 4401. He's not alone either. There's another man by the name of Viktor, but I didn't get his last name.'

'Yeah, his name is Viktor Dubcek. We found out they flew there together.'

'There appears to be other people associated with this staying at the hotel as well, but I don't know how many.'

'Don't worry, we can take if from here and find out. I'll notify the FBI. Thanks again for your help.'

'Good luck, Mr President. Let me know if I can be of any more help.'

'I suggest you keep an eye on them for us and let me know if there's any change whilst I contact the FBI.'

'Yes, sir.'

The American president rings the special agent in charge at the FBI and informs him where to find the Alexander Chenkov.

'We need to be diplomatic, but we can't fuck around with this because we don't have the time,' explains the president. 'Make it clear to . . . I believe they're called the Australian Federal Police (AFP) over there, that they need to detain them and not to let any of them get away. They need to find out where they've planted these bombs and see whether they can locate the detonation device, and for Christ's sake, make sure none of them press the bloody button.'

'Yes, sir,' replies the special agent. 'But how were you able to find out where they are so quickly?'

'Let's just say I know someone from the inside,' states the president. 'Now contact the AFP over there and make sure you give them clear instructions on how to handle this.'

Chapter 35

The headquarters of the Australian Federal Police in Sydney, Australia, is based only two blocks away from the Meriton World Tower. Within the hour, several units of unmarked police cars and vans make their way to the Meriton World Tower and park in the underground car park. Several of the police officers dressed as businessmen take the elevator and proceed to the front desk on the ground floor where they ask to speak with the manager in private.

'I'm Superintendent Stein from the Australian Federal Police,' says the superintendent, presenting his badge to the manager of the hotel. 'We've been informed that there may be several Russian terrorists staying in this hotel who may be linked to the threats being made to America, namely, the nuclear warheads they are threatening to blow up.'

'Fuck me,' replies the manager. 'How can I be of service?'

'We need to see a list of all the guests staying at the hotel and which rooms they occupy,' requests the superintendent.

'Certainly,' confirms the manager. 'Let me bring them up on the computer.'

The manager sits in front of his computer with a double screen and brings up the list of guests.

'May I?' enquires the superintendent, pointing to the computer.

'Certainly,' replies the manager as he stands up from the desk and the superintendent sits.

Using the computer mouse, the superintendent scrolls up and down the list until he found Alexander Chenkov. *The FBI agent was right,* thinks the superintendent. *He is staying in room 4401. How did the agent know that?*

The superintendent continues his search and locates Viktor Dubcek. He is staying in one of the lower floors, room 3711. The superintendent notes this down on his notepad and continues searching. He notes down several other room numbers of interest, all the occupants appearing to be staying on the same floor as Viktor Dubcek. In total, there are seventeen people of interest, apart from Chenkov and Dubcek, all of whom have arrived within the last twenty-four hours, staying in seven rooms on the thirty-seventh floor of the hotel. The superintendent notes their names and room numbers. He does a final search of guests who have arrived within the last forty-eight hours, their names, and their room numbers. None are found to be of interest.

'Can you provide me with keys to these rooms?' the superintendent asks the manager, presenting the room numbers he's recorded in his notepad.

'I'm sorry, but I can't do that,' replies the hotel manager, 'unless I get approval from the hotel owner.'

'Seriously?' questions the superintendent. 'You've got known terrorists staying at your hotel who are about to detonate nuclear bombs in the United States, and you want to get permission from your boss?'

'Well, I . . . ,' stammers the manager.

'I promise that you won't get into trouble,' continues the superintendent, 'and that the AFP will take full responsibility. Now can we please have the keys to the rooms?'

The manager, clutching the superintendent's notepad, proceeds to the front deck and returns several minutes later with eight key cards, each in a small envelope marked with the corresponding room number.

'I suppose you can't tell me whether these men are in their rooms or not,' enquires the superintendent.

'Actually, I can,' replies the manager. 'If you look at the room numbers on the computer monitor, there are two circles next to each number. You see, not only does the key card allow you access to the room, but you also need to insert the card in the holder just inside the door to activate power and lights in the room. When you insert the key card in the holder, one of these lights on monitor there turns *red*, meaning the room is occupied. When the other monitor light turns *green*, the *red* light goes out, meaning the occupants have removed their key card from the holder, meaning they have left their hotel room. We use this system to know when to clean the rooms. When the light is green, it's clear for the cleaners to enter the rooms to clean them.'

The superintendent scrolls through the room numbers he has recorded on both levels 37 and 44 and confirms all the lights are *red*, with the exception of room 3711, meaning that the rooms are occupied with the exception of room 3711. According to the hotel register, room 3711 has Viktor Dubcek staying in it, and as the FBI agent has reported, Viktor was with Alexander on the forty-fourth floor at the time the FBI agent had contacted the AFP. How the FBI agent had known this remained a mystery, and maybe Viktor was still there. The superintendent, however, doesn't know whether some of the occupants in the other rooms have gone out.

'Do you have any surveillance cameras up there?' asks the superintendent.

'We do, but not in the rooms, of course. Privacy issues and all that doesn't allow it,' replies the manager. 'There are three cameras on each floor, one at each end of the corridor and one next to the lifts. I can bring them up for floors 37 and 41 on the second computer monitor if you like.'

'Please do,' confirms the superintendent.

Well, the superintendent knows that he has no choice. It was urgent that this madman is stopped before he pushed the button, and since he appears to be in his hotel suite, the plan is to proceed.

'Sergeant Thompson,' the superintendent calls out, 'I want you to keep an eye on these computer monitors and notify me immediately if any of the lights from any of the eight rooms change from red to green or if you see someone in the corridors on those floors.'

The remaining three officers accompany the superintendent back down to the underground car park to coordinate the strike team. A further four officers and special response team members who wait in the car park surround the superintendent who goes over the plan of attack.

'I want each sergeant accompanied by three armed response members in front of each of the seven rooms on the thirty-seventh floor,' states the superintendent, handing out the key cards to each of the sergeants. 'I'll take the remaining two armed members to room 4401 on the forty-fourth floor.'

The superintendent looks at each sergeant who confirms they understand his instructions before he continues, 'It is now thirteen thirty-five hundred hours. I want you to synchronise your watches in "five, four, three, two, one, mark". I want you to be in front of your designated hotel rooms by thirteen forty-five hundred hours. You will use the key card to enter the rooms and locate all the people inside as quickly as possible. It is imperative that you don't allow them to ring or contact anyone, and you are authorised to use deadly force if needed to stop them doing so, or if they attempt to escape or attack you. Is everyone clear in what they are required to do?'

In unison, they respond, 'Yes, sir.'

'If what I have been told by the FBI is correct, we need to stop these guys and stop them now. Make sure that you have them secured as quickly as you can once you enter the rooms. Tie them up and gag them, and make sure they have nothing in their hands or be able to reach for anything, anything at all. Let's go.'

They head for the bank of elevators, commandeering all four of them. They hold the elevator doors open until all four elevators arrive. Three of the elevators are taken by the teams heading to the thirty-seventh floor and the fourth elevator by the superintendent and his team heading for the forty-fourth floor. By pressing the 'Bypass' button on the elevator control panel, they prevent the elevators from stopping at any other floor apart from the floor they are heading to.

Once the teams arrives on the thirty-seventh floor, they quietly proceed to their designated rooms. The corridor is ominously quiet, and no guests are visible. Once they arrive outside their designated hotel rooms, two of the four team members from each group comprising a sergeant and three armed members stand on each side of the hotel room door, with their backs against the wall, examining the time on their watches. The three special assault members are holding their M4 assault rifles across their chests, one hand on the pistol grip with their index finger resting across the trigger and the other hand supporting the hand guard. The sergeants are holding their Smith and Wesson pistols pointed at the ceiling in one hand and the key card in the other.

With ten seconds to go before thirteen forty-five hundred hours, the sergeants in unison move away from the wall and stand in front of the hotel room doors with their three special assault members turning towards the door as well.

At exactly thirteen forty-five hundred hours, each of the seven sergeants place their key cards over the card reader on the hotel room door. As soon as the card reader light turns green, the sergeant turns the door handle, pushes the door open, and steps back whilst the three special assault members rush in, yelling, 'Police! Put your hands in the air. Don't move. Police! Put your hands in the air. Don't move.'

The men in six of the rooms have no time to respond before they are overrun by the special response officers who have their rifles pointed directly at their faces. Most of the men are found lying in their beds, groggy from sleep because of their long flight over from the States. Within minutes, each man has their hands cuffed behind their backs and their mouths gagged. They are all searched, and their mobile phones confiscated. No weapons are found.

The seventh room, room 3711, is found empty. Either Viktor Dubcek was still with Alexander Chenkov on the forty-fourth floor or somewhere else.

Chapter 36

Whilst all this is taking place, Superintendent Stein is standing in front of room 4401 with his own key card. He taps the card reader, opens the door, and let his two special assault members rush in as he follows. The superintendent sees two men past the two special assault members, standing on the far side of the room. The older man whom the superintendent suspects is Alexander Chenkov has his back to the glass wall, overlooking Sydney Harbour. The other younger man whom he assumes is Viktor Dubcek is standing to Alexander's left, around six feet away. The older man has stood so quickly that the chair he has been sitting on topples backwards and clatters against the glass wall before coming to rest on its side. Because of the glass being toughened and shatter-resistant, it doesn't break. Although the special assault members are yelling, 'Police! Put your hands in the air. Don't move. Police! Put your hands in the air. Don't move,' Chenkov reaches into his bottom jacket pocket and retrieves what appeared to be some form of mobile phone and, with his other hand, produces a pistol from a shoulder holster hidden under his jacket.

The two special assault officers are yelling for Chenkov to put the weapon down and to put his hands in the air. Although Chenkov raises both his hands, they still hold his gun and mobile phone. The special assault officers continue to yell, but Chenkov remains motionless.

James is in the room and is observing what is taking place but not making his presence felt.

'I assume you are Alexander Chenkov,' says the superintendent, silencing the two assault officers. 'And this must be your accomplice Viktor Dubcek.'

'I am,' confirms Chenkov. 'And you are?'

'I am Superintendent Stein from the Australian Federal Police,' confirms the superintendent.

'So what is the meaning of this intrusion?' says Chenkov, appearing to be casual. Each of the two special assault members have their rifles pointed at the two Russians.

Trying to sound as casual, the superintendent replies, 'We've been informed by the FBI that you are planning to blow up the United States.'

'Not necessarily,' states Chenkov. 'If they give me what I've asked for, then I'll leave them in peace.'

'And what is that?' asks the superintendent.

'At trillion dollars,' confirms Chenkov, 'and their lives will be spared.'

'You're kidding?' says the superintendent. 'And you expect them to pay you?'

'I do,' states Chenkov. 'If I don't receive it within twenty-one hours, America will no longer be the superpower they are now. They'll be nothing, and they'll be blown to pieces—pieces that will take them years to clean up.'

The superintendent can see the crazed look in Chenkov's eyes. Although he's had a lot of experience negotiating with terrorists, would-be-killers, and people wanting to commit suicide, he knows this is going to be difficult, and he has to tread carefully.

The superintendent remembered a time, two years ago, in the centre of the city where a coffee shop had been taken over by three terrorists whom he had to negotiate with. Begin late morning, the coffee shop would have had a number of customers, not to mention the staff working there. The front glass of the coffee shop had been covered with newspapers so none of his men could target the terrorists or confirm how many people they held hostage.

The owner of the coffee shop, who had not yet arrived at the shop, was helpful in providing actual time CCTV footage which he accessed from his mobile phone. It showed that all the hostages were in the back room alone since the back door to the shop was locked. Two of the terrorists were standing on either side of the storage room, protecting the door, and the third terrorist, possibly their leader, was standing behind the counter.

The superintendent spent the next three hours negotiating with the terrorists whilst he coordinated getting the hostages out. He managed to organise a construction crew to set up half a block away from the coffee shop and use their jackhammer to pretend to dig up the street. The jackhammer was actually being used to mask the noise of the grinder cutting away the hinges to the back of the coffee shop door.

Once the hostages were removed, the superintendent encouraged the terrorists to surrender as they no longer had any hostages to bargain with. With the terrorist confirming that their hostages were indeed missing by opening the door to the storage room and finding it empty, they lowered their weapons and came out with their hands in the air.

'You do know that you can't get away with this,' says the superintendent to Alexander. 'All your accomplices downstairs have been captured, and I'm sure we can get them to tell us where the bombs have been planted.'

'On the contrary,' replies Chenkov, 'they're going to tell you nothing. They've all got genuine tourist visas, and all they're going to tell you is that they have come to Australia to see your beautiful country and feed your kangaroos, something I was planning to do once this was all over. You've got nothing to hold them with or threaten them with. The law is on their side.' Chenkov lets out a manic laugh to prove his point.

'I can't see why you would want to kill millions of innocent people,' says the superintendent, 'families, mothers, children who are going about their normal lives.' The superintendent is trying to get Chenkov to show his sympathetic side.

'Rubbish,' responds Chenkov. 'No American is innocent. They're all murderers and killers. Not only do they kill their own people because of their colour, or religion, or their origins, but they also invade other countries for their oil or beliefs or just to show off their strength.'

'That's not being fair,' counters the superintendent. 'Every country has good and bad people, and most of the people you will be killing are good.'

'Look, Superintendent,' spits Chenkov. 'You may be a good mediator, but it won't work with me. America has twenty-one hours to pay up, or they go boom. Now leave this room immediately, or I'll blow them up now.'

'And how do you plan to do that?' questions the superintendent. 'You make one move, and I'll have my officers shoot you.'

Chenkov tilts his head back and laughs. 'I thought you were a mediator, Superintendent,' counters Chenkov, 'but you're a fool. See this device I'm holding in my hand?'

Chenkov shakes the hand holding the remote control as everyone in the room looks at it. 'Well,' continues Chenkov, 'one push of the button, and you won't be able to stop those bombs from exploding.'

'No,' says Viktor. 'You can't do that. Give them time to pay the money.'

'You're as big a fool as the superintendent, Viktor,' replies Chenkov. 'If they leave me no choice or they try to threaten me, I've got nothing to lose. I'm certainly not going to spend the rest of my life in jail or, worse still, be sent back to America where they'll definitely put me to death, and you, for that matter.'

'What if I guarantee that you won't be put to death?' counters the superintendent.

'I know what you're trying to do, Superintendent,' states Chenkov, 'and it won't work. I told you that I'm not going to spend the rest of my life in jail. Didn't I just say that? And you're certainly not going to let me walk out of here a free man, are you?'

'No, I won't,' confirms the superintendent, 'but I can take you somewhere more comfortable to discuss this peacefully.'

'And what?' enquires Chenkov. 'I just hand over my remote control and gun, and we talk about this over a cup of coffee? That is never going to happen. Now I've done enough talking. Get out now, or I'll press the button. GET OUT!'

The two special assault officers lean forward and aim both their rifles at Chenkov as they can see Dubcek doesn't pose a threat.

'Please put down the remote control and gun, Alexander,' asks the superintendent as a last resort. 'Please don't do this.'

James tries to intervene, but before he can enter Chenkov's mind, Chenkov raises the hand holding the remote control up high as if he were holding a winning trophy, presses the button, and throws the remote control to the tiled floor with a crack. Before anyone can do anything, Chenkov raises his left foot and drives the heel of his shoe into the remote control, shattering it to pieces.

Viktor yells 'NO' and rushes towards Chenkov. Chenkov lowers his pistol and shoots Viktor in the chest once before a barrage of gunfire from the two special assault officers hit Chenkov and shatter the glass window behind him.

Chenkov falls back, trips over the fallen chair behind him, and goes through the shattered window to the ground, forty-four floors below.

Chapter 37

The superintendent rushes to the fallen Viktor, gets on his knees, and rolls him over onto his back. Viktor's shirt is soaked with blood around the bullet entry wound. His eyes are closed, and he has a calm expression on his face as if he were at peace. The superintendent presses his fingers on Viktor's neck and feels for a pulse. There is one, but faint.

The superintendent looks up and yells at one of the assault officers to call an ambulance before turning back to Viktor. He tilts Viktor's head back and opens his mouth to make sure he hasn't swallowed his tongue before pinching Viktor's nose and blowing several times onto his mouth. The superintendent tilts his head close to Viktor's mouth to see if he can hear any breathing before placing one palm over the other and pressing down on Viktor's chest, one, two, three, four, five, six, seven. The superintendent's hands are slick with Viktor's blood, but he continues blowing air into Viktor's mouth and pressing down on his chest.

James is shocked on how quickly things went south and is lost on what to do next. He finally enters Viktor's mind and finds it still active.

'Hello, Viktor.'

'Who's there? What do you want?'

'Let's just say that I've been watching you for the past few hours, and I'm disappointed that you have associated yourself with Alexander in destroying the world.'

'I wasn't my intention, but once I found out how crazy Alexander was, it was too late. I knew I couldn't make him change his mind, so I just went along. I was a fool to believe him, with his promises of giving me everything I've ever wanted, ever dreamed of. Now it's too late. So who are you? Are you . . . God? Have you come to hear my sins?'

'I don't believe God would be pleased with you right now on how you've helped to create something that is going to kill millions of people.'

'Did he send you?'

'Well, to be honest, I've been given this power to communicate with you by a being who helped nurture the world we live in. So in a way, I am here because of . . . him. So you must tell me how to stop the nuclear weapons from detonating and wiping out millions of innocent lives who don't deserve to die.'

'But God can do anything. Surely, he can make those bombs just disappear.'

'Viktor, it doesn't work that way. Otherwise, God would have stopped nuclear bombs from being created in the first place. He would have stopped famine and provided the world with an abundance of food and water. He would have stopped persecution and murder and racism and greed. The world belongs to everyone living on it, and it's up to us to make it a place of peace where we look after our fellow man, where we make sure every living creature can also live without being hunted or killed to extinction. We've made the world what it is today, and people like you are trying to destroy it faster. So tell me, how do we disarm those nuclear weapons?'

'You can't! Once Alexander pressed the detonation button, there is no way to stop them unless you enter the deactivation code on the remote control, which he's destroyed.'

'So why can't we use another remote control?'

'Because the nuclear weapons were linked to that remote control before they were packed. There's no way to link another remote now that the warheads have been activated. They can only be deactivated using the same remote.'

'*Are you sure the warheads received the signal from the remote control? Because they are so far away and he smashed the remote right after pressing the activation button.*'

'Once the button was pressed, the signal was relayed to the warheads by satellite, so yes, they have received the signal, I'm afraid.'

'*Can we deactivate them using the control panel on the warheads?*'

'You could if you knew what the deactivation code is, but it's a twelve-digit number, and I was never given that number by Alexander. He didn't trust anyone, not even me, completely, even though I did most of the dirty work for him, even activating and packing the bombs for him.'

'*Maybe they are the same numbers you used to activate the warheads.*'

'Impossible. Alexander would have entered them on the remote control before giving it to me to activate the bombs.'

James can feel Viktor's mind slipping away, so whatever information he could get from him, it had to be now.

'*Can you think of any way we can deactivate the nuclear warheads? Anything at all. Even if it sounds impossible.*'

'There is no way of deactivating the weapons without the remote control because it needs to communicate with the control panels on the weapons and turn them off. No.'

'*So where are the warheads? Where have you placed them?*'

'It doesn't matter anyway. Once Alexander activated the weapons, a sixty-minute timer was started. There's no time to do anything.'

'*So if it doesn't matter, why don't you tell me? Maybe we can try and evacuate as many people from those areas as we can. At least give some of them a change, for Christ's sake.*'

'Each weapon had been packed in the base of a gold-plated sphinx made of plaster that is six-feet long and the same high. They are in . . . the . . . foyers of the . . .'

'Viktor, Viktor, you can't let so many people die. Please tell me where these statues are.'

'They . . . they are in . . . the foyers . . . of the Bank of America Plaza . . . Dallas, Wells Fargo . . . Houston, US Bank Tower LA, Aon . . . Centre Chicago, the . . . Chrysler Building New . . . York . . . and . . . Bank . . . of . . . America . . . Atlantaaaaaaa . . .'

The ambulance officers enter room 4401 and quickly replace the superintendent who is totally exhausted from administering CPR to Viktor. One of the officers examines Viktor and checks him for a pulse and respiration but founds none. The other officer unpacks a defibrillator and hands the paddles to the first officer whilst he charges the unit.

Viktor's shirt is cut away from his chest, and a gel is applied to the surface of his skin, one area above his heart and the other below. The initial shock of 500 volts applied does nothing to revive Viktor's heart. Several further attempts are made, increasing the voltage to 1,000 volts, but with no effect. After a further examination of Viktor's vital signs, the officer looks up at the superintendent and shakes his head.

The superintendent turns away and faces the window. 'What the fuck am I going to tell the FBI?'

By this time, James had left once he knows Viktor is dead.

Chapter 38

'*I'm sorry, Mr President, but both Alexander Chenkov and Viktor Dubcek are dead.*'

'What?' asks the American president. 'How did it happen?'

'*Viktor tried to stop Alexander from pressing the remote control and was shot in the chest. Alexander was shot by the Australian Federal Police.*'

'You've got to be joking. Why didn't they shoot the bastard before he pressed the button?'

'*They didn't have time, sir. Alexander was holding the remote in his hand when they came in, and he refused to put it down. They didn't have time to stop him before he pressed the detonation button. I even tried to intervene, but I wasn't quick enough.*'

'Well, we haven't heard of any explosions going off. Maybe it didn't work.'

'*Sorry, sir, but the warheads are on a sixty-minute timer, so it's highly likely that they still will.*'

'So can we use the remote to deactivate the warheads?'

'*I don't know how to say this, sir, but Alexander smashed the remote control before he was shot.*'

'You're kidding! What the fuck were the officers doing whilst this was going on? Playing cards? Why didn't they shoot him when he pressed the button? I knew this was going to be disastrous once I heard Alexander had gone to Australia.'

James is silent. He has no answer for the president, no remote to even try and deactivate the warheads, nothing to communicate with them. In fifty minutes' time, there were going to be six massive explosions ringing around America and no way to stop them. *If there was some way to communicate with those warheads . . .*

'Mr President, I have an idea, but I don't know whether this will even work. We've got fifty minutes before those warheads explode. I need you to contact your best men, men whom you can trust. The warheads are in gold-painted plaster sphinx about six feet by six feet. They are in the foyers of the Bank of America Plaza in Dallas, Wells Fargo in Houston, the US Bank Tower in LA, the Aon Centre in Chicago, the Chrysler Building in New York, and the Bank of America in Atlanta. Get your best men to go there, and once they find the sphinx, take a selfie of themselves and text it to this number.'

James gives the American president his mobile phone number.

'They have to be trustworthy, sir. They must not leave once they are there and they've located the statues. It is important that they stay there, no matter what. Is that clear, Mr President.'

'If you pull this off, you can call me Donald from now on, young man.'

'We can talk about that later, sir.'

James opens his eyes, laying on the bed in the panic room, waiting for the messages to arrive. He hasn't made a note on when Alexander had pressed the detonation button on his remote control, so he doesn't know exactly how much time there is left, but he estimate it to be around forty-five minutes.

'Christ, I hope this works,' James says to himself, 'not that there is one, but I need all the help I can get right now.'

He sits up in bed and waits. Five minutes go by . . . ten minutes. The phone vibrates, informing him he has a message.

James unlocks the phone and opens his messages. He sees an image of a man with short-cropped greying hair, possibly in his fifties. The message read, 'I am at the Bank Tower in Los Angeles.' James takes a final look at the photo before closing it. The phone vibrates telling he had another message. That will have to wait until James visits the first man. How much time has he got? Maybe thirty-five minutes?

James is in an open space with a large reception area. The lights are on as it's late evening. He notices two men with similar stature standing next to the sphinx, pacing nervously, looking at their watch. There is no one else in the room.

James introduces himself to the man who has sent the text message, but he needs to be quick.

'Don't be frightened. I'm here to help. I know this is difficult to understand, but I don't have time to explain right now. Hopefully, I can after all this is over.'

The man looks around, frightened, but it appears that someone has told him to expect something unusual. The man touches his earpiece to activate it and says to the person on the other end of the line, 'He's here, sir.'

James doesn't have time to listen. He focuses on the sphinx and lets his mind flow past the plaster casing. It's totally dark and almost tranquil as he can't hear anything going on outside. His mind floats in the darkness and notices the lights from the nuclear warhead control panel. At least he now knows how much time he has. The display is showing

32:17

32:16

32:15

His mind pushes past the control panel and follows the electrical wires to the circuit board. This is all alien to him. 'What do I do now?' James asks himself. The circuit board gives off a faint luminescent green light highlighting the veins of solder which connects the circuitry together. His mind flows over the circuit board, and he feels a faint pulse similar to his heartbeat, but slower—a pulse beating every second, marching the countdown on the display board. James lets his mind follow the pulse as it appears to increase in vibration. All of a sudden, James is behind the display, and the pulse is again faint.

What the hell am I doing here? he thinks. *To think that I could do something to stop these warheads from detonating is ridiculous. It's nothing like a human mind. How the hell can I communicate with it?*

'Don't give up, idiot,' James tells himself. 'Do something. Everyone is depending on you. You wanted to die a year ago, so you might as well die trying. Even if your mind survives the blast, your body might not. You might be lying in your little bunker eighty miles away from Los Angeles, maybe clear of the initial blast zone, but the radiation might reach that far, so you're going to die anyway. DO SOMETHING.'

James's mind flows deeper into the circuit board and into one of the solder lines following the pulse. The pulse again gets louder until it appears to be ear-piercing. If James had hands, he'd have them over his ears. And then his mind in an open space. James doesn't know how big the space really is, but the pulse here is throbbing, possibly the origin. He lets the pulse take him and flow with it and is one with it. It's part of him as he focuses on the pulse, making it change and slow. The pulse continues to slow as one would be when dying. James focuses on further slowing the pulse, and it responds and slows and slows and stops.

James's mind moves out of the tiny box that he's been occupying and follows the circuit board to the electrical cables and to the display board. The screen is dark. No numbers appear on the face of the display. There is silence and darkness. James moves out of the sphinx.

'Tell the man whom you've been speaking to that the warhead is no longer active. I assume that means that it will not detonate. Tell him to tell the others to stay where they are and make sure they've all sent me their photos.'

James opens his eyes in the bunker and checks his phone. He has received five more text messages with photos. He opens the next message, looks at the image, and closes his eyes again.

James sees the man in the photo standing next to the sphinx. This one is in the Chrysler Building in New York.

James tells the man the same thing he's told the man in Los Angeles and lets his mind enter the sphinx.

Now that James knows what he's looking for and knows what to do, he deactivates the second nuclear warhead in under five minutes.

James proceeds to the third warhead in Chicago and disarms that one in just over four minutes.

James knows that he's running out of time. He's got less than thirteen minutes to disarm the remaining three warheads.

He views the final three text messages and memorises the photos of the men guarding the bombs. James proceeds to Wells Fargo in Huston and disarms the warhead. He has nine minutes left to disarm the remaining two.

James arrives at the fourth nuclear warhead in Dallas and disarms it. He has five minutes to disarm the last one.

James arrives in Atlanta, but he's not at the Bank of America Plaza. He's following the man in the text message who is sprinting down one of the main streets possibly away from the plaza.

James stops the man in his tracks.

'You fool, what the fuck are you doing? You can't escape the blast zone, so why are you running?'

The man looks around, frightened, but only sees the people who are walking past, and have now stopped to look at him with questioning looks.

'Who's there? Who said that?' the man asks no one.

'You know who I am and why I'm here. They've told you that I was coming.'

'But I was frightened because we were running out of time, and I didn't believe what they were telling me.'

The people around the man step back but continue to look at him as if he were crazy.

'We don't have time for this. We've got maybe four minutes before the bomb detonates. I need you to show me where the bomb is. I haven't been here before. Now run.'

The man reluctantly turns and runs the way he's come. The man turns the corner and points at a large white building with the lights on in the foyer.

'There, it's there!' he screeches.

James flows to the foyer of the building and enters the final sphinx. The display was showing . . .

2:44

2:43

James follows the circuit board and into the solder as he had done before. For some reason, the pulse in this warhead appears ominous, but he knows it's his imagination playing tricks on him. He reaches the empty space where the pulse is originating from and calms himself. His mind is the pulse, and he begins to slow it down, slow it down, slow it down. It stops with a click, something the others hadn't done. He waits and listens. Silence. James moves out of the space and follows the circuit board to the display which is till illuminated. The display is showing 0:09. For some reason, the timer has stopped but has not completely gone out. Maybe the control acts differently once the final ten seconds are reached and needs to be totally deactivated some other way.

James is concerned that the timer might restart if left in its current state, but he's not certain. He's worried that some external electrical device could reactivate it again or, if it's moved, the timer might start again. *If I can slow and stop the pulse, maybe I can reverse it,* he thinks, *but how can I do that? Maybe the count only works in one direction. I could blow up the place if I try.*

He's been lucky so far. Was he willing to take that chance?

James's mind flows over the circuit board again and re-enters the empty space he had occupied before. Silence. He concentrates on the pulse he had felt when the timer was counting down and takes charge of its movement. One pulse and then a click. Another pulse and another click. James wonders whether his idea is working or whether the timer was continuing to count down. His mind leaves the empty space and examines the display. The board was still illuminated, but it's now showing 0:07.

I can control the pulse, he thinks, *but I can't control the direction. Why? Maybe I'm thinking this all wrong.* James continues to analyse the possible reasons he can't control the direction of the timer. *I can slow down the pulse, and I can stop it, and I can restart it again. How do I reverse it? How can I make the count go the other way?*

And then he realises that he's only been restricting the pulse, the same way you could restrict or stop the flow of blood in an artery. By applying pressure to the artery and then clamping it off, there's no flow.

James focuses his mind on the display and envelopes the whole circuit board. He concentrates on taking control of its function, the pulse that makes the timer count down. His whole being is focused on the mechanism, making sure he's in control. He continues to think and wants the timer to move. 'Move, damn it.'

The display begins to flicker along with the pulse.

0:07

0:07

0:06

0:07

0:06

0:06

0:07

0:06

0:07

0:07

0:08

0:07

0:08

0:08

0:08

0:09

'That's it. Keep going,' James tells himself.

0:09

0:09

0:09

0:10

0:10

0:10

0:11

Click.

James stops the pulse by applying pressure with his mind. Instantly, everything goes dark. The display is no longer illuminated, and James can see no light omitting from it anymore.

James leaves the confines of the plaster sphinx and sees his contact outside the building, pacing back and forth, smoking a cigarette.

'Tell the FBI that all six nuclear warheads have been disarmed.'

The man is startled and drops what's left of his cigarette.

'What? How did you do that?' the man asks.

'It doesn't matter. All that matters is that we're all safe.' James is mentally drained, but there is one more thing he needed to do.

Chapter 39

'**Hello, Mr President.**'

'Thank God,' replies the American president. 'It's been over an hour since you told me that the warheads were activated. I assume, since I haven't heard anything from anyone, that you were successful?'

'*Yes, sir. I managed to disarm them although I was a little concerned with the last warhead. But they're all disarmed now, so you can decide what to do with them.*'

'I can't thank you enough for what you've done—on saving countless of lives and stopping the destruction those warheads would have caused.'

'*I still think that I'm to blame for all this, sir, because if I hadn't asked for nuclear weapons to be destroyed, none of this would have happened. I'm just glad that I was able to stop it.*'

'Nonsense, young man. As I said before, your reasons for doing all of this was to save the world from destroying itself, and I'm glad that I'll be part of this monumental event to make the world a better place for everyone.'

'*Thank you, sir. I hope that we succeed. Now if there's nothing else that we need to discuss right now, I'd like to leave and recover as I'm feeling rather mentally drained. Goodnight, sir.*'

'Goodnight, young man, and we'll talk soon.'

James opens his eyes in the panic room. He's shaking uncontrollably as if he's been out in the cold for a long time, although the room's thermostat keeps the room at a constant temperature of twenty-two centigrade. He leans over, grabs the corner of the bedspread, and pulls it over himself. Within minutes, he falls fast asleep.

***

The FBI organise the collection of the nuclear warheads disguised as a sphinx and take them to a secure facility in the Mojave Desert.

The technicians separate the two halves of the sphinx and remove the polystyrene pellets around the warheads. They notice the lead sheet surrounding the bases.

'Those cunning bastards,' says one of the technicians. 'We'd never would have located the warheads unless we were right next to them with this lead lining.'

The technicians remove the warheads from the bases and strap them to their correct holding cradles.

The next day, the American president rings the Russian president and informs him of the news.

'Hello, Vladimir,' he starts.

'I've been trying to find out what's been going on, but the information I've been getting has been scarce and contradictory,' replies the Russian president.

'Well,' continues the American president, 'I've got some of your misplaced nuclear warheads, and I was wondering what you want me to do with them. Would you like me to destroy them or send them back?'

'Your help has been more than enough,' confirms the Russian president, 'but I will organise for them to be collected and destroy them myself. I've put you in enough danger, and I don't want to impose any further. I assume then that you were able to disarm them.'

'It's a long story, but yes, our mutual friend was able to disarm them after Chenkov activated them,' replies the American president.

'What do you mean?' questions the Russian president. 'Chenkov was able to arm them? I hope you have him detained so that we can interrogate him.'

'That's part of the same long story,' counters the American president. 'Chenkov and his paid conspirators flew to Australia where we tracked them to, and the Australian Federal Police tried to stop him but not before he activated the warheads. Thankfully, our mutual friend was able to find out where the warheads had been placed and deactivated them before they went off.'

'To tell you the truth,' says the Russian president, 'I underestimated the capabilities of our friend. Now I know better, and I am pleased that he's asked me to help in his cause to save the world. I assume Chenkov and his conspirators have been captured because I want them to pay for the crimes that they had committed.'

'The only way you're going to get Chenkov and Dubcek are in body bags,' replies the American president, 'because Chenkov killed Dubcek before being shot himself by the AFP. As for the others, I'm sure the AFP would be pleased to hand them over to you.'

'That's some story you'll have to tell me in detail when we get together,' confirms the Russian president. 'In the meantime, I'll organise the collection of the warheads with your FBI and contact the AFP and have the men responsible returned here. Goodbye, Trump, and talk to you soon, hopefully only about good news.'

The news about the stolen warheads is relayed to all the countries that were in the process of disarming and disposing of their own nuclear weapons. The security and protocols are tightened by all the facilities responsible for handling these nuclear weapons so that this type of possible catastrophe could be averted from happening elsewhere.

Chapter 40

In the meantime, the change in the world is progressing at an impressive rate. By the end of the second year, the majority of the insurgents occupying countries, killing innocent people, and destroying communities are eradicated.

The combined force of army, air force, and navy personnel and their equipment volunteered by countries totalled nearly one million troops. Once an area is selected for assault, everyone in it is notified using flyers dropped from airplanes, broadcasting on radio stations, television networks, and all radio frequencies.

'You are all to leave through designated checkpoints surrounding the area. Those who leave the area and are verified at these checkpoints as being true residents will be temporarily housed and fed. Insurgents who surrender voluntarily will be taken to large prisons where they will be assessed for possible rehabilitation. Those insurgents who denounce their radical beliefs will agree to help rebuild their communities. Those insurgents who fail to leave will be wiped from the face of the earth.'

Once everyone in the area has left, including the sick and the injured, the combined army and air force begin eradicating those that remain, whilst the navy patrol the surrounding oceans and seas for anyone trying to escape.

The air force sweep over the land using radar, sonar, and heat-detecting equipment, and plot possible locations of where insurgents might be hiding and where bombs or landmines have been placed.

Using this information, the army, either by foot or by trucks or in tanks, sweep the land, removing landmines and blowing up ammunition deposits and bombs. Most of the remaining insurgents surrender without a fight, and surprisingly, there are very few casualties. There are times, however, where the insurgents have captured innocent people and use them as human shields to protect themselves from the troops who are overrunning the land. This is the most difficult part of the operation. More often than not, the negotiators are able to convince the insurgents to surrender peacefully. There are times, however, where the insurgents can't be reasoned with, believing that their afterlife will consist of everlasting happiness. In the end, the land is cleaned of the rubble of buildings because of constant and persistent bombings, and destroyed communities are cleared away and made ready to be rebuilt again, and the population returns.

Armed forces on mass deployed into countries where radical groups are plundering and killing innocent people repeat the cleansing process countless of times, leaving the land clean and ready to be moulded into thriving cities, towns, and villages.

Housing and roads and infrastructure and factories and offices and shopping districts and farms begin to rise from the ground. Wells are excavated, pipelines laid, and desalination plants built to provide water to these communities. Solar panels are assembled, wind towers built, and safe nuclear power plants constructed to provide the communities with electricity.

The surrounding lands are fertilised, and soil brought in to prepare the foundation to grow crops of wheat or rice or barley or corn or potato or high-yielding vegetables and fruits.

Displaced people are returned to these communities, jobs created, and government elected—governments that considered their people first before power or greed or money.

Countries which have shown animosity for one another join together in peace to help one another, and share in the natural wealth of the land.

Reforestation commences, and animals returned. Animals nearing extinction are protected, and teams of scientists and biologists provide environments where these creatures can survive and thrive.

***

James is enjoying a freshly brewed cup of coffee and reading the monthly report created by the 'Earth Committee' appointed to updating the world on the progress of change that was taking place.

James still lives in the house his mother and father had built, and has since added to by building his panic room. He goes to the panic room seldom nowadays, apart from when he's invited to speak with one of the leaders or attend their yearly meetings or be thanked for what he's done for them.

It's now been five years since James was first contacted by the being who has helped create the world he now lives. He wonders whether this being will return to see how much it has changed, hopefully for the better. James hopes the being will be pleased with what has been achieved if he ever returns, hopefully in James's lifetime.

In the meantime, James needs to find something to keep himself occupied with but, hopefully, not as stressful as his last venture.

After taking a year off, James manages to get into university and is in his third year of a four-year course in becoming a private investigator specialising in missing persons. He hopes to start his own company, but that's another story.

James takes another sip of his coffee, leans back in his favourite chair, and closes his eyes. He thinks, *Maybe life is worth living after all.*